MINE GAMES

MINE GAMES

A NOVEL

MEL LAURILA

TATE PUBLISHING
AND ENTERPRISES, LLC

Mine Games
Copyright © 2011 by Mel Laurila. All rights reserved.

No part of this publication may be reproduced, stored in a retrieval system or transmitted in any way by any means, electronic, mechanical, photocopy, recording or otherwise without the prior permission of the author except as provided by USA copyright law.

This novel is a work of fiction. Names, descriptions, entities, and incidents included in the story are products of the author's imagination. Any resemblance to actual persons, events, and entities is entirely coincidental.

The opinions expressed by the author are not necessarily those of Tate Publishing, LLC.

Published by Tate Publishing & Enterprises, LLC
127 E. Trade Center Terrace | Mustang, Oklahoma 73064 USA
1.888.361.9473 | www.tatepublishing.com

Tate Publishing is committed to excellence in the publishing industry. The company reflects the philosophy established by the founders, based on Psalm 68:11,
"The Lord gave the word and great was the company of those who published it."

Book design copyright © 2011 by Tate Publishing, LLC. All rights reserved.
Cover design by Kate Stearman
Interior design by Sarah Kirchen

Published in the United States of America
ISBN: 978-1-61346-448-9
1. Fiction / General
2. Fiction / Psychological
11.09.12

To my wife, Anna, who encouraged me countless times over twenty years to complete this book in your hands.

Silver occurring with Native Copper –
Wolverine Mine

Photo Credit: George Robinson

A. E. Seaman Mineral Museum,
Michigan Technological University

PART I

THE DREAM

CHAPTER 1

There is nothing darker than a mine shaft with no light or more disorienting than being in a cage that is bouncing up and down at the end of six hundred feet of cable after an abrupt stop when the power goes out. The three men lying on the floor struggled against the motion to stand up.

Gary Johnson turned on the lamp on his miner's hardhat as he asked, "Are youse guys okay?" His first concern was for his colleagues, the new owners of the Wolverine Mine.

Alan Larsson sputtered, "S—-! What just happened?" followed by a, "Sorry, Reverend."

Gary was a local pastor at Mohawk Methodist Church, an instructor in the mining engineering department at Michigan Tech, and maybe most importantly, the previous owner of the Wolverine Mine.

"No worries, just thought ya were describing the condition of yer Fruit of the Looms, eh?" He turned back to the other man. "Ya sure yer not hurt?"

Fumbling for the switch on the side of his lamp, Jim Taylor replied, "Yeah, I mean, yes, I'm not hurt... er, no, I'm okay."

Gary nodded as though he understood, his lamp blinding Jim as he pulled himself up using the wire mesh on the side of the cage. "Damn hoist motor tripped out the power again! Happens once in a while. I don't know how many more sudden stops like dat dis ol' boy can take. Youse young fellers can shrug it off. Now where are we?"

Three beams moved up and down the rock walls of the shaft, scanning for an opening to one of the mine's nine levels. They were almost impossible to find since the electrical trip shut down most of the power in the mine and the distance between levels was some one hundred feet.

"Looks like we're almost at level six," Gary announced. "Dat's good!"

"Why's dat, I mean, that?" Alan asked. "Less distance to fall when the cable lets go?" At only thirty-three, Alan was the junior partner in Wolverine Ventures, used to doing risk assessments, but not this kind.

"Nah. Less climbing down that ladder over there," he said, pointing with his miner's lamp by nodding his head. "If ya slip, ya fall to the bottom of the shaft."

Alan looked at the emergency hatch at the top of the cage and then over to what seemed like an endless line of round metal bars mounted between timbers in the wall of the shaft running into oblivion. He had already climbed to the top corner of the cage and had pushed the hatch open. "How does one get from the top of the cage to the ladder?"

"Ya jump."

"That's what I was afraid of."

"No need ta be afraid. I'll be praying for ya."

"I'll take whatever help you can provide." Pulling himself through the roof of the cage, Alan stood and caught his balance with the grease-covered cable. He looked from his hand to the slime-covered rungs. "Oh geez. You've got to be kidding."

"Fraid not, but I do have a rag for yer hand." Gary handed him the cloth he'd been carrying in his back pocket. "And Alan, don't think about it. Jump and grab the ladder!"

So he did. Then he screamed.

"Alan!" Jim watched him drop between the cage and the shaft.

CHAPTER 2

Scrambling to the top of the cage faster than a cat to the top of a refrigerator, Gary yelled, "Jim, can ya see 'im?"

"Nah, I can't see nothing through the bottom of the cage." Jim felt totally helpless. For someone used to being in charge, this was the worst feeling in the world.

Leaning dangerously over the edge of the cage, Gary removed his miner's lamp and used it like a flashlight to illuminate the side of mine shaft where the ladder ran. "Lord, let me find 'im alive," he prayed softly. In what seemed like eternity but was in reality just a few seconds, Gary exclaimed, "I see 'im, but he's not moving." This time Gary was pleading with God, "Alive, please let him be alive."

"What did you say?" Jim asked. "Where is he?"

"Hangin' on a loose piece of timber by his jacket. If he slips off, he'll be dead for sure."

"Can we get to him?"

"Yeah, but I'm not sure how we'll get 'im off and up to level six."

Both men made the big step from the cage to the ladder and descended as fast as possible. Gary was first on the scene. "Look like he's lost some blood and he ain't conscious."

Jim arrived out of breath, sporting white knuckles and a complexion to match. "Thank God he's alive." A wave of relief swept over him; then just as quickly panic ensued. "How are we gonna get him out of here?"

Gary's response was immediate and decisive. "On my back."

"Huh?"

"Slide by me on to da edge of da ladder."

Turning sideways, Jim managed to get one leg between the wall of the shaft and the ladder and, rung by rung, carefully edged past Gary and Alan.

"Position your shoulders under Alan's feet and hang on to his ankles with one arm." Gary slipped under Alan's body, and his feet landed right on top of Jim's hardhat. The extra weight caused Jim to buckle, nearly losing his grip on the ladder. "One step at a time when I say 'up.'" He was not certain of Gary's rescue method, but he couldn't come up with a better one.

Thirty rungs up the ladder was the longest climb of Jim's life. Nearly falling twice, covered with mud and slime, Jim pushed Alan's limp body onto the boards that formed the edge of the sixth level then stumbled over Alan, falling to the ground completely exhausted.

"Is he still alive?" Jim asked. Alan was like a younger brother to him. This was not just a business relationship. This was family.

"Shallow breathing, bleeding from the timber wound that kept 'em from falling to death." Pointing with his lamp, Gary said, "In the boss's shack is a first-aid cabinet. We gotta stop the bleeding, or he might not make it."

Jim caught his toe under the lip of one of the rails that ran to the shaft and was used for hauling supply cars up and down in the cage. He fell forward into the shack and knocked over a table, and a large, native copper specimen landed next to him, gouging his arm. "What the hell?" He briefly examined the rock with the jagged copper vein protruding from one side and noticed some blood, his blood, on the edge. His arm began to hurt. Focusing on the task at hand, he shrugged off his injury, got up, and headed for the cabinet on the other side of the room.

Opening the cabinet with his good arm, Jim found a box of bandages and brought them to Gary, who had started working on Alan.

"Put some pressure here to slow the bleeding while I wrap 'em up." Looking up and seeing the cut on Jim's arm, he asked, "Ya okay?"

Nodding, Jim asked, "What was that chunk of copper doing on the table I crashed into?"

"Took it out of the number-two crosscut here on the sixth level last week. Weighs near seventy pounds, and I almost got a hernia getting it to da shaft. When we get Alan patched up, go look on the right side, and you'll see part of a silver nodule where I broke it loose. The old-timers up here call these half-breeds. This was the only piece I could get loose. It's part of an outcropping dat weighs at least a ton. I figure it's gotta be a new vein between levels five and six nobody knew about, until now."

Alan groaned as he began to regain consciousness.

"We'd better get 'em to surface for some help," Gary said.

"Just how are we going to do that?"

"How far can ya carry da ol' boy?"

"About three more steps."

"Then we'll need a plan B," said Gary. "I'll go get some help."

"You're going to climb back up to the surface?"

"Go any better ideas?"

"How far is it?" Jim asked.

"'Bout six hundred feet."

"That's sixty stories!"

"Yep, so I best get going. Stay with Alan and keep 'im from bleedin' too much." At fifty-eight, Gary would struggle with the climb, but he was the only one who knew what to do to get power back on once he reached the surface. To reassure himself as much as Jim, he put on his best Austrian accent and said, "I'll be back."

Jim smiled and blew him a kiss. He then spent the next few minutes applying pressure to the gash in Alan's side and listening to Gary's boots scraping the rungs on the ladder as he methodically climbed up the shaft. As the footsteps faded to just little trickles of rock falling down the shaft, he became lost in thought, wondering if the pain was worth the gain.

He remembered Alan coming to him this past spring, all excited over a discovery he had made while trout fishing up here one weekend. Alan had heard about this gristly mining engineering instructor who was paying his students to collect native copper samples for local souvenir shops from an abandoned mine he owned with the same name as their venture capital firm. That must have been a good omen because in the process he came across an incredibly rich vein of copper ore, unheard of in over a century of mining history in the area. His problem was that he couldn't conduct an exploration program on a college instructor's salary. Alan had immediately looked him up and introduced himself. It wasn't long before they had a signed agreement for majority ownership of the mine and had brought Gary Johnson on to manage the project. This was by far the riskiest investment they had ever made, and with Alan lying next to him on a dirty platform, barely breathing, Jim was thinking this might have been one big mistake.

Alan opened his eyes. "Jim?"

Jim felt his heart skip a beat with excitement. "Yes, Alan?"

"What happened?"

"You missed a couple of steps."

Alan tried to chuckle but grimaced from the pain instead.

"Gary went for help, and my job is to keep you alive."

"So long as there's no mouth-to-mouth involved. Otherwise, let me die."

"I may just do that. Anyway, what was Gary bringing us down to show us?"

"He said he had a real find that could change our whole game plan for the mine."

"I think I literally stumbled across it."

Alan, the younger partner in Wolverine Ventures, gave Jim a puzzled look. "What are you talking about?"

Jim showed him his torn denim jacket and the cut on his left arm. "I fell over this huge copper and silver specimen that Gary had put in the boss's shack on my way to the first-aid cabinet."

"Did you say silver?"

"Yep. It occurs sometimes with the native copper. Gary called it a half-breed. He says there's a whole vein of it running between levels five and six and maybe all the way to seven."

"Really? If that's true, then this is a game changer."

"How so?"

Alan thought for a moment before responding. "All of the research I've done on electric motors tells me that silver is a far better conductor than copper, but it is also about six times more expensive. If we have it occurring naturally with copper in this mine and both occur at high enough concentrations, then our cost to produce a highly-conductive alloy is very small, and conversely, our gross profits very high. Think of all the hybrid and electric cars that are going to be produced over the next few years. Everyone focuses on battery life, but a higher efficiency electric motor is a simpler, more eloquent solution to extending battery life as well."

"I knew there was a reason I took you on as a partner."

"Who took who on?"

"What's the name of the firm?"

"Wolverine."

"What school did I graduate from?"

"Reform—I mean University of Michigan."

"Defense rests. So should you. You won't be any good to me if you're dead."

CHAPTER 3

Elizabeth MacIntyre woke to the sounds of a strong wind rustling the leaves on the oaks outside her bedroom window. She lay in bed gazing at trees whose leaves had just begun the metamorphosis to their autumn brilliance. Getting out of bed to look out the master bedroom balcony doors of her house set on a lush five-acre parcel of the most sought-after land in the Chicago suburbs, she vowed that today was going to be different. Ever since her mother had died last summer, leaving the family inheritance to Liz (as she affectionately used to refer to her daughter), there was something that Elizabeth had always wanted to follow up on, and now was the time. "I will not waste another season of my life not doing what I want to do," she said emphatically, if only to herself. Then she turned and marched into the bathroom to ready herself for battle.

After spending some time deciding how to put her plan in motion, she made a call to an old family friend in Michigan—Arnie Tyrronen.

Three rings later she heard a gruff, "Hallo."

"Hello, Arnie. This is Liz MacIntrye. How are you doing?"

"Well, Liz, good to hear from ya. I'm fine. Haven't seen ya since the funeral. Ya doin' okay?"

"Just fine. Hey, the reason I called is to check on the house and find out what it would take to turn everything on and move in for a while. I need a change of scenery, and with Mom gone, I wanted to come up and get reacquainted with the area again."

"The house is just as Marie left it. I can make sure all the utilities are on and working. When ya coming?"

"Don't know yet. I've got some loose ends to tie up here. Soon."

"Be lookin' forward to seeing ya. Look me up when you're in town."

An hour later, a limousine pulled up to the Black Hawk restaurant. There were enough limos in Chicago to change the state moniker from "Land of Lincoln" to "Land of Limos." Elizabeth stepped out curbside followed by Mary D'Andres, one of her closest friends who went back to her days at the University of Chicago's circle campus. The two women made a striking pair as they strolled up to the maître d' to claim their table.

Having patiently waited for Elizabeth to order a bottle of chardonnay, Mary decided it was time for her friend to let the cat out of the bag.

"Now that you've got my attention, Liz, let's hear what this big secret is."

"It's not really a secret," Elizabeth said, smiling. "I've just decided to make a few changes in my life and wanted to hear what you thought."

The puzzled look on Mary's face showed that she did not know what to expect from her friend, who was known to act on wild impulses in the past.

"I'm going to pack up and move to my great-grandfather's old house in Laurium for a while. You remember the place in northern Michigan I took you to see after we graduated? Well, I've wanted to get back up there ever since Mom died. Seeing all those old friends at the funeral made me homesick. It's been a long time, but I could use a simpler life right now. There's no one left except Andy, and the last I heard from him, he was going to contest the will. Can you believe that? I don't need that, and I don't need him. What I do need is a change of pace."

Tears formed in the corners of her eyes as she spoke. "I have no family left except an estranged brother who disappears after high school and shows up for the reading of the will. Does he think he can waltz right back in and stake a claim in the family mining business like the wildcatter that he is? Never mind, that was a rhetorical question."

Mary was obliged to respond in as gentle a manner as possible to the news that at first saddened her. "This is kind of sudden, isn't it?"

"Yes," Elizabeth admitted. "But if I don't do it now, I'll never do it, and I'm wasting away in my own little world down here. You know what I mean, don't you?"

"What about the family businesses?"

"They get along fine without me. Over the years, the businesses have evolved into passive investments, mostly minority stockholdings, and I have little to do other than act in an oversight role as chairman of the board. Philip Turner does a great job running the day-to-day functions. The consolidated P&Ls look great. Remember, I showed them to you after Mom died. You whistled at them in admiration and told me you wished the Continental Bank could see those kinds of returns on their investments. But I've not made any significant contributions since the last board meeting two months ago."

When the wine had been poured, Elizabeth continued, "Ever since I graduated, I've been doing what everybody, or I should say my mother, expected me to do. I've looked after the business, made my semi-annual trips north to see her, put up with her down here for three months at the beginning of every year, and the list goes on and on. It's so bad I don't know who Elizabeth Anne MacIntyre is anymore. I only know who she's supposed to be. Going back to where I grew up is the best way I can think of to figure out who I am and what I need to be doing with my life. This time, I'm going to do something for myself. I need some excitement in my life, a sense of adventure."

Mary was forced to conceal her worry. She knew Liz had been the good daughter all too long and there was a lot of resentment, besides her feelings toward Andy, buried deep within her. This change might not be for the best. However, she knew Liz was not in a mood to hear any contrary opinions. "You've got to do what you think is best for you. Be careful, and please stay in touch. You know I'll be your friend no matter what the distance is, and I expect to see you back in Evanston from time to time."

"Thanks," Elizabeth said. "I expect to see you in Laurium."

Mary furled her eyebrows. "Don't get your expectations up this winter. I've seen the picture of ten-foot-high snow banks."

CHAPTER 4

Alan awoke to the clamor of the surgical floor in the Calumet Public Hospital. A nurse was attending to the patient in the next bed. When he tried to sit up, the pain in his side caused a yelp that surprised even him.

Turning his way, the nurse said, "Easy on those stitches, Mr. Larsson. I'll be there in a minute to make you more comfortable."

Nodding his head, Alan lay back down until the nurse had time to raise his bed.

"You're the worst tree-stand accident we've had this deer-bow huntin' season," she said. "Good thing your friends went lookin' for ya, or ya might have bled to death out there. Ya came in with a half a tree branch in ya."

A bit puzzled, Alan decided to play along. "That's what friends are for."

"You betcha," said Gary as he walked in with a cup of coffee. The nurse looked over to Gary standing in the doorway. He looked a bit like a mountain man going to Sunday meetin.' His salt and pepper beard was neatly trimmed, and his long, gray hair was combed back. In fact, add a tie, and this was how he looked on Sunday mornings when he preached at the Mohawk United Methodist Church. The coffee cup was almost lost in his large hand, and as the nurse made her way to exit, she realized that he filled the doorframe. Stepping aside, Gary bid the nurse farewell with a nod of his head and then sauntered over to Alan's bedside. "How ya feelin'?"

"I've been better, but I guess I'm lucky to be alive, thanks to you."

Gary leaned over to whisper in Alan's ear. "I am so sorry I told ya to jump. I should've been the first one up there."

"That's okay," said Alan, checking to see if the nurse was within earshot. "I should never have gotten so excited over a six-pointer."

"Well, the Michigan Department of Natural Resources may think your stand is unsafe." Then quietly, Gary followed with, "But it's better than a Mine Safety and Health Administration investigation."

"Hmm, I might've fallen out of my blind, but now I see."

Now it was Gary's turn to groan.

"Where's Jim?"

"He's in the outpatient clinic getting stitched up. He wanted to make sure you were okay first."

"I heard he tripped over a large rock."

"We need to talk about that. Let me show ya something."

Gary proceeded to lay out a map on the bed showing the results of the drilling program in the abandoned Wolverine Mine. The isobars on the contour map showed large areas of high concentrations of copper located on the sixth level, some six hundred feet down, where the exploration work had begun. Occurrences of fifty to ninety pounds of copper per ton of ore were highlighted and showed a massive vein that ran parallel to the old workings.

"Whadaya think?" Gary asked.

"This is fantastic! The ore grade is at least as good as any mine that ever operated up here at the turn of the century. How many drill holes have we sunk in the last three months?"

"Thirty-two, of which twenty-five have assays complete, and seventeen of these intersected this vein, which averages seventy-two pounds per ton. That's better than anything that ever came out of this mine since it was shut down."

"So they completely missed this vein when they were mining on six?"

"The old geologist's reports and the shift logs described this find, which was too large to remove with the equipment of the day," explained Gary. "I've had the only copies of them for years."

"How about silver content?"

"Looks like about 6 to 7 percent of the copper content."

"That's perfect! I was looking at a report the other day that says the optimum range for a high-strength, high-conductivity copper-silver alloy is 4 to 32 percent."

Gary looked puzzled. "I thought we were after the copper wire market."

"We would be if all we had was high-grade copper in the ground. But we can do something with this ore nobody else can—smelt a high-conductivity copper-silver wire for electric motor windings that makes these motors high efficiency and save on battery life in hybrid cars. It can make electric cars go farther and faster. An electric motor will lose 20 percent of the energy put into it. If the copper-silver alloy wire produced from our ore improves this efficiency from 80 to 95 percent, think of the advantage it gives our customers. This gives us a specialty product, something nobody else has, and to even compete with us they have to produce it at a much higher cost than we can mine and smelt the native ore vein shown on your map."

Folding up the map, Alan asked, "When will we have the last assays done? You know, this still isn't a lot to bet the farm on."

"Alan, dese are old workings with over one hundred years of history. Dis ain't a Greenfield project. Back in da day, some of these mines were started with a one-drill hole."

"Yeah, and back in da day, I mean the day, many of them failed."

"That won't happen here," Jim said as he entered the room and pulled up a chair.

"Were ya eavesdropping on our conversation?" Gary asked.

"I was in the hallway talking to Alan's nurse to see if he was being a compliant patient."

"Don't talk about me like I'm not here," Alan said. "And what did the nurse say?"

"Do you really want to know?"

Alan hesitated then answered, "Yeah."

"She said she'd never seen anyone get that banged up falling out of a tree. I told her that when you do things, you do them right."

"Speaking of which, why don't you think this venture may fail? Because you don't want it to?"

"Well, that's one reason. A better reason is that while you were sleeping, I spent a bit of time with Jack Sanders, the geologist Gary hired for the exploration and feasibility study. He still has to log the last of the drill cores. Once he gets these logged and assayed, he'll map the vein for you and give you a reserve estimate. He's got a new kid working for him that's a whiz at geostatistics, so you'll get more numbers than you'll know what to do with." Jim turned to the door. "Hey, Jack, come on in and meet Alan Larsson."

Jack came up to Alan's bedside, and it was then Alan realized what a giant he was. After delivering a crushing handshake, he said to Alan, "Sorry to hear about the accident. Didn't know you Chicago boys liked to deer hunt."

"Oh, we're just full of surprises. But don't get me wrong, I really don't like them when it comes to investing my capital. So, Jack, I'd like to hear your estimates of grade and recoverable tons for that level now that you've had six months to study it."

"My best guesstimate at this point is that we've got eight million tons of seventy to eighty pounds per ton of ore on six."

"Let's see. At three dollars and fifty cents per pound or even just three dollars per pound, that's about $1.8 billion in revenues from that level alone." Alan gazed at the ceiling quietly for a few moments, trying to grasp the magnitude of the ore body they had found. "The old shaft went down nine levels, and who knows what is below that."

"Whadaya find on seven?" Gary inquired.

"Not too much yet. Just checking the accuracy of the seventh level plan and seeing if I could find the new vein on seven. Saw some similar mineralogy to what I'd seen on six where we intersected the seam. So far, so good."

"How does this compare to Kearsarge down the road?" asked Jim.

"Their quality is not near this good. Most of their ore is in the fifty-pound-per-ton range. Still very respectable."

Jim stood up and signaled for Jack to take his chair. "Just how big is the Kearsarge?"

Jack rubbed his chin while thinking about how to answer. "Last information I had was that they were up to twenty thousand tons per day and were still hiring workers for both the mine and the mill."

"That's unbelievable!" said Alan. "How did they get to that production level so fast?"

A big grin came across Jack's face. "Lots of money."

"It's gonna take a lot to get this thing up and running." Alan became concerned because he hadn't anticipated a project of this magnitude and having to move so quickly to compete for market share.

"Don't wait too long." It seemed like Gary had read Alan's mind. "When copper gets to four dollars per pound, this place will be hopping with activity. Orders for equipment will be backlogged for months, every qualified miner will have three job offers, and someone else will be ready to close dat big wire order youse guys been lookin' at."

"What have we got to go on?" Alan asked.

Gary had a confused look on his face. "I just showed ya."

Alan thought, *This guy's not getting it.* "What you showed me was a map that didn't even have all the drill core data on it."

Gary thought, *Dis guy has never done this before.* "You try gettin' a drillin' rig and crew any quicker, and I do have seventeen cores showing the best copper find up here yet."

Jim intervened. "Whoa, guys. Don't go busting any stitches, Alan."

"Look, I'm just having a hard time overcoming the 'too good to be true' syndrome."

"You still don't believe we've got the best find of copper up here and add to that a little bonus of some significant amounts of silver?"

"Well, the data's a little sketchy right now. I mean, this is the first time we're really seeing it, and it's not complete."

Eyeing Jack, Jim asked, "When can we get the reserve estimate complete with geostatistics?"

"Should have it for ya in two months."

"You've got to be kidding!" Jim exclaimed. "We've got to get some preliminary numbers to the investment bankers in a month if you want to see this thing in operation by next summer. If we're not shipping next summer, there's no Chicago Wire deal, which kills the project!"

Given that Gary had just heard the first commitment to reopen the mine by the senior partner of Wolverine Ventures, his enthusiastic response to the demand was, "You'll have the report complete with the geostatistics on your desk by All Saints Day."

Jack opened his mouth to object but opted just to stare at Gary. He'd tell him later about the fault line, or maybe not. No point in losing this high-paying gig.

CHAPTER 5

On the west side of Denver, Colorado, the growing suburb of Lakewood had become home to a number of small companies where many entrepreneurs would go for the gold, some literally. It was also home to James A. MacIntyre IV. True to his heritage, he worked in the mining industry. Unlike his namesake, he didn't own the company he worked for. In fact, Andy (as he was known to his friends and family) had been disowned by the MacIntyres some time ago. This was only after he disowned them first. He had gotten tired of his father controlling every aspect of his life, and when he rebelled and tried to make his own decisions, in his father's eyes, Andy became his one and only big failure. The only family appearance he made in the last twenty years was at his mother's funeral—and, of course, the reading of the will. The document reflected the hurt that she lived with for so long, and although he inherited a six-figure sum that most people would be rather comfortable on, he was essentially written out of the will. The rift between he and his sister became even wider, and now he had convinced himself that he should lay claim to his share one way or another.

His time spent at the Colorado School of Mines in Golden had forged his love of the west and the Rockies. When he graduated as a mining engineer after spending six years in a four-year program, he went to work for a large copper producer in Montana. When the bottom fell out of the market in the early eighties, he had come back to the Denver area and landed a job with a small engineering company that designed and engineered gold mines. Ultimately, he was offered a job by one of their clients and took it. Now, he headed up the mining department of North American Metals, one of the largest producers of precious metals in the United States and Canada.

On this particular morning, Andy sat with his feet up on his desk, his hands behind his head, and his leather chair leaned back as far as it would recline without tipping over backward. Fortunately, his cell phone was voice activated.

"Tom Baker." He was careful to properly enunciate.

"Hey, Andy," came a greeting in the best Barney Fife imitation Tom could muster.

"What's cooking?"

"Copper—closed at almost $3.53 a pound yesterday on the London Metal Exchange."

"You're kidding. Think it'll last?"

"As long as the Chinese keep needing wire and building supplies, it will. You thinking about expanding into copper?"

Andy never heard the question. As he stared out the window at the golden aspen that covered the foothills, he realized yet another season had come and gone since his visit to Michigan.

"Yeah, it's time." He wasn't about to let another season pass before he owned the company he worked for. He had already devised a plan. It was just as matter of executing it. After bringing his boss up to speed and booking a ticket and a hotel, Andy went home to pack his bags with warm clothes for his stay in Michigan's Copper Country during its brutal winter.

CHAPTER 6

Arnie Tyrronen loved to play pinochle with his friends at Shutes Bar, next to the Calumet Theater. In the town's heyday, the bar was packed three rows back from the bar on the nights when major acts would come to town, such as Douglas Fairbanks Sr., Lillian Russell, and John Phillip Sousa. Lately, the crowds had been returning due to the resurgence of copper mining in the area. The opening of the Kearsarge last year and two smaller mines before that had brought a lot of new blood to the old boomtown, and the spirit of the late 1800s was seen on occasion, especially on Friday nights.

As he walked in, Arnie surveyed the landscape. Over the bar hung a large canopy made from stained glass and copper that gave the establishment the aura and charm of a mining town that had known prosperity. He saw the old gang gathered around the small table in the corner, where a 1960s-style jukebox cast a myriad of colors on the woodwork. On his way to the table, he noticed two men at the end of the bar engaged in an animated discussion. At first he thought nothing of it, but then he recognized one of them.

"Andy? Is that you?"

Andy MacIntyre looked up to see the burly, retired mine captain approaching with his hand extended. "First, I don't see ya fer twenty years, and now I find ya up here twice in the last four months."

"I guess I forgot how much I liked the copper country. I thought I'd come back for a little while."

"Dat's funny. Your sister said the same thing to me two weeks ago."

"No kiddin'!"

"No kiddin.' In fact, I just opened up the house for her a couple of days ago." Already knowing the answer to the question, Arnie asked, "Ya talked to her lately?"

"No. When's she coming?"

"Didn't say exactly. Maybe ya should talk to her."

"Maybe I will."

Arnie stared at Andy as though trying to determine what he was up to. Reading between the lines wasn't getting him anywhere. The thirty-eight-year-old son of the man Arnie used to work for was obviously an outdoorsman, sporting the tanned, leathery skin of someone who has spent a lot of time roaming the wild west looking for wild game and most likely wild games in the mining towns he frequented. "Who's yer friend?"

"Oh, I'm sorry. Arnie Tyrronen, meet Jack Sanders."

Extending his hand, Arnie took a long gaze at Jack, sizing up the towering man who was crushing his hand. After Jack released it, Arnie couldn't help but rub his right hand with his left, thinking that this was a no-nonsense kind of guy. "So what mining company do you work for?"

Not wanting to be interrogated, Jack replied with a question of his own. "What makes you think I work for a mining company up here?"

"'Cause I've seen ya around the last few months, and what else is there up here?"

Shaking his head, Jack said, "Small town, big gossip."

Arnie raised his eyebrows. "What did ya say?"

"Now, now, old-timer. Don't get your Fruit of the Looms in a knot. I just meant it's hard to keep folks out of your business up here."

"Are ya saying I'm…" Arnie took a breath. "So, Jack, ya never answered my question."

"I think I did."

After an awkward silence, Arnie said, "See ya around, Andy." He turned and walked over to his friends. He greeted the three men already seated at their table.

"Wha' was dat all about?" asked one of his cohorts.

"Oh, just talkin' with Andy MacIntyre. Wonderin' what he's doin' up here."

The three men seated at the table just looked at him impatiently, waiting for a tidbit of gossip. What is often said about women applies doubly so to nosey old men with time on their hands.

"He didn't really say. Funny thing is his sister, Liz, is comin' to stay for a while in the Tamarack Street house. I opened it up for her and got everything workin' the other day."

"No kiddin.' How come she wants to move up here from that nice place they got down in Chicago, especially with winter settin' in?"

"She didn't really say either. I guess she misses this place even though she ain't been around too often since they moved after the mines closed. Ya know, that's the thing about the copper country—once you've lived here for a while, there's just no place else like it. A lot of folks have moved back lately, and a lot more will come when this place is the copper capital of the world again."

"There ya go dreamin' again, Arnie. Now shaddup an' let's play."

CHAPTER 7

On the corner of North Wacker Drive and Madison, one block north of what used to be called the Sears Tower, stood a glass office building not all that different from the hundreds that populated the loop. The only unique characteristic was the sloping glass sides that caught the afternoon sun as it rotated around the Chicago River.

A month after being discharged from the hospital, Alan still limped while walking across the Madison Street lift bridge as he returned from an early lunch with Pete Singer, Wolverine Ventures' resident engineer. He had spent most of that time working on the business plan for the proposed mining operation. Turning to Pete, he inquired, "What do you think about this one? Is it worth going after, or do we pull the plug?"

They came up to the corner next to the Civic Opera House. Pete used the time waiting for the walk signal to carefully formulate his response. "I'd wait another month before I made that decision. Everything we've got so far says it's a go, but my experience is that you can never overdrill or collect too many samples in a mining venture."

Alan hobbled across both lanes of Wacker Drive and the median as fast as his injured leg would allow. Once safely across, he resumed the conversation as they entered the lobby of the ubiquitous office building that housed their offices. "Well, we don't have the luxury of time. Things are moving quickly up there, and Kearsarge recently doubled production. I can sign a long-term contract for supply of at least fifty million pounds per year of copper to Chicago Wire tomorrow with options for another fifty. At one dollar and fifty cents per pound with an escalation clause, that guarantees an income stream of 75 million dollars. Problem is, the contract has got to be signed before the end of the year, with deliveries starting July one next year."

Getting on the elevator, Pete offered Alan his best pained expression. "Ouch! But then again, those are the good kind of problems to have. I understand you wanting to move this. It'll be tight even if we get started now. Just be careful. I haven't seen enough to give it my stamp of approval yet."

"All right," Alan conceded as they got off the elevator. He really didn't appreciate having the wind taken out of his sails, but that was what he paid Pete to do. "I've got to get ready for the bankers. They'll be here in forty-five minutes. Thanks, Pete."

Sitting in their conference room, Jim and Alan reviewed the presentation that Alan had pulled together that morning based on the information that Gary had given them just days before. The forty-page document looked good off the color printer with all its charts and tables, but both men knew it lacked substance. They also knew that the trick to getting this particular deal off the ground was to sell the risky venture as a sure thing. Fortunately, they had a good track record to fall back on.

"What'd Pete think?" Jim asked as he looked up from behind the final version of the plan.

"He says the jury's still out on this one."

"What does he want?"

"Three more months, double the number of drill holes, and a pilot plant test program to verify recoverable copper and silver."

"How does half the time, no more holes, and three weeks in the pilot plant sound?"

"He won't like it." Alan reflected on Jim's suggestions on how to proceed. "But I guess he'll live with it and wouldn't expect anything else from us. I believe it's a good compromise, and that means we'll be ready to ink a supply contract by mid-December."

"What's the sell to the bankers?"

"Proven reserves of eight million tons at seventy-five pounds per ton. For starters, a five-year supply contract with a guaranteed income stream of 75 million dollars per year. Mine production design capacity of ten thousand tons per day. Initial capital investment of 28 million dollars in a new plant, and 20 million dollars in the mine reopening. Operating costs are thirty dollars per ton; amortized capital is eight dollars per ton. Gross profit is sixty dollars per ton, if our estimates are correct. Even if they're not, there's a lot of room for error."

"This looks good, Alan. How much are we putting up?"

"We've got $1,065,000 into it already. I think we should put in 5 million dollars for operating capital and go for a 50-million-dollar finance package for the construction."

Jim took one last look at the numbers and took a long, slow drink from his coffee cup. He knew that a failure on this one would wipe out all of their liquid assets, 40 percent of which belonged to him. He also knew that payback on the investment was easily less than a year. As with most large business transactions, timing was everything. There was not enough time to turn over every stone to minimize risk, and this could cause the analysts at Continental Bank some heartburn. If they didn't act, Kearsarge could take the contract right out from under them. Finally, he looked Alan in the eye and responded, "I told Gary this was a go, and as far as I'm concerned, we're in for the ride. Let's do it as proposed."

CHAPTER 8

Jim woke early the next morning. He stared at the ceiling, replaying the previous afternoon's meeting with the investment bankers over and over, trying to analyze what went wrong and, more importantly, how to fix it. The quandary he found himself facing was how much risk he was willing to take on. It was painfully apparent that the investment bank thought it was too much even though the upside was very profitable. There simply wasn't enough time to reduce the risk with more drilling and testing. He would have to assume more of it to get this project off the ground and to ink a supply contract with Chicago Wire by year end. Was this the best use of his firm's limited resources? No answers would come, or at least ones he was satisfied with. Frustrated, he rolled over and gazed at Anita, his wife of nineteen years, watching her sleep as he had done so often on sleepless nights after a rough day in the high-stakes venture capital business.

Her steady breathing caused her breasts to rise and fall. He had always enjoyed her ample breasts and loved the way the twins always responded to his gentle caress. As his hand was about to try his luck with one of them yet one more time, she mumbled, "What time is it?"

"Time for you to enter paradise with the world's best lover."

"Okay." She rolled on her back, propped her hands behind her head, and waited.

Jim took a moment to admire his wife's physique. He loved her olive complexion and how it went so well with her dark hair that fell across her shoulders. She had managed to stay fit and trim despite having two children. Twenty years after they first slept together, she still stirred such desire within him. *I wish everything was this easy,* Jim thought.

Later, as they both lay awake, Anita asked, "Feel better?"

"For now."

"What's bugging you this time?"

For the most part, Jim didn't discuss business matters with Anita. It was just easier not to have to explain all the interactions that took place while trying to put together a business deal. There were always nuances that could not be explained, and even a wife couldn't really understand how one felt without having similar experiences. When you are the head of your own firm, sometimes it is lonely at the top. "Our proposal for capital funding for the Wolverine Mine was turned down by the bankers yesterday."

"Does that surprise you? Money is a whole lot tighter these days."

"That doesn't matter. This is a great project with huge returns."

"Not huge enough for the Continental Bank."

"Well, the problem is that the risks are just as big, and this is the biggest project we've ever done. If we go forward and the mine fails, then Wolverine Ventures fails."

"What does that do to us?"

"How does moving from Barrington Lake Estates to the YMCA sound?"

Anita sat up and pretended to be upset. "Wouldn't be my first choice."

"Don't worry."

"I'm not. I believe you will find a way to make it happen. You always have in the past." She had never had reason to doubt Jim's Midas touch because nearly all the deals he had put together had turned to gold. Anita enjoyed living in a gated community in an exclusive suburb of Chicago and all the amenities that came with it, such as the country club and her social network.

"Yes. But Alan's handling this one. Maybe that's the problem. The bank questioned our estimates, and we had little to fall back on."

"Can I ask why you're letting Alan handle the most important project you've undertaken?"

"Because he's the one who brought it to us. He found Gary Johnson and the old mine workings with, coincidentally, the same name as our firm."

"He knew you'd like that! But when it comes to closing the deal, you have much more experience, and you should be the one doing it."

Jim was worried about this one. He had obtained financing for more questionable deals than this in the past, just not as big. Anita was right. After yesterday, he was going to need to be more hands-on, especially given all that was at stake. "I guess you're right. I was letting him run with it because he's so enthusiastic about this one."

"And where has that gotten you? You know I'm right." Anita rolled out of bed. "Come on. You want some breakfast? The kids will be up soon."

Jim sat up and said, "You know what this will mean?" Anita turned and looked at him. "It'll mean I will have to spend a whole lot more time up at the mine for the next several months if I'm taking over the lead managerial role."

"That's not the only thing," Anita replied. "It will mean we can do anything we want once Wolverine Ventures makes its exit from a successful start-up. It will mean a whole lot more mornings like this because you won't have to go into the office."

CHAPTER 9

Jim was studying the borehole map of the sixth level when Pete Singer strolled in to his office. Recognizing the footsteps and expecting a visit since dropping off an updated copy of the Wolverine Mine report early that morning, Jim addressed Pete without even looking up. "Did you get a chance to do a cost/benefit analysis yet?"

"The first thing I did was to calculate payback."

"And?"

"And I decided that if Johnson's numbers are correct, you've paid back your initial investment—both phases—in a matter of ten to twelve months. If you use the Singer estimates and assume worst case, you're covered in eighteen to twenty months. All in all, I'd now go so far as to give you my stamp of approval contingent upon my visiting the place."

This was good news from Jim's perspective. Pete was a tell-it-like-it-is kind of guy. He didn't care what your title was or if you signed his paycheck; what you got was his unvarnished, and usually accurate, opinion. "In that case, what are you waiting for? Catch tonight's flight. I'll have Gary pick you up, and you can have a look around. Find out how the pilot plant tests are going and let him know that we'll be willing to commit the first 5 million dollars next month to get the first mining section up to begin development work the first quarter of next year. You might help him get some lines on used equipment. We'll never get any orders for new loaders or haulers filled in less than two months."

"Yes, boss." Pete saluted. The enthusiasm of the project was catching up with Mr. Keep Your Feet on the Ground. "I'll see you in a few of days."

"Oh, Pete, one last thing. Find out what Kearsarge is up to and who they're selling to on the spot market these days. You need to plan on more than a few days. I want you to oversee the testing and drilling and get the mining equipment ordered."

"No problem. I'll get my 007 watch back from the jewelers and pack my snowshoes."

As Pete turned to walk out the door, Alan walked in. He looked angry. The winkles on his forehead showed prominently below his receding hairline. His lips were pursed, and despite his smaller stature, he walked up to Jim for a nose-to-nose confrontation. "What's going on here?"

"I'm sending Pete up to Calumet to speed things up. Why?"

"I thought I was handling this one."

"You were."

"And you're saying I'm not anymore." Alan started to get red in the face.

Not wanting to get into the fray between the senior and junior partner of the firm he worked for, Pete headed for the door. "I've got things to do, and you guys need to sort this out."

Alan focused his anger on Jim. "I'll ask you again. What the hell is this all about?"

Jim had not wanted to get into this first thing, but now it was inevitable. He tried to keep his temper in check, not liking the way Alan was challenging him. This was one of the few times they disagreed on how to proceed with an investment, and he was going to have to assert his authority. "It's about winning. We couldn't get approval on the 50-million-dollar finance package we proposed to the Continental Bank. We didn't even get a counteroffer. They just weren't interested. The clock is ticking, and we've got to get some more information together on our reserves and mining plan."

"You just saw the latest numbers from the drilling on level six. The geostatistics confirm our earlier projects."

"What about level seven?"

"That's been started."

"If we sign the supply contract with Chicago Wire, then we've got something, even though we're practically giving it away. A contract that covers our operating and start-up costs should get us financing. The only issue then is cash flow."

Alan threw up his arms. "I know all that! What else do you think we can do?"

Jim leaned closer to make sure Alan knew he had already made a decision and the decision was final. "Just what I did. We send Pete up to light a fire under Gary, and then we commit the capital we were going to use for working capital to start-up until we can get financing."

"That's pretty risky, Jim."

"I'm not going to lose this order!"

"I don't want to lose this business!"

Jim saw the concern on Alan's face. He lowered his voice and backed off. "I don't either, and we won't. This is one of those times when you grow some *cojones* or you get out of this business. We're committed."

Alan resorted to some humor to break the tension. "I may need to have you committed."

"You do what you have to. Just don't look over your shoulder because the competition is waiting for us to stumble."

CHAPTER 10

In the late 1800s, Calumet was the copper capital of the world, producing some 13 percent of the world's copper. James MacIntyre Sr. was one of the pioneers who gave it that name when he and a handful of investors formed the Tamarack Mining Company in 1882. By 1909, the Tamarack was famous as the world's deepest copper mine. This massive operation covered a tract of over one thousand one hundred acres and employed more than two thousand men in the early 1900s. The lode proved to be both rich and extensive, earning the shareholders millions by the turn of the twentieth century.

Such wealth was not unusual in those days. The Tamarack Mining Company was the sixth largest producer on the copper range for many years. Calumet and Laurium knew their share of James MacIntyres one hundred years ago; however, what differed about the MacIntyres was that their fortune did not die when copper mining did during the mid-1900s. Other wise investments paid off well, and the MacIntyre mansion on Tamarack Street had stood for one hundred and six years as a monument to that success.

Thus, when Elizabeth moved in to the residence, she felt a sense of home that she had not known for some time. Arnie had made sure all the utilities and appliances were on and working. On the kitchen table was a brass tag with the Tamarack Mining Company and number 662 stamped on one side. A note explained that this was Arnie's tag that he took into the mine every time he went underground to indicate his presence in the mine. After each shift, the men would return the tags to their proper place on a peg board by the cage, indicating they had safely returned one more time. *Thought this would make a nice memoir of your family's mine. It was a great place to work, and the MacIntyres were great people to work for,* the note read.

Despite having not lived here for over twenty years, the memories of her childhood came back that first week as though it had only been yesterday. Her room on the second floor of three-story, sixteen-room structure was as she remembered it when she was twelve and her father used to tuck her in every night under a heavy quilt beneath the canopy. There she felt safe from what was sometimes a hostile world to a little girl whose parents were wealthy and whose friends were jealous. Now she experienced a different type of feeling—the safety of the familiar.

It had taken a week to unpack the small load the movers brought. It had also taken a week to redo the master suite from her parents' room to hers. The suite consisted of a large bathroom, complete with a claw-footed tub, the bedroom with a curved wall of windows looking out over the side yard and the carriage house, and a sitting room with a fireplace. With the fall chill setting in, she had purchased a hot tub and had it installed in the corner of the room by the fireplace. She had changed all the bedding and draperies to something more of her liking to add her signature to the place. Packing up her mother's clothes and personal items had been a sad but liberating experience. She had always been independent, but until now, she had never been truly alone. A new day was dawning, and with the morning sun, that too would change.

Walking down the large staircase that was lit from behind by brilliant sunlight, casting hues from the stained glass windows on the landing, she recalled how she had practiced drifting down the stairs into the waiting arms of her date for the prom. Alas, it never came to pass since she moved to Evanston when she entered high school.

The kitchen in the back of the house was also a large room. Ceramic tile lined the walls, and again, the warmth of the sun was reflected from its surface. As Elizabeth sat at the round oak table in the center of the room, she drank in the pleasant surroundings along with her morning coffee. Afterward, she headed out back to the carriage house, where her mother's Mercedes was lodged. She had ten minutes to make her morning appointment.

CHAPTER 11

The farm sprawled over a hillside on the east end of Torch Lake. It overlooked the ruins of the old stamp mills across the lake where the sandstone and brick buildings blended in with the brown hillsides as the barren ground awaited its covering of a white blanket of snow. As Elizabeth pulled into the drive, the back door flew open, and Tina flew out, barely touching the steps as she raced down to the car to greet her.

"Wow!" Elizabeth exclaimed. "I remember when we used to get all excited about going riding together when we were teenagers and I'd spend the summer up here, and that was the last time I've had anybody jump in my car before I got my feet on the ground."

"Geez, it's so good to see you again, Liz. I was hoping you'd be back. Come on in. Let's make this one like it used to be."

Inside the kitchen of the old farmhouse, Tina had prepared a coffee cake along with a fresh pot of coffee. She ushered Elizabeth to a seat that produced an excellent view of the countryside and proceeded to serve up an enormous slice of coffee cake.

"Whoa, Tina. This piece is large enough to choke a horse."

"Well, I'm not feeding it to the horses; I'm feeding it to you. They've already been fed this morning."

"Speaking of horses, I'm looking forward to a ride. It's been a while since I've had a chance to go for one."

"They're ready. Eric brushed 'em down last night and even cleaned out their stalls." Eric was Tina's husband and a classmate of theirs. They had married the summer they graduated from high school and eventually settled on the family farm after Tina's father died when a tractor he was fixing fell on him. Her mother needed help to keep the farm going, and they needed a rent-free place to live.

"How is Eric these days?" Elizabeth had spent some time catching up with Tina and Eric at her mother's funeral. She remembered that the farm had not been doing well, so Eric had to find other work.

"He's doing fine. Still working for the county road commission, although he's turned in an application to work underground at Kearsarge." After thinking for a moment, Tina added, "I'm not so sure I like that idea. The pay may not be as good at the road commission, but fixing trucks and driving a snowplow has got to be safer than working as a mechanic underground."

"I wouldn't know about that. But I do know that it's a lot safer mining today than when the mines closed years ago. Mining technology has come a long way in four decades."

"How did you come to know so much about mining? I didn't know the MacIntyres were back in the mining business!" Tina's cheery disposition had disappeared. Her old friend had not been sympathetic to her concerns about her husband. It made her begin to wonder if their friendship could be rekindled after all this time.

Well aware that she had touched a nerve, Elizabeth backed off. "We never left the mining business. When the mines closed up here, we picked up some properties out west. Anyway, whether or not Eric takes a job with Kearsarge, it's good to see the area picking up again."

The two old friends smiled at each other, both realizing that the conversation was going nowhere and neither wanting their different backgrounds to get in the way of what had become an important friendship and a lasting one, despite the distance and time factors working against it.

Tina broke the silence. "Whadaya say we go out to the barn and saddle up the horses?"

"Let's!" Elizabeth replied, glad to get out of an uncomfortable situation. Coming back home was not going to be as easy as she had first imagined.

Once on the trail, Tina turned to Elizabeth, pointed to the top of the ridge that bordered the valley, shouted, "Race ya," and was gone, her horse at full gallop. Not to be left behind, Elizabeth snapped the reins, and with a gentle kick from the stirrups, the race was on through the meadow, over the old fence, and along the tree line. Pulling up at the top of the ridge, the women and their steeds caught their breaths.

"Remember doin' this in eighth grade?" Tina asked.

"How could I forget? I ended up with a broken ankle when a tree branch got me. I remembered to keep my head down this time." Elizabeth laughed. "It's really good to be back."

"Whadaya goin' to do? Are you staying for a while?"

"Yeah," Elizabeth said absentmindedly, gazing on the lake below and noting the new shipyard and buildings. "When did they start shipping copper again?"

"This past spring. You should see all the new businesses that have filled up old vacant buildings around here."

"I saw some last summer when I was up for my mom's funeral. What a turnaround. Remember when we were going into ninth grade and I moved, the mines had closed, and so had many of the businesses in town. Twenty years later it's all starting to come back."

"There's a lot more activity now. New people are moving in every week. I've never seen anything like this. It's funny. A few years ago the National Park Service made Calumet a national industrial park to tell the story of the copper boom, and now the copper boom is happening all over again."

"Leave it to the government to screw up their own park."

"No, the park actually raised awareness, and when copper prices shot up, three mines reopened. I hear there are plans for a couple more."

"I heard about the mines reopening. What do you know about the Wolverine Mine?"

"Well, a fair amount since Eric's been lookin' for work in the mines." Tina paused. "Why ya ask?"

"Truth is, I've been planning on moving back up here and getting back into the copper mining business since last summer. If you know of something about to happen, I'd appreciate you telling me. If Eric wants to get into the mining business, maybe I can help."

☙

Calumet Avenue was the main thoroughfare that led from the mine offices on Red Jacket Road to the mines scattered on the northern perimeter of the town. Lining the north end of the avenue were rows of large company-built homes, with the eloquent mine captains' homes on the east side and the not-quite-as-eloquent assistant mine captains' homes on the west side. Three houses north of the company-built school on the east side of the avenue, Arnie Tyrronen's house was nestled among several large balsam trees. Elizabeth rolled her mother's Mercedes up to the garage door, put the top up to protect the interior from the partly cloudy afternoon sky, and made her way to the back porch. She couldn't remember ever using the front door at Arnie's house.

Arnie's massive frame filled the doorway as he opened the etched glass door to let her in. "How ya doin,' Liz?" His embrace was suffocating but welcoming. The giant of a man didn't know his own strength. No wonder he was so well respected by even rough and tough miners in his days underground.

Catching her breath, Elizabeth answered, "I'm fine. Just coming from a brisk horseback ride and an even colder ride up here with the top down."

"You crazy girl! You haven't changed a bit. If Marie was around, she'd have a fit 'cause you're bound to catch a death of a cold." Realizing what he had said, he quickly added, "I'm sorry, Liz."

"That's okay. You don't have to apologize about teasing me. I've always loved it, and so did my mother." Elizabeth gave him a reassuring look and continued. "I want to thank you for opening up the house and making sure everything was working. It's been nice to stay there again."

"That's the least I could do. After all, you're family. Your parents were always so good to me and my own family, and I certainly can never repay them for the house and all the company provided."

"Come off it, Arnie. You were the reason the Tamarack ran so well. I used to hear Dad say that all the time."

"So what ya plan on doin' back home now that you're here?"

"Well, I've started to do some catching up, and I want to find out what the commotion is all about up here. I've even heard about the reopening of the Kearsarge back in Evanston. Tell me, has the copper come back here to stay?"

"You bet it has. In fact, there's a Chicago company goin' to open up the ol' Wolverine Mine. They've had a dozen guys out there already pumping the thing out and doin' some drillin.'"

"Oh really? From Chicago? What a coincidence. Know who they are?"

"No, but if ya wanna take a ride out there, we can find out. I heard Reverend Johnson is runnin' the show out there. Also heard they've found a lode that's as rich as any Calumet and Hecla used to mine up here. The reverend used to own the place. Remember him?"

"No, I don't, but I'd love to meet him."

This time, Elizabeth elected to leave the top up on the Mercedes. With Arnie's guidance, they drove past the gate at the Wolverine

Mine seven minutes later. Just as Arnie had said, there were several cars in the parking lot and some men loading ore into a dump truck from what appeared to be a fresh stockpile. She parked the car, and they got out and strolled in the direction of the loading operation.

"Reverend Johnson around?" Arnie shouted over the noise of the front-end loader. One of the men pointed to the building adjacent to the shaft house. "Thanks!" Arnie waved.

In the miner's dry stood a bearded man with a tattered jacket, obviously busy explaining the fine points of mining copper with his hands to another gentleman who was much cleaner and wearing a new set of coveralls.

"Hello, Reverend!" Arnie hailed as they approached.

The gruff-looking one turned, held his hand over his eyes, and finally asked, "Is that ol' Arnie Tyrronen I hear?"

"You betcha! How ya been, Reverend? Heard you're back in the mining business."

"Dat's right. Oh, by da way, Arnie, I'd like you to meet Pete Singer. He's a technical advisor for da owners of the mine. Arnie here's a former mine captain of da Tamarack Mine."

Arnie shook hands with Pete and, with a boyish look (if that's possible for a seventy-eight-year-old man) resulting from his forgetfulness, inserted, "Oh. Almost forgot. Please excuse me, Liz. This is Elizabeth MacIntyre. Her family owned the Tamarack. She's also a neighbor of yours down in Chicago."

Pete's gaze shifted to take in her beauty. "I normally don't get to meet a baroness in the business I'm in." The questioning expression on Elizabeth's face caused Pete to rephrase his initial comment. "Please excuse me. That came out wrong. What I meant to say was that it's unusual to find such a fine-looking lady in the mining business. That didn't work well either, did it? I guess I'd better shut up before I dig an even deeper hole, if you'll also excuse the bad pun."

Elizabeth was obviously amused with Pete's antics. "Apology accepted, Mr. Singer. Actually, I'm not in the mining business like my family used to be. We only have a small interest in a couple of gold operations out west; however, I'm very interested in what you're doing here and would like to be involved in a profitable copper mining operation again. I believe that would be in the best tradition of the MacIntyres."

"Oh really?" Pete said. "Then it must have been fate that brought you here."

"No, she brought me," Arnie interrupted with a roaring laugh that could mask even the loudest underground blast.

"Well, if you're Mr. Fate," Pete continued, "then you've done your job because we're ready to start development work and we're just finalizing our financing now. If you're serious about becoming an investor in this operation, I'm sure my bosses would like to talk to you, Mrs. MacIntyre."

"It's Miss MacIntyre, Mr. Singer, and I am serious. Tell them J. A. MacIntyre Inc. has investment capital available and would be interested in a controlling interest."

Pete's jaw practically dropped to the ninth level. He looked first at Gary, whose eyes showed disbelief at what had just transpired, and then at Arnie Tyrronen, who had the dumbest-looking smirk on his face. "As you wish, Miss MacIntrye. I'll phone them now and discuss the matter with them. Where can you be reached?"

"I'll be at our family home on Tamarack Street." She pulled a notebook out of her purse and wrote her phone number on a piece of paper, giving it to the astonished technical advisor. "I can be reached at this number tomorrow morning. It's been a pleasure meeting you, and I hope to work with you on this project. Reverend Johnson, I look forward to seeing you again too."

Arnie bid farewell to the reverend and Pete and joined Elizabeth, who was already halfway to her car. "Why didn't you tell me you were going to pull a stunt like that?"

"Why? Would you have done anything differently or not brought me here?"

"Of course not. It's just that I rarely get to see the reverend go into shock like that. Besides, you don't know nothin' about this mine."

"Not yet, but if what you heard is correct, then I'm about to make a very good investment. What do you think you can find out?"

"Well, I've heard some pretty impressive numbers from a couple of the guys who are doin' the drilling. You'd be best to get the information straight from the reverend and the guys who bought him out."

"Good advice. I'll do that. When I get it, will you help me out and tell me how good it really is?"

"My pleasure! Oh, this is goin' to be fun."

"More than that. We'll be back in the mining business in a big way. My father would've liked that."

"I'm sure of it. I think you will too!"

"I hope you're right, Arnie. I could use a few things to go well."

"It'll happen. This is your heritage, your destiny. Fate brought you here, remember?"

ॐ

"Mr. Thomas, you've got a call from Mr. Singer," said the voice over the intercom on Alan's desk. He picked up the receiver and pressed the button above the flashing red light. "What's up, Pete? Got the scouting report on Kearsarge yet?"

"No, but I've got something even better for you. The strangest thing happened to me this afternoon. You're not going to believe this."

"Try me," Jim shot back, getting impatient when what he thought was a pressing issue had been ignored.

"Just by chance, a young woman named Elizabeth MacIntyre strolled into the dry today as I was going over some things with Johnson. An old miner who used to work for her dad brought her there trying to find out what was happening. The next thing you know, she's offering to invest in the mine and asks for a controlling interest. Johnson tells me she's worth millions. How do you like that twist?"

There was silence on the other end of the phone as Jim pondered what he believed was more than mere coincidence or happenstance. Or was it?

CHAPTER 12

The unmistakable sound of the gunshot echoed across the water. Andy smiled as he lowered his rifle. "Perfect," he whispered to himself as he began to head down the hill to his target.

Not even taking a step, the ten-pointer had fallen right where he paused to look back, a bullet through the heart turning the new-fallen snow crimson. "I guess you are quite the marksman," said a voice from the bushes behind the quarry. Jack Sanders emerged with his hand extended. "Congratulations. Nice kill. I was trying to follow him but couldn't get a good shot from down here."

"Well then, thanks for chasing him my way," Andy said.

"I owed you one. Remember a few years ago hunting elk when we were working on getting that gold mine going? You spooked that six-by-six bull, so he trotted past me and then stopped to look at you. That was his last mistake. Now, let me get your picture with your trophy. This one's nice enough to go on the wall over the fireplace. Look at the spread on those antlers," Jack said as Andy picked up the deer's head by its antlers and posed for the shot.

"Yeah, I think it would look good in that cabin I just bought with my inheritance. Thanks, Mom," he said sarcastically.

Jack looked surprised. "I didn't know you bought a cabin."

"I had my eye on a hunting cabin up by Steamboat Springs. There's great elk and mule deer hunting up there. It will be a good place to spend hunting season with a few friends when I retire."

"You always were good at long-range planning."

"Good things come to those who wait." Andy smiled and nodded at the trophy buck. "Case in point."

"The last time we did this, it netted us some real nice stock options at North American Metals. I see you've got a nice little copper company in your sights this time."

"Yes, I do."

"Just like this deer. I'll leave it to the expert marksman to take his best shot."

"Supply me with what I need, and it'll happen."

"No problem. I'm looking forward to also retiring well."

CHAPTER 13

Pete was in the process of guzzling his third cup of coffee as he sat around the conference table with Jim and Alan. His flight back last night had gotten in very late.

"How long until the pilot work is complete?" Alan asked.

"If we're lucky, they'll have it done by Thanksgiving," Pete informed him. "I wouldn't count on it though. From what I've been able to gather, Johnson does good work, but he ain't too fast at it."

"You've noticed," Jim said, laughing. "We've had to really push this guy to get anything done on any kind of a schedule. If we're going to finish this and try to lock up the financing by Christmas, you may have to camp out at the mine."

"I was afraid of that. But it'll take someone more senior than me to keep Gary on track. In case you didn't notice, he doesn't take orders too well."

Jim was no longer laughing. "I did notice, and it looks like I might be joining you for a while."

"Great. We can go snowmobiling and Christmas shopping together."

Alan resumed his line of questioning. "What else have they accomplished with regard to dewatering and further exploration since Gary's last report?"

"They've got the water down to nine hundred fifty feet, and the eighth level can now be entered. Sanders has mapped out a plan for another forty core holes on seven, and I gave him the go-ahead to start drilling. The seam we mapped out on six extends down to seven, but it disappears at the third crosscut, where there may be a major fault line. Sanders hasn't punched enough holes to tell what happens there, but it may make mining a lot tougher on seven than on six if we want to be selective."

Jim was less worried about exploration and more worried about getting production started to have some cash flow to offset the costs they were incurring. "Have we ordered the equipment for the development work on six?"

"Not yet. I brought back a list of equipment for your approval. Gary hadn't thought that far ahead, so he and I spent most of the evening preparing the equipment list. I still have to get a few prices, but it looks like we can get one section up for 2.6 million dollars."

Jim changed the subject. "How about Kearsarge? Did you find out how much they're now producing and who they're selling to?"

"Sorry, boss. Ran out of time. After talking to Elizabeth MacIntyre, I wrapped things up with Gary and got my smiling face back here ASAP to fill you in on what had transpired."

Jim sat back and contemplated what he had been told over the last few minutes. "Looks to me like we're pretty much on track. I've called a half dozen potential customers, and I believe I can lock up a couple more contracts. If I can do that, it might mean expanding our original production schedule and putting in more capacity. So tell me about Ms. MacIntyre's offer."

"Don't go getting ahead of yourself, boss. We still don't have the money for our existing plans; however, this may be our saving grace because she's looking to invest in a copper mine but wants controlling interest. I told her I'd discuss it with you. She said to call her this morning."

Jim turned to his partner. "Well, Alan, how do we field this one? We've been turned down by an investment bank, but all of a sudden we have a private investor willing to get into bed with us. Do we play hard to get?"

Alan was still smarting from the rejection by Continental Bank and his demotion from the lead on this project. "I guess the first thing we do is see if she's interested in something less than 50 percent of the outstanding shares. If not, we find out how much she's willing to pay to run the show. It might be enough that you won't have to think twice to take the money and run. Isn't that what you want? Financial freedom and not having to worry about a thing?"

Jim was astounded. "That's a pretty drastic tact, isn't it? Besides, how do we value what a controlling interest is worth?"

Alan was beginning to lose his temper. It seemed Jim was questioning him at every turn. "You call yourself a venture capitalist and yet ask me how to pin a value on this asset! Why do you think we spent so much money on reserve estimation? What about the copper and silver sitting in the ground that we've quantified as minable reserves using all those fancy geostatistics programs?"

"Don't get all bent out of shape, my friend. I was simply pointing out that this is a venture still in the embryonic stages of development, it hasn't produced a single ton of ore other than a test sample, and now you believe we can sell it for a profit to some millionaire's kid who comes out of the blue wanting a romantic adventure in a copper boomtown?"

"Yeah, that sums it up pretty accurately. Why not?"

Alan had won this one. Jim found himself at a loss to answer the last question posed to him. There was no reason they shouldn't sell out now if they could make a profit doing so. All that remained was to map out an approach and make the phone call.

A few minutes later, Jim picked up the phone and dialed the number Pete had given him.

"Good morning, Miss MacIntyre," Jim began. "My name is Jim Thomas, and I'm the president of Wolverine Ventures Inc. With me in our conference room is Alan Larsson, executive vice president, and Pete Singer, one of our technical advisors, whom you've met."

"Good morning, gentlemen."

"I understand from Pete that you're interested in our operation at the Wolverine Mine."

"Yes, I'm sure Mr. Singer relayed the extent of my interest. The question is, are you interested in my offer?"

"We most certainly are and would be willing to entertain another investor in this project."

"Surely Mr. Singer must have told you that I am not interested in a passive investment; I'd like a controlling interest."

"He did tell us that, Miss MacIntyre; however, you should know that Wolverine Ventures currently owns 100 percent of the operation and looks to manage this particular investment."

"Do you have all the capital you require to own and operate, including working capital?"

"We're, ah, working on that."

"If you're interested in managing this operation, I'm interested in owning it and leaving you a large enough piece for you to keep it very interesting."

Alan didn't hesitate. "We're interested. What information do you have on the mine?"

"Only what I picked up during my visit this week."

"I'll e-mail a confidentiality agreement to you now. Once signed, I will arrange for Gary Johnson to drop off copies of the reserve estimate and mining plan as we have it so far. Are you available to meet on Monday if Jim and I fly up that morning?"

"Sure. That'll give me the weekend to go over the plans."

"We're looking forward to meeting you. Please make whatever arrangements are convenient for you with Gary. He'll take care of everything."

Jim sat in silence after Alan hung up the phone. By the way Alan took over the conversation, it was apparent that he was not going to relinquish control of this project easily.

CHAPTER 14

Monday's itinerary had been arranged by Gary. Jim and Alan's flight was due in at noon, and he had made lunch reservations at the Hut in Kearsarge. He found them waiting outside the airport and braving the snow flurries that had been coming down since early that morning.

As the '66 GTO approached, they picked up their bags and hurried over to the curb where Gary had parked. Gary hopped out, grabbed the bags, and threw them in the trunk. Being the senior partner, Jim chose the front seat, where he could warm his hands over the defroster.

"You didn't pick a very good morning to be late," Jim scolded. "It's mighty brisk out there. Our pumping operation freezing up yet?"

"No. The water coming out of the mine is at a constant ten degrees centigrade. No way dat will ever cause freezing problems. Der hasn't even been any ice on the pond. Besides, with the quantities we're pumping, there's little chance that the water in the pond is stagnant enough to form a good layer of ice. We'll have a good skating rink out there for ya once we slow down though."

"You mean a good ice rink for Elizabeth MacIntyre," Alan said.

"Ya really going to sell out to her?" As the original owner of the property, Gary was visibly upset. He had his own vision for what the Wolverine Mine would become, and he had no idea what would happen now.

Jim tried to reassure Gary. "No, not sell out, but we may agree to her having majority ownership if we can work out an amicable management agreement and the price is right."

"What about my options? If she gains the controlling interest she wants, then she is calling the shots."

Jim knew he needed to win over Gary to make this deal work. "Don't worry, your stock options will be part of any deal. You know they're written into the security holder's agreement. Furthermore, it is not my intent to sell out. I plan to see this project through start-up to the production goals we've talked about."

"Just checking."

Jim paused and looked out the window at the evergreens getting their first deposit of snow to trim their branches, making a perfect setting for a postcard. Upon resuming the conversation, he changed the subject. "So tell me what you know about Elizabeth MacIntyre. You were at her house Friday night. What's she like?"

"Elizabeth MacIntyre is the only great-granddaughter of James A. MacIntyre, who was one of da original investors in the Tamarack Mine. From da time it opened in 1885, the Tamarack produced ten to fifteen million pounds of copper per year. It was also the deepest mine in the world in its day. When James Sr. died in 1924, James Jr., her grandfather, ran the business until 1959. When he retired, her father, James III, ran the show until it and all the other mines up 'ere closed in the late sixties. They stayed hoping for a return of da King Copper days, but after her dad died in the late eighties, she and her mom moved to Evanston, Illinois, where she lived with her mother until she went to college in the Chicago area. Her mother moved back up here then. This past summer, Marie died, and Elizabeth became sole heir to the family fortune. James Sr. made their initial millions on dividends paid by the Tamarack, but I understand the family's real money was made on investment income in a few closely held companies. If she wants to buy a majority of the shares in da Wolverine, I'm sure she can afford it. What I don't understand is why you'd want ta sell after you insisted on 100 percent ownership when you bought it from me."

Gary had a legitimate argument and was about to get his first hard lesson concerning venture capital. Jim began slowly. "When we bought the property from you some fifteen months ago, it was nothing more than an old mine with a great degree of potential. Even this was pure speculation since it was based on old mining records, the accuracy of which was questionable. Now, after having pumped over a million dollars into this thing, you've been proven correct in your original assessment. Our intent has always been to develop and operate the mine, particularly since we may be able to sign an excellent long-term contract within the next month; however, we are venture capitalists, and that means that we are always looking for the winning investment with a good return. Normally, we'll stay in an investment for at least three to five years and then look for a way to either sell out at some multiple of the original investment or get our money back out and maintain some equity ownership. Normally, we don't own 100 percent of the company as we do in this case."

Alan jumped in. "The reason I want to seriously consider any offer is that this could be the largest moneymaker in the history of Wolverine Ventures. If we can get our money back out after fifteen months, use someone else's money for the largest upfront capital investment required for a mining operation, and still manage the project and at least share in the profits, then it's a good deal for everyone involved. We've assumed all the risk at this point, and we're ready to unload even a majority of the company for a guaranteed return and a shot at an even larger operation and greater cash flow and profit potential than we or you have ever imagined."

They were now in the parking lot of the Hut, and Gary was beginning to wonder whether or not he had done the right thing by getting involved with Wolverine Ventures. He wasn't all that interested in quick paybacks. He had sold the property to them because it was a chance to get back into operations in the Keweenaw Peninsula.

Another mining company up here meant much-needed jobs and a chance to do something worthwhile for the region. Obviously, his goals were long term and theirs shorter term than he'd been led to believe. Oh well, he'd listen to what was going to be said over lunch, and then he'd decide if he'd been shafted or not.

Jim, Alan and Gary walked up to the hostess and inquired if the rest of their party had arrived. "Yes, they have. Please follow me."

Through a wooden arch and past a waterfall was a table with an attractive young lady and two gentlemen seated at it. One was an old man well into retirement; the other was a fortyish-looking businessman with an expensive suit. Gary stepped forward to make the introductions. "Elizabeth MacIntyre, I'd like ya to meet Jim Thomas, president of Wolverine Ventures, and Alan Larsson, executive vice president. Youse guys, this is Arnie Tyrronen, who brought Elizabeth out to da mine last week."

As the handshaking ritual rotated around to the other gentleman at the table, Elizabeth interjected, "And this is Phillip Turner, president of James A. MacIntyre Inc."

With the preliminaries now over, they sat down to order lunch and to get down to the nitty-gritty. At first Jim was a bit taken aback by Elizabeth's natural beauty and charm as well as the fact that she had brought reinforcements to the business lunch. He chided himself for losing his focus and for not anticipating her being prepared and ready to bring some outside help into the negotiations. No doubt this woman was full of surprises.

When they had ordered, Elizabeth wasted no time to get on the offensive. "I spent the weekend reviewing the information you provided to me Friday. I also took the liberty to ask Arnie to dig up some historical information on the mine. Meanwhile, Phillip and I have been over our financial status, and we are prepared to make a substantial investment in this property, but first, we have a few questions."

"That's why we flew up as soon as possible," Jim said.

"Good. First of all, who is the customer that will purchase fifty million pounds at one dollar and fifty cents per pound?"

"Chicago Wire. Are you familiar with them?"

"Yes, we are," Phillip replied. "They are a reputable firm and have become one of the largest suppliers of copper wire in the world."

"Very true," Jim added. "Then you can understand why we are pursuing this venture and trying to get the mine online by next summer. The contract must be signed by the end of this year, and we must make our first shipment by July first. So as you can see, this single contract provides the justification for the entire project, but the timing is such that we must not waste a day. If we are not able to meet their requirements, they will look to Kearsarge, who just doubled their capacity and could supply at least half of the fifty million tons per year with what they currently have uncommitted and are selling on the spot market."

Arnie held up his hand to stop Jim and ask, "Why wouldn't they just go to Kearsarge?"

Jim smiled because Arnie played right into his presentation. "With the volatility in the copper market these days and Kearsarge getting a high price for their copper, they couldn't lock in the quantity at the price they want from them. Kearsarge has a much lower grade of ore than what we've found in the Wolverine Mine, and they couldn't afford to commit such a large percentage of their production to a fixed price. If we mine even half the grade that the geologist's reports Gary brought you show, then we can undercut anything Kearsarge can do because our costs per pound of copper recovered will still be 30 or 40 percent less than theirs."

Once again stopping Jim, Arnie was the one asking the tough questions for which there were no solid answers. "How sure are you that you can mine seventy-five pounds per ton ore? When the mine operated twenty-five to thirty years ago, the best they were pulling out was half of that, and they averaged twenty-four." Before Jim could even answer, Arnie continued, "I know you've identified a new seam, but I'm only aware of one or maybe two other operations on the range that were ever even close to these kinds of numbers consistently."

"I knew you were going to ask me that." Jim was tiring of Arnie's line of questioning and thought it better to bring Arnie's counterpart into the conversation. "I'd better let Gary field that one."

Gary began, "Old-timers like us remember the day when ya mined a vein by following it, taking the occasional channel sample across da face to check what ya already suspected. I know ya can still look at a sample and give me a pretty good guestimate of the copper content."

"Yer givin' me too much credit," Arnie said.

"We'll see. Anyway, there's dese new mathematical methods for estimating reserve grades on hard to quantify ores like native copper and gold because it occurs as nuggets or mass copper in basalt fissures and is unpredictable. Developed for gold and diamond mining in South Africa, it's called geostatistics. My geologist, Jack Sanders, and his young whippersnapper number cruncher have used dis method to allow Wolverine to be far more selective in da mining process and plan production to avoid large swings in grade due to the inherent variability of da native copper conglomerate. We can pinpoint where dese high concentrations of copper are most likely to occur. Without such tools, you are just guessing. Dis was the reason so many mines failed one hundred years ago despite the fact that rich pockets of ore remained in close proximity ta where they had been mining and coming up empty-handed. Dis was also the reason why such a rich vein had gone undiscovered at the Wolverine Mine."

When they had finished lunch, Jim ordered a round of coffee and tea to be served with apple pie for dessert. Then he began to outline the deal. "You've had a chance to go over our reserve estimates, mine and mill designs, and our cost/benefit analysis. I know you probably have a few more questions, and I'll answer them as I go along." He was determined to get back on the offensive. "This afternoon, I'd planned to take you over to the mine to meet with Jack Sanders, who has the reserve estimate for seventh level ready. As you may know, we have just recently begun a core-sampling program on the eighth level. All our data is based on the sixth level alone. If we operate at our design capacity, we will exhaust the known reserves on six in a little over three years. Chicago Wire has committed to at least one-third of the annual production, and I'm working on signing up one or two more customers in the near future."

"Who are you talking to?" Phillip asked.

"I won't give you my whole list of leads at the moment, but I can tell you we have opened discussion with Ford Motor Company and one of their major suppliers of electric motors for their new hybrid cars. Alan can tell you a whole lot more about this."

"So Alan, you're looking to sell copper to a car manufacturer?" Elizabeth asked.

"Well, not exactly, although that would not be so unusual. You see, Ford has owned mineral holdings in the Upper Peninsula of Michigan for years. In fact, their River Rouge plant has its own steel mill and takes in iron ore pellets at one end of the plant and produces cars out the other end."

"But why would Ford want to contract directly with us?"

"Because we have a high-grade deposit of copper and silver occurring together in such quantities that the resulting alloy off the smelter can be used to create highly conductive windings for electric motors. Silver has the highest conductivity of any metal, copper is second, and the combination can improve motor efficiency significantly. This, in turn, means the car can go farther on a charge-saving, critical battery life. In the new plug-in electric or pure electric cars, this efficiency is even more important because it will extend the range the car can run on electric power alone by at least 15 percent. That's a significant improvement."

At this point Jim picked up the conversation to present and negotiate the deal. "Timing is everything! Should we be online next summer, I don't think sales will be a problem. Besides, all our costs are covered by this one contract alone. Therefore, I would look to James A. MacIntyre Inc. to supply additional monies for working capital and possible expansion should our marketing efforts prove successful. I would be prepared to offer you a fifty-fifty partnership for fifty million dollars, which will fund operations from this point forward, with at least one-half up front in cash."

Jim had done his part well. Elizabeth stole a glance at Phillip, looking for any sign of support to counter within the limits they had discussed earlier. "I did request majority ownership, and I recognize that you are proposing a compromise that may be workable, but before we go any further, there are a couple of things you should know. First, your estimate of how much money it would take to get up to your design capacity of ten thousand tons per day is low. We believe you'll need at least thirty million dollars in the mine and another thirty million dollars in the plant and surface facilities. You should also be prepared to invest at least ten million dollars into working capital. Secondly, if we enter into a partnership, we would expect Wolverine Ventures to match dollar for dollar anything we put into operation after we've paid you for half the existing net asset value. Our preference is to fund the entire operation from this point on and give you an equity position with a management agreement that places Gary Johnson in charge of the operation."

Having expected as much, Jim was prepared with his response. "We'll have nearly four million dollars into it once the first mining section is up and running early next year. The only reason our costs have been this low is that Gary agreed to sell the mine to us at a very attractive price in return for stock options. If you want to own this operation, then I suggest an eighty-twenty split with one-fourth of our shares assigned to Gary. James A. MacIntyre Inc. then pays a price of sixteen million dollars now to Wolverine Ventures for 80 percent of what we know to be at least nine hundred million dollars worth of reserves with a guaranteed revenue stream of 375 million dollars over five years from Chicago Wire alone. You pay eighty million to bring this operation online. I'll continue to do the marketing, but I want two seats on the board of directors and veto powers in all matters concerning ownership of the company. Is this acceptable?"

This time, Elizabeth took a couple minutes to think it over, jotted some numbers down on a piece of paper, and passed it to Phillip. He nodded, and she replied, "You have a deal in principle."

"Very good. I'll have my attorney draft an agreement when I get back."

Nobody could have been more pleased to hear those words than Gary or Arnie, whose pasts and now futures would be closely linked to the copper mining heritage of the area.

CHAPTER 15

"Welcome to the Wolverine," Jack said, greeting them as they stepped off the cage on the seventh level. *Quite an unusual crew to have underground,* he thought as he ushered them into the boss's shack. Even decked out in coveralls, hardhat, and other ancillary mining paraphernalia, Elizabeth was still an attention-getter.

Gary made the introductions. "Jack Sanders, dis is Elizabeth MacIntyre, da new majority owner of the Wolverine, Phillip Turner, who runs da show for her in Chicago, and Arnie Tyrronen, former mine captain of the Tamarack, servin' as their technical advisor."

Arnie snarled. "We've already met."

Jack diverted his attention to Elizabeth and Phillip. "Pleased to meet you."

Without waiting for any further pleasantries or snarls, Gary completed the roster of visitors. "You already know Jim and Alan."

"Yes. Alan, you're looking a whole lot better since the last time I saw you." Jack did note that Alan was walking with a noticeable limp and he was actually much smaller than he looked propped up in a hospital bed.

"Thanks, I'm doing better since I swore off deer hunting."

Those not privy to Alan's hospital stay last month gave him a puzzled look.

"That's too bad," Jack said. "I was out hunting this past weekend. My buddy got a trophy ten-pointer, but I came up empty-handed except to share a couple of fresh tenderloin steaks with mashed potatoes, gravy, and gooseberry trimmings."

"Doesn't sound too bad to me. Better than getting speared by a branch," Alan said.

"Hate ta interrupt yer huntin' stories," Gary said, "but let's get started. Over here is da boss's shack. Da foremen would come down on da first cage and prepare assignments for each crew of men, which were handed out from the window of the shack as they got off from the second and third cage down. They would then head off in different directions along the haulage ways to their assigned raise or drift. With dat, I'll let Jack go over the new reserve estimate for the seventh level."

The group turned to Jack, only to find him staring at Elizabeth. Trying to make light of an embarrassing moment, Jack quipped, "You put me to sleep with one of your sermons again, Reverend. Sorry about that. Guess I'll have to go to confession this week."

"Wrong church," Gary said. "However, I will take ya up on coming to church with me this Sunday."

Did it again, ol' boy, Jack admonished himself, cringing at the thought of going to church with the reverend. He decided it was time to get on with it. "The map I've laid on the table shows the plan view of the seventh level and identifies the thirty boreholes we've taken and had analyzed. The contours on the map are isobars that indicate the grade of the ore. As you can see, the new vein, which we will mine on six, extends down to seven and splits at the number three crosscut, where there is a major fault in the ore body. On this side of the fault, the average grade of the minable reserve is the same as on six, approximately seventy pounds per ton. On the other side, the vein becomes more disseminated, and the grade drops considerably to about forty pounds per ton, still high grade, just not exceptional. The good news is that there's more of it; the bad news is that the fault will prove to be very problematic. Roof support will be crucial, and it will be expensive. It can be done, but it will increase mining costs 20 percent."

"What is the reserve estimate for the seventh level?" Gary asked.

"We've got about two million tons of seventy pounds per ton ore and nine million tons of forty pounds per ton ore."

"How many more levels do you think still have these kinds of reserves left?" Elizabeth inquired.

"I think we can still recover considerable quantities from eight and nine, but I'm bettin' we've seen the best of it here at six and seven. Everything above six has been well mined out. The one question is, what's below nine?"

It was Gary's turn to make a sales pitch. He'd been holding back all day. "Regardless of what's below us, dat makes a grand total of over a billion pounds of recoverable copper."

Jack resumed his presentation. "If there are no more questions, I'd like to take you over to the number three crosscut and show you a solid wall of copper where the fault is. We blasted away a short twenty-foot section into the side of the crosscut, and there it was. The old miners were right on top of a body of mass copper they didn't even know about, and even if they did, they wouldn't have gotten it out of here seventy years ago when they mined this level."

The tour party trudged down the north-south haulage way toward the number three crosscut. The sound of mining boots displacing the mud between the tracks as they stepped in the soft spots and the sound of the air rushing in to replace the void as their boots separated from the mud made sort of a cadence that echoed in the tunnel. Elizabeth tried walking one of the rails, but the oversize mining boots robbed her of any agility she might have displayed without them. When she slipped on the mud, she felt a pair of arms close around her chest as she fell into Jim, who had been walking alongside her.

"Oops, I'm sorry. I can never resist a balance beam. Must go back to all those years I spent training in gymnastics. My mother always thought I'd be an Olympian. She was severely disappointed when she discovered my two left feet."

Jim laughed and set her down gently next to him. "The last time I had someone as pretty as you fall into my arms was during my football days at the University of Michigan. One of the cheerleaders was doing backflips off the brick wall that runs around the stadium and needed a little assistance. I gave her some. I married her."

This time they both laughed, but Elizabeth was a little uneasy at the mention of his wife.

Jim noticed her reaction and thought, *She's trying to flirt with me.* "I guess the only thing standing between you and the gold was a little sliver of wood."

She gave him a big smile. "Well, Mr. Thomas, this time we're going to turn copper with a little sliver of silver into gold."

"As they say up here, you betchya." Jim stopped and looked straight ahead. Her eyes followed his. Simultaneously, they gasped.

The number three crosscut was not what any of them had expected. Despite the fact that the group contained members who knew nothing about mining and experienced veterans, they were all taken aback by a solid wall of native copper that appeared as though it had been sheared off. The surface was relatively smooth, with striations that ran parallel across the face all at the same angle. It was as though an earthquake long ago had cut off this rich vein and then buried it for them to find.

"What do you think?" Jack asked.

"This is unbelievable!" exclaimed an astonished Arnie. "Never in all my days underground did I come across a formation like this. I mean, I've seen faults before, but never one where mass copper had just been cut clean and moved elsewhere. What do ya make of it, Jack?"

"Not too sure yet. Many of the faults in these mines were caused by settling land formations that shifted on weak fissures in the brittle basalt so prominent in this area. This one looks like a tremendous force just shifted a whole mountain range. It certainly was not glacier activity. Maybe a quake. The whole character of the strata changes on the other side of this fault. It's as though a whole other piece of the earth was moved in to replace this one. Looks stable, but we won't know until we finish our compression testing."

"Does that mean it's unsafe to mine?" Phillip asked.

"No, it just means that we'll have to be careful," Gary replied.

"Well, I can't wait until we're loading this stuff into ore cars," Jim said. "When it comes out the other side of the smelter is when it'll look best."

CHAPTER 16

The MacIntyre estate was neatly tucked between two rather innocuous houses and nestled behind a row of maple trees that towered over Tamarack Street to form an arch with the neighboring trees across the street. When the house was built by James Sr. in 1886, it was the largest residence in Laurium.

Jim followed Elizabeth up the walk to the enormous front door, which was framed in sandstone, as were the windows and foundations of this brick structure. The entry was tiled in white, and the chandeliers in the front hallway were simply breathtaking.

"Let me take your coat." Elizabeth directed her comments to the ceiling so that she might catch his attention.

"Oh, excuse me. I was just admiring the lights and the marvelous work lining the ceiling in this hall."

"Come on. I'll give you a tour of the rest of the house if you'd like."

"Yes, I'd like to see it."

After wandering through fifteen rooms on three floors, they came to the ballroom on the top floor. A large room with hardwood flooring and stained glass lights around the perimeter, it was often the site of many a party during the turn of the century.

"This is wonderful," Jim said. "Do you ever use this room anymore?"

"Not much since my grandfather entertained here. It was updated twenty years ago with a sound system. Small orchestras were harder and harder to come by. Let me show you."

She walked over to one corner and placed a disk in the CD player. Over the four speakers mounted in the corners of the room came the charade waltz.

"Do you know how to waltz?" she asked. "My mother made me take ballroom dancing classes, but I never found any partners who really could dance well."

"I don't know how well I dance, but I can manage to get across the floor with the right steps. Shall we?"

He took her hand and placed his arm around her small waist. She moved effortlessly across the floor, and he marveled at her graceful moves. Certainly this was a remarkable woman.

Elizabeth broke the silence. "I hope you don't think I'm too forward. This seemed like a lovely way to conclude the house tour. In fact, it seemed like a good way to close a good deal. If you'd like, I've got a twenty-five-year-old bottle of black plum port in the wine cellar, which I've wanted to open since I've been back up here, but I haven't had anyone over to share it with. We can toast our success, and I can give you the banking information you'll need to effect a money transfer for the purchase. That will be a fine way to consummate the deal."

By this point, Jim was no longer thinking of the deal. He was preoccupied with the smell of her perfume and the light scent of her shampoo that lingered on her soft blonde hair.

Downstairs, in the front parlor, Elizabeth placed a pile of papers on the coffee table in front of Jim. "Take a look at these while I get the port."

When she returned, Jim remarked, "You've got a fine-looking company with an impressive array of diversified investments. I think the Wolverine Mining Company will make an excellent addition."

"So do I." Elizabeth beamed. "Everything you need to verify our financial status is in the package. Now to more important matters."

She handed the bottle and two cordials to Jim. "My dad brought this back from a business trip before he died. He had made a couple of investments in west Australia that have since paid off well. Hopefully, this will do the same. To the beginning of a long and fruitful relationship."

She raised her glass to meet his and savored the first sip and the moment. Jim looked over the top of his glass and saw her sitting there with her eyes closed and a look of contentment across her face. He was tempted to kiss her but instead asked, "What are you thinking about?"

Opening her eyes, she gave him a warm smile and said, "I just can't believe how quickly and how well the whole deal came together. The MacIntyres are back in the mining business in the Copper Country. Dad would be pleased. I know I am, and I'm looking forward to building our relationship."

Jim found himself mesmerized by her blue eyes, which matched the blue diamonds in her earrings and necklace perfectly. This girl could be on the cover of *Glamour* magazine. Not knowing whether she was talking about business or something more personal, Jim decided he should be leaving before something happened that he might regret. With an eighty-million-dollar cash infusion, he had everything he needed to go forward with the mine and plant development. Continental Bank had turned down his request for fifty million, and a couple of weeks later, he had an angel investor put in one and a half times as much money. It cost him 80 percent of Wolverine Mining, but now there was more than enough money to get the operation up and running, even on such a tight schedule. His share should return a handsome profit, and his risk was minimized. Of course, Elizabeth MacIntyre stood to gain four times as much. Maybe she really was more like a shark than an angel.

Standing up, Jim said, "I should be going. I need to prepare for my meeting with Kearsarge Mining tomorrow morning."

A pouty look came across her face. She gently patted his arm. "I understand. Please stop by tomorrow and let me know what happened."

CHAPTER 17

Gary met with Jack in the old mine captain's office. Jack had pulled up a chair to Gary's desk, and he proceeded to unwrap the package of baked goods he had brought along.

"Dese look mighty good," Gary observed. "Thanks for bringing in breakfast."

"No problem. Usually by this time of the morning, I'm eatin' dust from the drills. This sure beats a mornin's dose of heavy metals."

"Whadaya think of the deal an' the new owner?"

"I think they both look good." Jack leaned back and roared at his own joke, almost losing the doughnut he was chewing on at the same time.

"Yep, ya sure took a hard look at both of 'em yesterday. But I have to admit, it turned out a lot better than I thought it would."

"So what's this do to our agenda around here?"

"Looks like it'll speed things up. I've already got some equipment on order for the start-up of the first section. I need you to get movin' on eight so we can have a decent reserve estimate done by Christmas. I'll have development started after New Year's."

"How many more men you going to give me? For that order, I'll need another crew and another drill."

"You got it. Just make sure I've got da numbers da week before Christmas."

Jack feigned cleaning his ears. "I'm sorry, Gary; you know, they say your hearing is the second thing to go. Did you tell me to hire a second crew after all the complaining you did about the overtime we put in last month?"

"Don't piss me off and make me change my mind or say something I shouldn't. We need more people to make dis happen, not more time an' a half." Gary was feeling the strain of now having to make things happen all of a sudden. In the past, he had the luxury of complaining about not having the money to bring production on schedule. Now there was money, and the pressure was on him to deliver.

"I guess this means we've got some serious money coming in."

"Ya only need to worry about how serious this deadline is. Git me da estimates I need when I need 'em an' I'll git ya da crew an' drill ya need. Now git outta here."

Jack stood up and grinned. "I'm real serious about making things happen. I'm not one to leave things up to fate. Count on it!"

CHAPTER 18

"Mr. Thomas is here to see you, Mr. Grossman," the Kearsarge chief's personal secretary announced. She hung up the phone. "Right this way."

Robert Grossman's office occupied the northwest corner of the five-story modern office building that Kearsarge Mining had erected on the north end of Calumet. Sitting on a hilltop, the view was one of the best in the area. It overlooked the Calumet dam, built during the first mining boom, and beyond that, Lake Superior. The Kearsarge shafts and the mill buildings could be seen in the distance.

"Please have a seat." Grossman motioned to the corner of the office, where a small conference table and chairs were. As Jim took a seat facing the west windows, Grossman took the seat opposite him. The conference room was adorned with photos of old and new mining equipment working underground at Kearsarge. One wall displayed a sign that read "Our Past" and the other wall "Our Future." Grossman extended a slender hand for a handshake. He was a businessman with an MBA from the Wharton School of Business hanging on the wall.

"Some view."

"I've heard a lot about your acquisition of the Wolverine Mine," Grossman began, not responding to Jim's small talk. "Sounds like you've hit upon one of the best lodes in the Copper Country."

"So far it appears to be a rich vein. We're planning to be in operation next summer."

"That's fast! How much are you mining, and where's it going?"

Grossman's bluntness caught Jim unprepared. He should have expected these kinds of questions. "We'll be opening at ten thousand tons per day, and I can't disclose my customer just yet."

"What can I do for you besides compete for sales?"

"We don't mind a little competition. Besides, I understand there'll be two smaller mines going just down the road next year."

"That's true. One's slated for two thousand tons per day, the other five thousand."

"If you don't mind me saying so, none of the local competition has me concerned. What bothers me are the western producers. With the pending strike in Chile and futures on the rise again, now would be a good time for us to grab market share if we can fill the orders. I've been shaking the bushes and have come across some large potential orders. We can't produce enough copper quickly enough to meet what may be a large backlog, but together, we could probably do so and get an excellent price locked in the process."

Such remarks earned him a long look. Grossman scratched his chin before responding. "I like the way you think, Mr. Thomas."

"Call me Jim, please. We've got the ideal situation to go after those guys. You've got a tremendous quantity of known reserves; ours are limited. You can meet a production quota with your expanded capacity; we can produce a specialty silver and copper alloy by high grading our reserves. Between the two of us, we're as big as any of those guys out west, but we can produce more than one product. They may be able to produce molybdenum as a side product, but our high-conductivity alloy will sell well to the up-and-coming hybrid and electric car market. If we wanted to expand in the near term, we could do that without too much difficulty. As a force in the market, we'd be hard to beat."

"Call me Bob, and I think you've got yourself a deal. I would be willing to go after any of those orders in partnership with you, and I've got one here in our backyard you may be interested in."

"Excellent!" Jim stood up to shake Bob's hand to consummate his second deal in as many days. He would work out the details at a later date. The meeting culminated what had been an eventful two days. The stage was now set for bringing his plans to fruition. His actions on this trip would transform Calumet. Conversely, Calumet would also change Jim Thomas.

CHAPTER 19

The doorbell had taken Elizabeth away from her favorite pastime: reading. This time, it was not a mystery; rather, it was the feasibility study on the copper city mine Jim had left her.

She opened the door to a pleasant surprise. "Why, Tina, it's good to see you again. Come in."

"I was running some errands today and thought I'd stop by to see how you're doing."

"I'm glad you did. You got time for a cup of tea? I'll put some on. It'll only take a minute."

Tina glanced at her watch. "Sure, I've got time. I need to be home by three thirty. That's when Eric gets home. He got the job at the Wolverine Mine. Thanks for putting in a good word for him with Jack Sanders to get him the offer."

"Thanks for your help in getting me the lowdown on the Wolverine and Kearsarge. Tell me, are you still concerned about the hazards underground?"

"Yeah, it still bothers me. But I'm learning to live with it. The pay is very good, and Eric seems to like what he will be doing."

"Good. I think a guy like Eric could have a real future there." Elizabeth stopped to hang up Tina's coat in the hall closet and motioned for her to follow to the kitchen. "I'm glad you came. I was thinking of calling you to ask if we could get together, and here you are."

"How are things with you, Liz?"

"Well, it's a bit lonely not knowing too many people up here. However, the owner of the venture capital firm that we're now in business with is at least as good of a find as the high-grade ore at Wolverine. He lives in the Chicago area, and last night, I found out we've got a lot in common."

Tina was beginning to get interested. "How so?"

"He dropped off some papers at the house last night, and I invited him in for a toast. His name is Jim Thomas and we hit it off well."

"How well?" asked Tina.

Liz put her hands on her hips. "Not as well as you're thinking." After taking Tina through most of the details, the doorbell rang once again. "That's probably Jim now. He said he'd stop by after he was done with his meeting today. Come on, I'd like you to meet him."

Elizabeth opened the front door to a blast of cold air and even a more numbing surprise. "Why, Andy, what are you doing here?"

"Is that any way to welcome your brother?" he asked as he let himself in. "I was just thinking about Mom this morning and decided right then and there that I'd jump on the next plane and come over to see you. Good thing I called ahead. Shirley, at your office in Chicago, finally told me where you were. I told her it was a family emergency. In a way, I guess it is. I came here to bury the hatchet, sis. If the ground out there's not too frozen—whadaya say?"

Elizabeth turned to Tina. "Andy, you remember Tina, don't you?"

"Sure I do. How are you?"

"I'm fine." Tina tried to cover up a scowl. "You haven't changed much in twenty years."

"Not too much, but I'm taking after my dad. Getting a little thin on top. Hats are now a must in this weather."

Just as they were settling in the front parlor, another car pulled up. Relieved, Elizabeth went to the door to let Jim in.

"Hi, come in. How did your meeting go?"

"Really well. I was able to strike a deal with Kearsarge where we would jointly go after sales and increase our planned production."

Elizabeth took Jim's coat, and as they walked toward the coat closet, he realized they were not alone. "Let me make some introductions," Elizabeth said. "This is my good friend, Tina Kramer. And this is my brother, Andy." Motioning to Jim, she added, "This is Jim Thomas, president of Wolverine Ventures."

"Pleased to know you," Jim said politely as he shook Andy's hand and then extended his hand to Tina.

Tina, sensing that this would be a good time to depart, said, "I should be going. Eric will be home in a while."

"What about the tea?" Elizabeth did not want to be left alone with her estranged brother and new business partner.

"I'll take a rain check." Tina grabbed her coat from the closet and headed out the door, leaving Elizabeth standing in the room not believing what had just happened.

Andy broke the awkward silence by asking, "What did I hear you say about Kearsarge? You and Liz are going into business together with them? Someone on the way up told me that they had really started moving copper back up here again."

Jim wasn't sure how much he should disclose, so he glanced at Elizabeth for a little guidance. Her cross look told him that he should be careful. Unfortunately, Andy caught the look as well.

"We've gone into the copper mining business together at the Wolverine Mine. Your family business owns a majority interest, and I'm acting on the marketing side to line up initial contracts. It looks like we may be able to partner with Kearsarge, which is much better than cutting each other's throat."

Satisfied that he had gotten as much information as he was going to get, Andy replied, "That's very interesting. You see, I haven't been involved in the family business for years, but the purpose of my visit back here is to change all that."

That remark earned him a sharp glare from Elizabeth. She found herself in a difficult situation. How do you tactfully slit your brother's throat and tear off his head with somebody you are trying to impress with your warmth watching? If this was going to persist, she'd have to find a way.

Changing the subject, she asked, "When were you planning on taking off tonight?"

Jim was puzzled by the question at first; then he understood. "I can leave anytime I want to. I've got the corporate plane standing by. Why don't we grab a bite to eat first?"

"That would be nice. Andy, would you excuse us for a bit? I've got some things I'd like to run over with Jim before he leaves. If you don't mind, I can get you a room over at the Michigan House. It's been a long time, and I think we ought to start slow."

His temper almost got the best of him, but after thinking about it for a moment, Andy decided to cool down and accept his sister's suggestion. After all, a sweet attitude was going to be necessary here. "No problem. You probably don't have any beer in the refrigerator anyway. What time you want to meet me there?"

"About nine o'clock."

"Fine, see you then."

Jim knew he wouldn't have to ask what that was all about because as soon as they got in the car, Elizabeth proceeded to vent her anger at her brother. "You know what he's doing here, right?"

Not wanting to even speculate, Jim nodded.

"He knows about this deal. Why show up now as though this is a peace-making mission? He even filed a lawsuit contesting my mother's will but was later convinced he couldn't win and dropped it."

"Hear him out. You're going to meet him later. It won't cost you anything but time to listen. Then you can decide if he is trying to pull another fast one. You might even be able to throw him a bone and make him happy enough to stay out of the way."

"You know, he just walked out over twenty years ago, and we hardly ever heard from him. That devastated my mother."

"What about your father?"

"They had a rough relationship. He never wanted to do what my dad wanted him to do, so they would clash all the time."

"Let me guess. You, on the other hand, were Daddy's good little girl."

"Of course. Compliance is a lot easier than rebellion."

"I need to think about that one for a while," Jim said. He had pegged Andy as a troublemaker from the beginning, and now Elizabeth had confirmed his motives. This might become a problem he'd have to deal with at some point. The past two days had been a couple of the most exciting in his life. How he was going to let such experiences affect his future was something he would have to ponder for some time.

Jim's thoughts were interrupted by Elizabeth saying, "Stop here!"

Pulling the car to the side of the street, he asked, "What for?"

Pointing to the building next to them, she said, "The restaurant, silly! Lindell's—it's right there."

Relieved that she was hungry and not angry over something, he said, "Sorry. I was just lost in thought."

As though she could read his mind, she asked, "Your wife and family?"

"Well, yes. A lot of things just transpired that will change our future. I want to tell them the good news in person."

"They sure are lucky to have a guy like you in their lives."

"Thank you," Jim said.

"No, thank you for rescuing me from my brother. Now let's go inside and enjoy a great meal together before you go."

Right on cue Jim's stomach growled. "There's one vote in favor. Come on." He strolled around the car to open her door and escort her into the restaurant. "I don't recall ever having enjoyed living in the moment than the past couple of days. What an exciting time. I can hardly wait to see what fate has in store."

"Me neither." Elizabeth smiled. She knew that planning trumped fate any day.

CHAPTER 20

By the time Jim drove home from the air terminal, it was late. Anita had already gone to bed. Poking his head into John's and Julie's rooms, he found them both sleeping. He quietly got ready for bed and slipped under the blankets without waking his wife.

Even though he was exhausted, Jim couldn't fall asleep. His mind kept running through the events of the last couple of days, marveling at how things had turned around so quickly. Anita had advised him to take control. He did, and now they had the backing to make this venture a success. If they met their deadlines and fulfilled even the contract they had now, it would be a money maker. A couple more supply contracts and it could be a wild success. Then they could afford to do anything their hearts desired.

He turned on his side and watched his wife sleep. Next summer they would celebrate their twentieth wedding anniversary, and now they would celebrate the Wolverine Mine coming up to full production and meeting the Chicago Wire order. Nearly twenty years they had been at this. They were getting to the end of their child-raising years with John, the oldest, going off to college next year. After twenty years they would finally make it big. There would be no more worries about college expenses; they could take exotic cruise vacations. Jim fell asleep dreaming about the view from his stateroom on his around-the-world cruise.

It felt good to sleep in. Jim awoke to the sound of the shower running. He strolled into the bathroom and studied the silhouette of his wife through the fogged glass shower doors. She was washing her shoulder-length dark brown hair and had her arms raised to reach the back of her head, which accentuated the curvature of her body. Jim could make out the streams of water trickling off her body, and that was all it took to bring him into the shower stall.

Later that morning, the family gathered in the breakfast nook for their Saturday morning ritual of having brunch together and planning their weekend. John, their eighteen-year-old son, was going to the Northwestern game against Michigan. Like Jim, he was a good athlete and had already received offers to play for either of the schools competing in Evanston today. Jim was proud of his son's achievements and had no doubt he would follow in his footsteps to play in the Big House at the University of Michigan. However, John showed up at the table sporting a Northwestern jersey.

"What is the meaning of this?" Jim tugged on John's sleeve. "Wearing the enemy's colors in my castle?"

"Don't get too bent, Dad, I mean your highness. I just don't want to get beat up by my friends when I'm sitting in the home student section."

"Good point."

"How about you, Julie?" Anita asked. Their fifteen-year-old daughter had no interest in sports other than chasing boys. Although, she didn't actually chase them; they just flocked to her because she had inherited her mother's good looks and athletic body. She and her mother spent a lot of time together when Jim was out of town, and they enjoyed a close relationship. "Are we going to enjoy the pleasure of your company today?"

"Well, Lisa wanted to go down to Deer Park to look for a new sweater. Thought I'd go along and look for some new shoes."

"I knew that was coming. Plan on being home tomorrow, and by the way, home tonight by eleven."

"All right, Mom."

"I'll see you after the game," John said. "Don't plan on me for dinner. I'm going out for pizza with Rick and Bob."

"Whoa there, son," Jim said. "Before anyone goes running off to the game, I wanted to tell you about what has happened this week that will change our lives over the next few months."

Since they usually didn't carry on serious family meetings, this took everyone by surprise, including Anita. Jim waited a moment until the stunned looks on their faces disappeared and began. "Just two days ago, I closed the biggest deal in the history of Wolverine Ventures. We were able to sell 80 percent of the Wolverine Mining Company to a private investor for eighty million dollars."

Anita looked at him as if to say, "I told you so."

Julie wasn't quite sure what all this meant, so she asked, "Does this mean we're millionaires and I can have more money for shopping today?"

"We're not personally, or at least not yet, but the mining company that my firm still owns 20 percent of has all the money it needs to get up and running by next July. By that time, we very well could be." Jim gave his daughter a little smile. "But I am in such a good mood, I will give you some extra shopping money today."

John stood up. "Congrats, Dad. I know you and Alan worked hard on this one."

"Before you go, that reminds me of one other thing I wanted to tell you." Jim motioned for John to sit for one more minute. "This will take a lot of time on my part between now and next summer to pull this off. I will be gone much of the time to the mine site. I need you guys to help your mom out around here and to not give her any grief. Understood?"

John stood up again. "No worries, Dad. We understand. Now may I be excused?"

"One more thing." Jim held up his index finger. "It's been a good week for the Wolverine name. Go blue!"

Without bothering with a response, John was out the door.

CHAPTER 21

For the past several days, Elizabeth had tried to keep things distant and did not want to open up to her brother, but this was the first time she had invited him to the house for a meal. Up until that point, she had visited with him on neutral ground, doing some sightseeing and showing him the Wolverine Mine. At first she wasn't sure how wise of an idea that was, but since Andy was a mining engineer, she knew he'd be at least partially interested from the technical side. She already knew how keen his interest was on the financial side. To her surprise, he had taken a sincere interest and even made what seemed to her a couple of good suggestions about how productivity could be improved with minor modifications to the existing mining plan.

The past four days had been the most time Andy and Elizabeth had spent together since Elizabeth was fourteen. Starting with the night Jim went home, he had bent over backwards to be nice and understanding. This was not the brother she had known growing up or even the one that came back a few months ago for the reading of the will. Although she had tried her best to retain the hard feelings that she'd harbored for him for so long, Elizabeth couldn't bring herself to do so. With Mom gone, Andy was the only family she had left.

"Why the glum look, sis?"

"I had hoped to hear from Jim, but he hasn't called."

"Why don't you give him a call and find out when he's coming back?"

"I can't do that."

"Sure you can. Tell him about my idea for a belt haulage way. That'll give you an excuse to talk to him."

"I suppose I could do that tomorrow."

"Why put off till tomorrow what you can do today?"

"I know. Dad used to say that all the time."

"Speaking of Dad, and only if you want me to, I can stick around to help you open this mine. I'm not just another pretty face, you know. I do have some good experience, and I'd like nothing more than to get involved with J. A. MacIntyre Inc."

She knew it would come sooner or later. He was taking the sweet and gentle approach. Elizabeth might have been down, but she was not stupid. In fact, she had already figured out how she could use him.

Elizabeth wasn't going to make this easy for him. She wanted to hear him beg to get back into her good graces. "I don't know, Andy. I want to trust you and welcome you back, but it's been so long. You walked away from us twenty years ago, remember?"

"Of course I do. It was a mistake. I was a rebellious kid. I still am somewhat of a maverick, but not enough that I don't recognize when I've been foolish. I'm not here to force my way into an inheritance I didn't get. I don't need all that money. I'm comfortable with where I'm at. I want to claim my heritage. I've got the same name as the one on the door of the company in Chicago that our great-grandfather started. You're the executor of the estate and chief executive of the company. I'm asking that you forgive me and give me a chance to prove myself. I'm qualified to run the mining operation or any of MacIntyre's mining interests, for that matter. I could do the company good. I'm not expecting to waltz in here and claim my birthright, but I do ask you to consider letting me in the door."

"All right. I hear you. You want to run the company. I'll give you a chance. However, you've got to know that Gary Johnson runs Wolverine Mining Company and Phillip Turner runs J.A. MacIntyre Inc.

Right now, you run nothing. I'll ask the board of directors to make you a vice president in charge of mining operations. You'll report to Phillip."

It was just what he had been waiting for. Andy smiled and asked, "What about stock options?"

"Don't push your luck."

CHAPTER 22

The receptionist's voice came over the speaker on the phone in Jim's office. "Mr. Thomas, I've got a call for you on line three."

"Who is it?" Jim asked, a little annoyed that the call had not been properly announced.

"Elizabeth MacIntyre from Wolverine Mining."

It had been five days since he was up there. The papers for the stock sale had been duly executed and the money transfer made. What could she possibly want? After a couple moments of silence, Jim responded, "Thanks, I'll take it." He pressed the button with the flashing light above it. "Hello, Elizabeth. How are you doing? Did you have a good weekend?"

"It was okay. I spent some time catching up on things with my brother."

"How did it go? I knew you were pretty apprehensive about it the last time I saw you."

"Things turned out better than I thought they would. We patched up a few things from our past, and then he asked for a position with MacIntyre Inc."

"Oh yeah? What did you tell him?"

"Oh, I decided to give him one. I made him vice president of our mining operations. At the moment, it's a harmless position and a way to get him into the company and prove himself. He is a qualified mining engineer, and he did give me a couple of good suggestions for improving the mining plan at the Wolverine."

Trying not to lose his temper at the thought of Elizabeth and Andy making modifications to Gary and Pete's mining plan, Jim responded, "Are you sure this is a good idea?"

"No, I'm not sure, and I know I'm taking a big risk."

"As one who's in the business of taking risks, let me tell you something. This is not a big risk. This is a foolish risk!" There was silence on the line. Jim found himself thinking about how he was going to get rid of Andy, but when he heard her crying softly, he toned down his response. "I'm sorry, I just can't believe you let him manipulate you like this."

"He's my only family anymore." She paused. "Anyway, I was wondering if you'd be interested in hearing about them before we got too far on the development of the first section. Thought maybe I'd come down there and go over them with you." Another pause.

"You won't have to come here to outline your brother's ideas. Alan and I were just going over our plans for Wolverine and related ventures the other day. I've set up some meetings for us next week in the Copper Country. We'll get together with Alan then. He's going to be overseeing a new project Bob Grossman at Kearsarge has come up with for the partnership. I plan on spending the week up there. I'll call you back with an itinerary when we finalize it."

CHAPTER 23

Boston, Massachusetts, had historically been connected to Calumet, Michigan, since the copper boom of the mid-nineteenth century. Unlike their predecessors who had provided much of the capital required to finance many of the mining operations in the copper country, RE Associates was not interested in such capital-intensive ventures. They were interested in financing ancillary businesses, and thus, they had made their first investment in the old Michigan House restaurant, bar, and hotel and then expanded across the street, opening up a four-story hotel with the top two floors having nothing but the finest suites reminiscent of the late 1800s.

Jack Stallworth had skillfully made RE Associates a bundle of money in the past twenty-four months by buying up these properties at fire sale prices, investing five million dollars in the best renovations and then installing some of the best management he could find. The dividends were just now being reaped. On many nights, all the rooms were full, and the Michigan House was gaining a reputation as one of the best—if not the best—eateries in the area.

Two years ago, Jack had met two young entrepreneurs who had come up with a patented process for silver-plating copper to yield a product with exceptional conductance, energy storage, and heat-resistant capabilities. Unfortunately, these two Einsteins didn't even have enough money between them to rent, let alone assemble, a laboratory to test the process. Four hundred thousand dollars for an 80 percent interest in the process was also beginning to pay off. A large order for silver-plated wire windings had just been placed with a joint venture between Ford and General Electric to make their first low-cost, electric-powered cars for the 2012 model year. Jack had been able to bring in the order with RE Associates paying only half of the twenty-million-dollar investment required to build the processing plant. Since RE Associates normally didn't make such capital-intensive investments, he had accepted a ten-million-dollar investment last summer from J.A. MacIntyre Inc. Five months later they had begun to set the equipment in the plant, and it would be ready to commission next spring. No doubt this could be the start of something big. He couldn't wait to see his Christmas bonus this year. On the corner of his desk was a Hatteras boat catalog with the page showing the forty-four-foot convertible dog-eared.

That afternoon, Jack had received a call from another investor in the latest copper boom. "Hi, Jack, my name is Alan Larsson, and I got your name from Harold Peterman, CEO of Ford Motor Company. He thinks we have something in common that we should be talking about."

"Oh really?" Jack said.

The best way to get an executive's attention was to drop a big name, like a CEO of the big three domestic car manufacturers. "Yeah. He tells me you have a patented process for producing a copper-silver alloy wire that they'll be buying from you for their new line of electric cars with General Electric motors."

"That's right."

"If I understand correctly, you need to buy silver to add to your process, and it's very expensive—about ten times the cost of copper."

"Uh-huh."

"What if I could offer you a copper-silver alloy right out of my smelter for just slightly more than the cost of copper because I've already got 6 to 7 percent silver in the ore going in?"

"You would have my attention."

"When can we meet?"

Jack scheduled a flight with RE's private jet to the Houghton County Airport for the following Wednesday. When he set down the phone, he couldn't help but think how well his investments in Calumet had panned out. Maybe he was destined to be the one with the Midas touch who turned copper into gold, or was that alchemy?

CHAPTER 24

Jim and Alan surveyed the winter landscape as their plane made its final approach to land. The last time they had flown into Houghton together, it had been autumn, and they were just getting the news on the first of several drilling campaigns at the Copper City Mine. Now, just three months later, things had changed quickly. They also knew that they were not the only investors looking to make some very attractive returns in what was fast becoming the Midwest's first boomtown of the twenty-first century.

"Did you make arrangements with Gary to pick us up again?" Jim asked.

"S—-! No, I thought you had talked to him."

"I didn't even try to get a hold of him," Jim responded curtly. "You're the one dealing with the partnership, remember? Don't you think it would be nice if our general manager was involved in the discussions?"

"Me? Hey, bud, don't you remember throwing me off the job when you decided to step in and consummate the sale to Elizabeth and the partnership with Bob? Now I'm what? The office manager making travel arrangements?"

"Sorry, I didn't mean to come across that way. We have both been pretty busy with this investment. Tell you what: I'll rent us a car when we land. It'll be faster than waiting around for Gary anyway."

Jim's solution cooled down Alan, who was looking out the window to see how much snow was on the runway. "By the way, what's eating you these days? You've been awfully testy since you came back to work after Thanksgiving."

"Nothing. I didn't mean to snap at you," Jim said. But he couldn't seem to get his mind off of Elizabeth. He had phoned her yesterday to let her know what time they'd be arriving. She had set up a dinner engagement for this evening. He wasn't sure this was a good idea, but he succumbed to her insistence that they meet alone so she could explain to him what had happened with Andy. Their last dinner out had been enjoyable, so he agreed to a social get-together with his majority owner. There were no good reasons, business or personal, why he should turn down her request.

The two businessmen walked from the plane toward the terminal with their heads down to avoid facing the westerly wind that buffeted them as they emerged from the aircraft. Jim shouted over the wind, "I don't think Al Gore was ever up here, or he never would have thought about global warming."

"Yeah, the documentary would have been called *An Inconvenient Ice Age*."

"In fact, I think I just saw a wooly mammoth."

"No, Jim, that was the hood of your coat in your face."

After a good laugh, Jim procured a car and led Alan into the parking lot, where they tried to identify a new Ford Escape Hybrid underneath the mounds of snow where the rentals were parked. Upon finding the correct license plate, Jim opened the door of the SUV only to find himself the victim of an avalanche. "I'll bet the guy at the rental counter is having a good laugh right now," he muttered. "This thing better have heated seats."

After starting the SUV to let it warm up, Jim brushed the snow off. When he was finished, he asked Alan, "Did you hear that?"

"Hear what?"

"Exactly! Nothing. Everything on this hybrid runs off the battery when the engine shuts off. Even the heater."

Jim got in and drove out of the parking lot before the gasoline engine kicked back in. Alan said, "This is our future, partner, making these more efficient so that they run on the electric motors longer. You know, Ford Motor just announced that 20 percent of their fleet will be hybrids and electric cars by 2020."

"That's a lotta cars," Jim said in his best Italian accent.

"That's a lotta copper and silver."

"You know what else?" Jim said, motioning out the window. "That's a lotta snow. No need to ever worry about not having a white Christmas. Not when the annual snowfall is three hundred inches per year."

Ten minutes later, they were in the parking lot of the Kearsarge Mining Company. They found Bob Grossman waiting in his office for them.

Jim began with an introduction. "Bob, this is my partner in Wolverine Ventures, Alan Larsson."

"Pleased to meet you. Larsson—that is either of Swedish or Norwegian origin, isn't it?"

"Very observant. Swedish."

"Around these parts, it's a safe guess with all the Scandinavian descent; however, given that you're not from here, I find it interesting that you're braving our winter to do business up here. Certainly there must be an easier way to make a living."

Alan laughed. "I don't know of one if there is, but you've made a connection regarding my background. My father used to work for Cleveland Cliffs Mining on the Marquette iron range thirty years ago. He was promoted to a position in Cleveland in the early eighties; therefore, I spent my early years in the UP and have many fond memories. When I heard of the new mining activity up here, I decided to do a little exploration myself. It was then I met Gary Johnson, and a few months later, we purchased the Wolverine Mine.

Things have ballooned since then to the point we're at today, and I'd like nothing more than to see this area boom once again. I, for one, am bound and determined to participate in this boom."

"Likewise," Bob reassured. "I can see we're going to get along very well. As far as prospering from the boom is concerned, the partnership that we've formed will be the major driving force behind it. Let's talk about how we're going to make that happen."

CHAPTER 25

Jim had dropped Alan off at the Michigan House and was on his way to pick up Elizabeth when he came across an old Mercedes off on the side of Fifth Street with its flashers on. He coasted to a stop behind the car and recognized Elizabeth behind the wheel trying to get it started.

It had started to snow. Jim turned up his collar on his overcoat and pulled on his gloves as he made his way over to her car. She opened her door because her power window wouldn't go down.

"What are you doing out here stuck in this stuff?"

"Jim, is that you?"

"I don't have a twin brother, so it must be. I was just on my way to your house to pick you up."

Elizabeth got out of the car and gave him a hug. "Am I glad to see you. I thought I'd run to the store to pick up a couple of appetizers, and on my way back, the car stalled and I couldn't get it started."

Releasing himself from her embrace, Jim said, "Let me give it a try." The starter ground briefly when he turned the key, and the interior lights dimmed. "Your battery is run down. Do you have any jumper cables?"

She gave him a puzzled look. "I don't know."

Removing the keys from the ignition, Jim got out and opened the trunk. Inside was a road emergency kit complete with jumper cables. "Yes, you do." Jim held them up so she could see what they were.

Insulted, she replied, "My limo driver normally takes care of these things."

"Okay. Why don't you get back into the car and I'll hook these up to the SUV I'm driving. When I motion you to turn the key, try starting the car."

Jim made the connection, waited a couple of minutes for her battery to charge somewhat, and then signaled her to start the Mercedes. It started on the first try. By this time Jim was freezing, and after disconnecting the cables and storing them, he came up to the driver's side window, which rolled down this time. "It looks like it's okay now. I will follow you home and meet you in back at the carriage house so you can stow this ol' carriage."

"Thanks, Jim. I don't know what I would have done without your help. You look cold. Get back in your SUV, and I'll find a way to warm you up at the house."

He nodded, wondering how she was going to make it through the winter up here. Ten minutes later they pulled around the MacIntyre mansion to the carriage house in the back. Jim had Elizabeth back the car in so if it didn't start again, the battery could easily be connected to another vehicle. He took the two bags of groceries from the backseat, and she led him through the back door into the kitchen. By this time the snow was beginning to accumulate rapidly.

Elizabeth took his coat and hung it with hers to dry in the coat closet down the hall. She ushered him to a seat at the kitchen table next to a warm radiator so he could unthaw. "I've got some Woodford Reserve bourbon that my father had blended just for his taste by the master distiller at the distillery in Kentucky. It has aged well and is very smooth and will warm you up in no time."

"Your father had quite a collection of fine wines and liquor."

"Yes, he would bring them home from his travels all the time."

Jim did not hesitate. "If it's as good as the Australian port you served me a couple of weeks ago, I'll try it."

After disappearing for a couple of minutes, she came back with two tumblers and a clear glass bottle with a cork stopper. She poured them both a drink then sat next to him and proposed a toast. "To our partnership. May it grow and prosper."

Jim took a big swallow. "Wow, this is good, and it definitely warms you up from the inside out." Looking at the label on the bottle, Jim read the most impressive part out loud. "Small batch number 1045, crafted for James A. MacIntyre III."

Elizabeth proceeded to put away the groceries. "Do you like fresh smoked salmon?"

"Is the pope Catholic?"

"I've got some dill dip in the refrigerator and crackers in the cupboard. I picked this up from the fish market while I was in town. You'd have to catch it yourself to have it any fresher."

"I'd really like to try that," Jim said.

"Hold on, I'll get it for you."

"No, I mean, yes, I'd like some. But I would really like to try my hand at salmon fishing on Lake Superior."

Elizabeth chuckled at their lack of communication. "I guess it's true. Men are from Mars and women are from Venus. It does seem a bit cold to be going salmon fishing."

Shaking his head in disbelief, Jim said, "Next summer. After we make our first million. I'm buying a nice-size boat and going fishing up here."

Noticing his drink was empty, Elizabeth offered Jim a refill. "No, I'd better not if we're going out to dinner and I'm driving."

"Tell you what," she said while filling his glass. "I've got some lake trout to go with that salmon. It won't take me long to season it, put it on the broiler, and whip up a salad and some veggies to go with it. Besides, it's snowing like crazy out there."

Picking up the glass, Jim agreed without saying a word.

As Elizabeth busied herself making dinner, Jim sipped on his second drink. "What about Andy?"

"Huh?"

"You said you wanted to have dinner so you could tell me what happened with your brother."

All of a sudden Elizabeth's cheery mood turned sour. "Do we have to talk about that now? I already told you I offered him a position as vice president of mining operations. He accepted. I'll keep his direct involvement with Wolverine to a minimum, but he does have some good ideas that are worth consideration, like using belt haulage instead of LHDs. Enough said. How about you going down to the wine cellar and finding a good bottle to go with dinner?"

Wisely deciding not to push the issue, Jim headed to the basement to find a walk-in cellar lined with bottles, reds on the right and whites on the left. The arrangement cut his search considerably because he was after a white and they were not as plentiful because of their shorter shelf life. It also gave him some time to recollect his thoughts since he had come over to tell her she had made a big mistake taking Andy back into her good graces. She was playing some sort of a game with him, and he didn't like it. However, she had her own agenda, and talking about Andy hustling his way back into J.A. MacIntyre Inc. was not on it. Finding a German riesling, Jim brought this up to the cook for approval. Getting her nod in the affirmative, he made himself at home as she directed him to the corkscrew and ice bucket. He set two place settings at the end of the large dining table, finding everything he needed in the butler's serving pantry between the kitchen and the dining room.

"You are a man of many talents," Elizabeth said. "First you prove to be a mechanic and get my car running, then a connoisseur of fine wine, and now a gentleman who prepares my dining table in the finest fashion."

"I'm just a Jim of all trades." He smiled.

They sat down to a nice dinner served up by Elizabeth. She found some Sinatra music left behind by her mother and put it to play on the stereo in the parlor.

The ambiance was as soft as her touch. Jim loved the way she touched him gently on his arm when she talked to him. "So what was it like to grow up here?" he asked.

"I loved the small-town atmosphere and the fact everyone knew you. I also hated it because they all knew your business, and when your daddy owns the biggest house in town, people talk."

"How long are you planning on staying up here?"

Elizabeth thought about the question for a while. "I'm not sure. It really depends on how things go."

"What things are you talking about?"

He was prying too much now. Elizabeth simply said, "Relationships."

When they finished dinner, Jim helped her clean up. "I should probably get going back to the Michigan House."

"Are you sure you're okay to drive? The weather is not good. You could just stay the night here. You have a choice of rooms on the second floor."

"Thanks, but I'm okay. That's why I've rented an SUV. It'll go through the snow without any problem. You might want to consider getting one rather than relying on that old Mercedes if you stay through the winter."

"Don't change the subject," she said. "You had a bit to drink. I think you shouldn't drive."

Jim looked at his watch. "It's been over three hours since I took the first one. I feel fine. Thank you for dinner and a nice evening."

She looked at him, debating whether or not to continue to argue. "If you insist, please be careful."

As he went to hug her good-bye, she kissed him. He was taken aback at first, but when he felt her lips against his, he kissed her back. Tasting the wine in her mouth and feeling her body against his, he wondered if he was making the right decision. She could ensnare any man with her charms, and he was no exception. Having such a glamorous and wealthy heiress dote on him and invite him to stay with her in a mansion on a snowy, cold night was almost enough to make Jim forget his marriage vows. "I, uh, should be going. I'll see ya tomorrow at the meeting with Northern Michigan Refining."

When he closed the door, the snow in his face was a good wakeup call. Standing on the edge of the wraparound porch, he looked to the heavens. "Thanks, I needed that," he said just as the drift on the porch roof let go and buried him under an avalanche.

CHAPTER 26

Gary had joined Alan and Bob Grossman for breakfast. They had just placed their order when Jim hurriedly entered the dining room at the Michigan House.

"Well, look who decided to show up after all," Alan teased.

Gary got right to business before they got any further. "I believe we should get to the business at hand, and dat's how much copper and silver we can provide to Ford Motor through whatever channels we can. The prelim' projections I've put together for level eight show dat da high-grade seam we've identified on six an' seven continues down to eight, but at a much steeper slope. This will make mining more difficult, but the good news is there's more of it der than we found on seven. When ya go down some two hundred feet, it changes direction and doubles back from the fault in a southeasterly path. Nine out of thirty-three core holes intersected the high-grade seam, and I've had dose assayed. The copper content is again seventy to one hundred pounds per ton. Jack Sanders will have the reserves quantified for me next week. I'm guessin' we're looking at three million or so tons of this stuff. With eight million on six at seventy-five pounds per ton, another two million on seven at seventy pounds per ton, and adding three million on eight, we're lookin' at least thirteen million tons of seventy-five pounds per ton reserves. That's almost one billion pounds of high-grade ore. Quite a find, huh?"

"I'd say," said Grossman, a little green with envy. "I wasn't aware of how rich you guys had struck it until now. I'd heard some things through the grapevine, but you've really got yourself one nice ore body I'd love to help you exploit."

"That's why we're here," Alan said. "At the moment, we've got a long-term contract, which I will finalize when I return to Chicago next week. That will dedicate a minimum of fifty million pounds per year for five years. The customer has options on up to another fifty million per year if they exercise it by year-end next year. Therefore, some 250 to 475 million pounds of reserves are committed."

"Don't forget about da nine million tons of forty pounds per ton ore on seven," Gary interjected. "That's 360 million pounds right there. Dat alone could almost fill that contract. In fact, dat's where I plan to start the development work next month, rather than on six where we originally planned. That way, I can begin shipping by July; however, Bob, if things get a little dicey or if I need some additional ore to meet our requirements for this lower grade stuff, then dat's where you come in."

"Dat's, I mean, that's true." Alan turned to address Grossman. "Your involvement in this partnership allows us to focus on the electric motor market."

Gary couldn't stand it any longer. "If I hear ya say partnership one more time, I'll go nuts. Can't youse guys come up with a name for it?"

"Got any suggestions?"

"Sure. How about Red Metal Sales? Dat would be appropriate for a company that does nothing but broker copper."

"Not bad," Grossman said. "What do you think, Alan?"

"Red Metal Sales it is. With all these new companies I've been involved with over the past six months, I'll have a hard time keeping them straight."

"Isn't that what the venture capital business is all about?" Grossman asked. "I thought this was the kind of stuff you guys thrived on."

"It is," Jim said. "But before we get caught up forming any new companies, I've got something I need to relay to Gary. Remember I told you that Andy MacIntyre was made the new vice president of mining operations for MacIntyre Inc.?"

"Yeah."

"Well, I found out from Elizabeth last night that he's got a proposal he'd like you to look at for conveyor haulage that he thinks will save us a lot of money in the long run, especially if we expand the operation."

Gary rolled his eyes. "Great. Now I've got ta take this kid seriously too?"

"I'm afraid so. You're going to have to at least humor Elizabeth. I guess he's a pretty good mining engineer. You might be able to put him to some good use."

"We already looked at dat option and ruled it out for capital cost reasons. But if ya want to commit to an expansion plan soon, I'll give it another looksie."

"Fair enough," Jim said. "What time is the meeting with Stallworth?"

Alan pulled his smart phone out of his pocket. "Ten o'clock."

CHAPTER 27

The executive conference room at Kearsarge Mining stood off Bob Grossman's office. His secretary, Jane, had just brought in a pot of coffee on a silver service. Jack Stallworth sat on one end of the table with Elizabeth sitting next to him, chatting him up like they were old friends. It was after ten o'clock, and Bob excused himself to call Alan, Gary, and Jim to find out where they were.

Bob came back in the room shaking his head. "They claim to have been held up at a breakfast meeting. I was at that meeting, and it was wrapping up when I left. Anyway, they're on their way, so help yourself to some coffee and we'll get started shortly."

Five minutes later, the Wolverine Mining executive team showed up. After profuse apologies, Gary started by giving Jack Stallworth a quick history lesson on the origins of the Wolverine Mine. "Da mine was originally opened in 1908 on a ten-acre parcel of land dat contained the outcrop of the Kearsarge Lode. Dis is da same body of ore that Kearsarge Mining worked then at its number-four shaft, and it's the same one that Bob Grossman oversees now from the number-six shaft. Da Wolverine Mine was not a real deep mine by copper country standards. Da ninth level was only one thousand feet below the surface an' had barely been worked. Da first five levels had pretty much been mined out 'bout a hundred years ago."

Alan could tell by the expression on Jack's face that he was having a hard time understanding Gary, so he took over the discussion.

"Last summer, Gary discovered an exceptionally rich vein of ore in his exploration of the sixth level. This was found to extend down through the seventh and eighth levels, where drilling programs had been completed. The mine contains nearly one billion pounds of copper along with sixty million pounds of silver, which could be processed to form a copper and silver alloy that exceeds the specifications you are seeking to make the highly conductive electric motor windings. A twenty-to-one or better ratio of copper to silver in the ore should enhance the conductivity of the refined alloy without having to seek out a second source of silver, and we can supply it at a very attractive price."

When Bob entered the conference room fifteen minutes later, he found Gary and Jack poring over site maps and geologists' reports. It was apparent the Gary had done most of the difficult work of the initial sell. Before long, it would be up to Jim to close the deal and bank the first contract for Red Metal Sales.

Jim already knew this would be one of the easiest deals to put together because their ore coupled with Stallworth's refining process was like a marriage made in heaven. In fact, it was a marriage facilitated by the CEO of the Ford Motor Company. Why he would be calling Alan Larsson was still a mystery to Jim, but it really didn't matter. The only thing that mattered to Jim was that next model year, the electric motors in the Ford hybrids like the one he was currently driving would be wound with wire that was produced from the copper-silver alloy they would be producing at costs no competitor could beat. This put a smile on his face as he waited for Alan to finish going over the reserve estimates, which were also growing with each new exploratory drilling campaign.

CHAPTER 28

Christmas at the Thomas household was more like a homecoming. Jim had spent the better part of the last month in the Copper Country putting together the Red Metal Sales partnership with Kearsarge Mining and the supply contract to Northern Michigan Refining, whose ultimate customer was the Ford Motor Company. Furthermore, he already had a contract in place with Chicago Wire that was driving the whole schedule. Never before had he orchestrated so many pieces that had to come together at the right time. He was down to six months to make it all happen. He found all the challenges to be exhilarating. His family found them exasperating.

John's football team had made it to the state finals last month. Unfortunately, Jim had not. The only thing more disappointing for both of them was that John's team lost. However, that was not the only loss in the process. John was much more distant from his father, and the time they did spend together over the holidays was strained.

Jim had found the time to go Christmas shopping. He lavished Anita, John, and Julie with expensive jewelry and electronics. To his dismay, they were not impressed. Life had changed in one month's time. His newest challenge was to win back his family.

On Christmas day, they gathered for their traditional dinner together. Anita's parents were visiting from the Detroit area, and John had invited Melissa, his new girlfriend, to join them. Jim carved the ham while Anita put together the rest of the meal. John put on some Christmas music in the background, and they all sat down to enjoy the feast.

"Before we all begin, would you mind if I said grace?" Melissa asked.

Jim looked at Anita, and she returned a smile that meant she knew something he didn't. "Please do."

Melissa waited until everyone put down their silverware. "Father God, we give you thanks for this day. We are especially thankful for your Son, whose birth we celebrate. Bless this food, this family, and bring them through these trying times. Amen."

"Thank you, Melissa. That was very nice," Anita said. She obviously liked John's choice in girls.

The prayer had gotten Grandma's attention. "So what church do you go to, dear?"

"We go to Willow Creek, the big nondenominational church in South Barrington. They have a great youth program and a fantastic praise band. John's been going with me on Saturday nights."

Jim cast a sideways glance at John. He grinned. "You're going to church on Saturday nights?"

"Yep. You should come with us. Last night's Christmas Eve service was awesome."

"Really?" Jim was astonished. He had been out on the last-minute man's Christmas shopping run last night, so he had no idea of John's whereabouts. During the pause in the conversation, he also noticed that the music John had selected was not the traditional *I'll Be Home for Christmas* that had become his theme song of late.

"While we're on the topic of what I've been doing with my life lately, I have an announcement to make." John now had everyone's undivided attention. "I am planning on signing a letter of intent to play for Northwestern next year."

At first, Jim thought John was going to say he and Melissa were getting married next summer, or worse. For that he was relieved. After that he started to get angry. "Northwestern? What? They don't have a team. They can't compete for a national championship. They might not even make a bowl game."

Anita raised her voice. "Jim, settle down. He's got a full scholarship, and Northwestern is a fine school."

Jim was still stuttering. "But…"

John stood up. "I knew this is how you'd react. You and all your Wolverine s—-!"

Jim was pointing at him now. "What did you say? Sit down!"

"No. I knew it was too much to ask you to respect my decision, much less be happy for me. All you ever wanted was for me to go to your alma mater. Well, I don't give a s—- about Michigan or what you think."

Anita intervened before it went too far. "John, watch your language. Don't talk to your father that way."

Jim was about to say something further, but Anita's look stopped him before a single word was uttered.

"Sorry," John said as he left the house with Melissa in tow.

That evening, John called to ask if he could stay at Melissa's house that night. Jim figured it would be best for both of them to cool down and they could talk tomorrow. As he got into bed with Anita, he let out a big sigh. "I guess I ruined Christmas, huh?"

"It wasn't one of our best."

"I'm sorry. I was shocked, and I reacted badly."

Anita rolled on her side to look at him. "You reacted horribly. Football doesn't mean as much to John as it does to you. Winning doesn't mean as much to John as it does to you. Don't you see? He doesn't want to be a benchwarmer for Michigan when he might have a real chance of playing for Northwestern. John wants to make a difference, not watch. Furthermore, he has a new interest that will keep him here in Chicago."

"Yes, she got my attention too. But what's with this church stuff?"

"Maybe you should ask Reverend Johnson when you go back."

Jim felt himself getting angry again. "That's not fair. You told me to take charge of this, and I did. We have exceeded all expectations. I told you this was going to take up a lot of my time, and it will continue to do so, at least until we're up and operating. What do you want me to do? Turn it back over to Alan? Quit?"

She rolled back over and turned off the light.

Jim lay there wondering what else could go wrong. "Aren't we going to—"

"My parents are across the hall in the guestroom."

"That never stopped us before."

"Goodnight, Jim."

Wolverine Mine Shaft and Dry

Credit: Curt Gillespie – original artwork

PART II

THE DREAM BECOMES A NIGHTMARE

CHAPTER 29

A long winter had finally passed. The airport weather station at the Houghton County Airport had recorded three hundred five inches of snowfall for the season. Elizabeth MacIntyre had found that the Copper Country winters were definitely not to her liking. However, she knew the best way to ensure the success of her investments was to oversee them herself. This could not be done as effectively from Evanston. It required a more personal touch. She had established a rapport with all the key players from Wolverine Mining and Northern Michigan Refining, especially Jim Thomas and Jack Stallworth. However, neither knew of her involvement with the other because both were privately held companies, so shareholder information was not publically available.

Things had kicked into high gear at Wolverine Mining in late spring when Gary Johnson had finally received all the equipment he needed to get the first section of the mine into operation by starting development of a drift on the seventh level right off the number three crosscut where the outcrop of what had now been named the Wolverine seam occurred.

Next weekend was Memorial Day, and it appeared that the mill would be ready to begin commissioning with at least one line of process equipment. This was all good news because it meant that the July first deadline for the Chicago Wire contract was going to be met.

Wolverine was panning out to be everything the investors thought it would be. The second section would begin work on level seven next week, and the first section was ready to start hoisting ore out of the mine.

All of the partners had scheduled a meeting that day in Wolverine's offices to lay down some plans for both short- and long-term production at the mine. Bob Grossman had flown in to review with Wolverine Mining what Kearsarge would be able to do to cover shortfalls in production as development progressed. These certainly were exciting times to be in the mining business.

The conference room at Wolverine Ventures buzzed with excitement as Gary Johnson, Elizabeth MacIntyre, Andy MacIntyre, Bob Grossman, Jim Thomas, Alan Larsson, and Pete Singer sat down for an all-day strategy session. It was the first time this group had been together since before Christmas. A lot had happened since then.

Success is contagious. Even though the Wolverine Mine, mill, and smelting complex had not produced a single ingot, the group gathered in the conference room was elated with how well things had progressed. All in all, it was remarkable that they had come to this point in less than a year. Now it was time to plan production to meet the first series of required shipments. It was also time to plan for the formal reopening of the mine.

Wolverine had received a lot of press over the past few months, not only locally, but on a national scale as well. Copper prices were firm, and even the *Wall Street Journal* had reported on the success story taking place in Calumet, revolving around the rebirth of copper mining and, in particular, the two major players in the game: Kearsarge and Wolverine.

"So, Bob," Alan began, "how are you going to spend your share of the profits from Red Metal Sales?"

"I'm going to buy a new continuous miner and tunnel into the Wolverine from Kearsarge number six."

"Wouldn't it just be easier ta let the experts move the ore?" Gary rebutted. "Ya gotta be better off sellin' what we hoist. Ya know, leave the minin' to us."

"That's a pretty big boast from someone who's only hoisted one little pile of ore so far."

"Yeah, but give it time. That little pile is going to be worth a lot of money soon."

"Okay, boys," Elizabeth interjected. "When the first shipment to Chicago Wire is on the road, then you can puff up your chest, Gary. In the meantime, I want to know when we can start stockpiling the high-grade ore for Northern Michigan Refining to produce the copper and silver alloy wire for GE electric motors that will eventually go into all of Ford's hybrids, plug-ins, and pure electric cars and trucks. That's where the real money is! I should know. I paid the premium for a hybrid Ford Escape last winter. It's a great vehicle. Got well over thirty miles per gallon all around and kept me between the ditches all winter."

"Well, boss," Gary replied, "you can expect the first shipment to arrive on surface by the Fourth of July."

That comment opened some eyes. Nobody was expecting production from the number two section this quickly.

"Are you sure you can meet such a tight schedule?" Jim asked, wanting to give Gary an out if he was still caught up in bragging about his performance thus far.

Gary looked at him over the top of his glasses. "Have we missed any deadlines yet?"

Jim narrowed his eyes and then answered, "No, but you have cost me some extra money in meeting a couple of them so far."

"Look, my job is ta move the dirt. I've given ya the best cost information I can all along. We've been pretty close, but we have missed on a couple of occasions. My impression is dat you want this thing producing as soon as possible. Dat you've got. July fourth. No later."

"Great," Jim reassured Gary, who seemed to be on the defensive. "Now let's have a look at the production plan, and I'll start scheduling shipments."

As the meeting wore on, Elizabeth became bored and decided that it was not really necessary for her to be there. She caught Jim's attention and with a tilt of her head motioned him out of the conference room.

"I don't think there's anything I can contribute to this get-together; however, I did have something else I wanted to discuss with you. We want to borrow Pete Singer for a while to look into an acquisition we're looking at. Remember I told you that Andy had proposed buying North American Metals?"

Jim nodded his head, knowing what was coming next.

"He's put together a package with his former boss for the acquisition. I like the prospects, and so does Phillip Turner. You know the situation with Andy. We'd both feel better if we had a second opinion on this one."

"Sure thing. I don't think there's a problem. The only thing I'm not certain of is his schedule."

"Whatever is good for you is good for me." She smiled. "We'll pay you whatever consulting fees you require."

Jim poked his head into the conference room and asked that Pete and Andy see him in his office for a few minutes. When they had gathered around Jim's small conference table, he reviewed what he and Elizabeth had just discussed. It was agreed that Pete and Andy would fly out to Colorado next week to check out North American Metals and their operations.

After a full morning of reviewing production schedules and shipping requirements, they adjourned for lunch at the Berghoff. The German restaurant was one of Jim's favorite haunts; he always liked finishing off deals over a good German beer.

Grossman was obviously pleased with how things were working out. "It appears as though we've got everything under control. Once we're in full production, I think we should go after the western producers. Fifty years ago, they put the Copper Country out of business. I think we could muster enough production, and our margins are high enough to shift market share our way and make these guys feel a bit of pain."

"If it means more sales, I'm all for it. We've got plenty of reserves to service more contracts with," Jim knew he was committing to spend even more time in a management role, but the returns would be huge. "Maybe you'd like to turn this partnership into something more than that. Ever considered a merger between Kearsarge and Wolverine?"

"Now that you've mentioned it, yes, I have," Bob said, grinning as though he had planned such a turn of events.

This immediately got everyone's attention and changed the topic of the discussions for the afternoon. Elizabeth opted to throw another curveball into the game by outlining what MacIntyre Inc. was into in precious metals out west and what they were considering with North American Metals.

CHAPTER 30

It was just a few minutes before five o'clock, and the daylong meetings at Wolverine Ventures had broken up half an hour ago. Everyone had departed in good spirits since the events had culminated in an agreement in principle to merge the mining interests of MacIntyre Inc., Kearsarge Mining, and Wolverine Ventures. This had included the Wolverine Mine, Kearsarge number four and six and two small gold mines, one in Colorado, and the other in the Canadian Rockies (in which MacIntyre owned a minority interest). It was also decided that the expanded Red Metal Sales (from now on to be known as RMS, to deemphasize the focus on copper) would purchase North American Metals and attempt to gain majority interest in the gold mining interests. Andy and Pete were to look after the precious metal side of the business; Grossman would oversee copper.

Jim had stepped into his office to place a call. "Hey, honey, you'll never guess what happened today. You know we had this all-day strategy meeting, and well, one thing led to another, and guess what? We've ended up merging all the partners together into one company and acquired a couple of gold mines in the process."

"Really?" Anita said in a sarcastic tone. "What does that mean?"

"Well, for now it means I've got to work out some of the details tonight, so I won't be home until late."

"That figures. You can't do that tomorrow?"

"No, babe. Everyone's heading back, so I've got to do it now."

"All right then. See you later." The phone went dead.

Jim looked at his receiver as though it had burnt his ear. Once again, it had been a while since he had been home for any length of time. *Oh well, I'll deal with this later,* he thought.

Later that evening, as they dined on some of the best Italian food in all of Chicago, Elizabeth was ecstatic over what had transpired. Her majority interest in Wolverine Mining had just expanded into a substantial minority interest in RMS. Coupled with a significant share of Northern Michigan Refining, whose process plant was just commissioned, it was only a matter of time before her entire plan came to fruition.

In a high-backed booth in the back of the Como Inn, Jim and Elizabeth toasted the formation of RMS with the last of a second bottle of reserve Chianti. The layout of the dining room gave them a great deal of privacy, perched in an elevated booth overlooking a decor overflowing with parrots.

"I don't know which is better," Elizabeth said. "Putting together deals or celebrating them with you."

"You really can't decide?"

"It's like baking a cake, frosting it, and eating it too!"

"I'm afraid you have your clichés a bit mixed up."

"You think I'm the dumbest rock in the box?"

Jim couldn't tell if she was serious. "Are you just trying to paint me into a corner?"

"A painting's worth a thousand words."

Now he knew she was just having fun with him, coming up with every cliché she could think of. He shook his head in disbelief over this amazing woman with a twisted sense of humor.

They walked out of the restaurant at 8:00 p.m. It was but a twenty-minute drive to the MacIntyre estate. Jim turned his Jaguar XJ-S into the drive and watched the electronically-activated iron gates close behind him. Despite his devotion to Anita and the kids, Elizabeth provided him a newfound sense of purpose. He enjoyed being with her and appreciated her intelligence. Likewise, she seemed to appreciate anything he did for her. He pulled around the circular drive in the front of the house.

Elizabeth leaned over and kissed him on the cheek. "Come on in for a nightcap before you leave."

After their little celebration dinner, Jim was feeling no pain and had no inhibitions. He reached over and pulled her back to him. This time it was a passionate kiss. "Yes. I'd like that very much."

The trail of clothes started at the front door and led to the master suite. At first the satin sheets felt cool, but body heat wasn't a problem.

She rolled over on top of him and smothered him with a passionate kiss. Her mouth tasted like the wine, and her body was warm and soft against his. He could feel each contour of her back as he ran his hands down the length of it, caressing her smooth skin and moving with the motion of her pelvis as they engaged in a fervent episode of lovemaking.

CHAPTER 31

By 11:40 p.m., Jim had exited the Route 53 and found himself ten minutes from home and thinking up a story to tell his wife because she was undoubtedly still up. Certainly the ol' dinner-and-drinks routine was appropriate for this occasion. In fact, it wasn't too far from the truth since he had celebrated with one of the participants in the meeting.

Walking into the house, he heard the television on in the living room. He hung his keys on the rack near the kitchen door and made his way down the hall to the living room. Anita was up watching one of the late-night talk shows.

"Looks like you had a very successful meeting today," she greeted him as he sat down next to her.

He wasn't sure whether the comment was sincere or if she was being facetious because of the late hour. "You might say that. We've got a merger between Kearsarge and Wolverine Mining Companies. I kind of thought the partnership we formed last year would lead in this direction, but I never thought it would happen this quickly."

"It's not the only thing that's happened quickly as a result of this copper mining venture of yours."

"I don't get it," replied a puzzled Jim, although he did have some inkling of what was to come.

"You do too. When was the last time you had the time of day for John or Julie, or even for me, for that matter? You work late hours.

You do more entertaining than you ever used to do. You're always going out of town. Is the business worth all of that? Or is there something else going on that I should know about?"

Jim was beginning to sober up now. "No, there's nothing going on." At least that was the case until just a few hours ago. Did it ever feel funny lying to her! He couldn't recall the last time he'd done that, other than the little white-lie cover-ups he did for her birthday or when he'd been out with the guys. "It's just that this has been the biggest thing Wolverine Ventures has been involved with, and it's taking up a lot of my time."

The explanation appeared to appease her. "I understand. And no, I'm not accusing you of anything. But you've got to understand. You've put a big strain on this family over the past few months, and it's time to do something about it."

Instead of sitting next to her, he sat down opposite her, not wanting to risk her noticing Elizabeth's perfume. "I'm sorry. I guess I've been so caught up in this venture that everything else has taken a backseat. I'll make some changes starting tomorrow. You're right. This one has gotten out of hand. Alan and Pete will pick up some of the slack. I wanted to personally handle many of the details because this thing is so big, but now that it's come this far and is doing well, I'll make sure I delegate more. In fact, I had planned to go up to the mine for the grand opening next week, but I'll back out of it if you want me to."

"No, I don't want you to do that. I just want you to be a husband and a father again. Sometimes I think you've been hanging around those single business associates of yours too long. They never made vows to love and cherish for better, for worse, for richer or poorer, and I wouldn't mind the latter if it meant having you around more."

Jim tried to focus on what she was saying. "I always thought of myself as a good provider. We are one week away from opening the mine, and as of today we'll become part of a company that's a serious player in the mining business. We are on the verge of becoming seriously rich. Think of the security this will provide. Think of never having to worry about money or risking it all again. That's what I've been spending all this time trying to do. And guess what? We're almost there. There'll be no poorer in this scenario."

Anita stared at him for a long time. "Just don't count your chickens before they're hatched."

Jim groaned at yet another cliché. He couldn't tell if she was still angry.

She didn't give him much time to think about it. "It's late. I'm going to bed."

"Okay. I'm going to take a shower." He waited until she was up the stairs and then started turning out lights.

The cool shower brought him to his senses. He ran through the evening and tried to decipher what had just happened. One more incredible business score. A one-night stand? And one pissed off wife. This was almost more than one guy could take.

CHAPTER 32

Jack Sanders strolled out of his office in the new wing that had been added to the old miner's dry at the Wolverine Mine. The chief geologist made his way down the hall to the general manager's office and poked his head in the outer office.

"Hi, Debbie. How goes it?"

"Just fine, Mr. Sanders, but it's pretty busy around here with last-minute preparation for the grand reopening ceremonies this afternoon."

"I suppose so. Where's the reverend?"

"He went over to the plant to make sure Don Nelson was up and running. They'd been having some problems over there, and he wanted to make sure the mill would be running for the tour today. He said he'd be back in a half an hour."

The news put a scowl on Jack's face. "Yeah, I'd heard about some of the problems. The mills don't do well with the large chunks of native copper and have been tripping out. If that's the case, he won't be back in thirty minutes. When he does come back, tell him I'm looking for him."

"I'll do that. Will you be in your office?"

"Yeah, for about an hour or so. But then I need to go back down on level nine to check something out. Make sure he gets a hold of me. It's important."

Jack went away wondering how best to break the news to Gary. No doubt he would be running around like crazy trying to get all the last-minute details for the tour in order before he had to appear on the platform for the governor's speech after lunch. Gary always ran around with too much to do in too little time. Jack was amazed that they had stayed on schedule for the mine development over the last nine months. Maybe he shouldn't mention it at all.

CHAPTER 33

Pete turned to Andy, who was sitting next to him in the first-class section of a United Boeing 777 en route to Denver International Airport from Chicago's O'Hare field. "Tell me about Ray McKinnen. What kind of a guy runs North American Metals?"

"For starters, a very energetic guy. Ray is always on the go. I'm surprised we were able to schedule a meeting with him this quickly. He's gone more than he's in the office."

"Why?"

"North American owns and operates five properties in two states and Canada. Ray keeps a close rein on the operations. Nothing major is ever purchased without his approval. He just doesn't sign the purchase orders either. He insists on knowing every detail and having personally reviewed the bids."

"Wow. Does he ever sleep?"

"Sometimes he does. At the office, that is. This guy is the living definition of a workaholic."

"Then what's his motivation for selling the company?"

"Money, of course. North American is a good moneymaker, but Ray wants to move on to bigger and better things. I know he's been talking to DeBeers in South Africa about a senior management position there."

"How much of North American does he own?"

"I believe the number is around 75 percent."

"Who owns the rest?"

"The other senior managers."

"Including yourself?"

"Of course." Andy didn't tell him that he had used the balance of his inheritance and whatever else he could borrow to acquire a 15 percent stake in North American. His shareholdings would be revealed soon enough during the due-diligence process.

Pete looked out the window at the mosaic patterns the farmlands made when viewed from thirty-five thousand feet. "Doesn't that present you with a conflict of interest?"

A look of concern came over Andy's face. "What do you mean?"

"You're a vice president of mining operations for J.A. MacIntyre Inc., and I presumed you have just resigned from a similar position for North American Metals."

"That's right, but why is that a conflict? I'm not negotiating the deal, nor am I the buyer. I don't hold shares in the company with my name on the door, and I have but a minority shareholding in the company being acquired. It's not my decision."

Andy had made a persuasive argument. Nonetheless, Pete was bent on playing the devil's advocate. "Yes, but you can greatly influence what happens."

A smile came across Andy's face. He knew he had him now. "Since when is being in a position of influence illegal?"

Not giving up, Pete countered, "It may not be illegal, but it could be unethical."

This time Andy gave him a look of disgust. "Give me a break. And try not to be so conflicted over this yourself."

CHAPTER 34

"Oh, Mr. Johnson, Mr. Sanders has been looking for you. He says it's important," Debbie half-yelled at Gary as he rushed into his office.

"Yeah. Dat figures. Everything's important today. Just had a shutdown in the mill, and now I suppose he's gonna tell me that the mine's had a cave-in or somethin.'"

Gary glanced through the stack of messages on his desk. He returned one phone call to the governor's office confirming the arrangements for the governor to deliver the keynote address at 2:00 p.m. that afternoon. Then he stomped down the hall to Jack's office.

"What can I do ya fer?" Gary said as he was still coming through the doorway.

"I came across something in our exploration efforts on nine that I thought you'd be interested in."

"Can't it wait until tomorrow? I'm pretty busy puttin' out fires at the moment."

Jack thought for moment trying to decide whether or not to add another complication to Gary's day. He pursed his lips because he had become concerned about the tour arrangements and Gary needed to know. "It can if you want to risk a roof failure while the governor's here."

Gary actually took a step back. Jack was not known for melodrama. "Say what?"

"You heard me. The core holes we took out of nine indicated the fault along which we've started mining in section one on seven changes direction again."

"So?"

"That means we've been eroding a major portion of the roof support structure. Basic rock mechanics, my friend. I don't believe the rock strata is stable enough to withstand further mining unless we go back in and condense our roof bolting pattern and add some steel where the number three crosscut makes the northeast turn."

"Geez, Jack. Do you know what that'll do to my production schedule? We will lose days." Gary wondered why Jack was taking up his time telling him this now. He couldn't understand what it had to do with the tour this afternoon.

"Yep. But I'd recommend you do it. You could probably get by for now, but if you go any farther without additional roof support, you're asking for trouble."

"I hear ya. What's this got to do with this afternoon?"

"You were planning to blast a fifteen-hole pattern to show the governor some fresh ore."

"Yeah. But I was going to do it on six where we've just reached a working face even quicker than I thought we would. I'd rather show 'em the high-grade seventy pounds per ton ore."

"Okay. My mistake. I thought it was scheduled for seven. You should be all right then."

"Good. I wish all my problems today were that easy. See ya at the tour. Remember, six, not seven."

"Glad somebody bothered to tell me!"

CHAPTER 35

The top executive of RMS had just finished a luncheon with the governor of the state of Michigan and was leaving the Miscowaubik Club to head to the mine. One couldn't have picked a better day, with but a few small clouds dotting an otherwise clear June afternoon.

Elizabeth glanced down Calumet Avenue on her way out of the front door of the club toward Arnie Tyrronen's house. The garage door had been left open. Obviously Arnie had already left to take his place on the speaker's platform after having been invited as a special guest by Elizabeth. After all, she would not have even become involved in the venture had it not been for Arnie.

A motorcade had parked in front of the club, waiting to take the governor's entourage to the reopening ceremony. Elizabeth looked in the direction of the governor's car when she heard her name called and saw Jim motioning for her to get in. She hadn't realized that she had been given such a place of honor, but then again, she owned 80 percent of Wolverine Mining.

Elizabeth had not paid much attention to the governor at lunch; rather, she was preoccupied with Jim's demeanor. He had been distant for the past week, and she hadn't yet had a chance to find out why. She suspected it had something to do with the night they had celebrated the formation of RMS and some flack he must have subsequently faced from Anita.

Again, her mind had drifted, and she heard Jim saying, rather annoyingly, "Liz, the governor asked how you got caught up with us band of swindlers."

The governor interjected. "Well, those weren't my words exactly, but Mr. Thomas has the gist of what I asked. How does a pretty girl like you become a partner in a mining venture?"

"I'm sorry. I was just taking in the gorgeous day outside. As to how I got involved in this venture, you might say it's in my genes. You see, my great-grandfather was an early investor in the mining industry up here, and last year after my mother died, I became interested in it once again." She went on to relay a bit of her family history and the sequence of events that led to her involvement.

Upon their arrival at the Wolverine Mine, they found a crowd of a couple thousand people who had gathered for the festivities. A miner's band was playing old tunes from the early 1900s. There was barely room for all the people in attendance, and many had to be bussed in for lack of parking. The crowd was in good spirits. A second major mine reopening was welcome news, signaling a boom to an area that had been bust for four decades. It was like the fourth of July come early, including the band. Red, white, and blue banners were everywhere, including some from the Society of Mining Engineers that read, *If it can't be grown, it has to be mined.*

Everyone took their place on the speaker's platform. Bob Grossman addressed the crowd as the master of ceremonies. Arnie was introduced to the governor as one of the prominent members of the old regime of mine management. This was a proud day for Arnie. He wished his wife would have lived to see this.

The governor then began his remarks. "It is indeed a notable day in Michigan when once again the vast natural resources in the Upper Peninsula are to be used in producing more efficient, less polluting automobiles in the Lower Peninsula. I plan to own one of the first models that come of the line next year using the high-grade copper-silver alloy windings in the electric motors. As I understand it, not only will the car go farther on electric power, but it can go faster with the added horsepower. We might need a new bill to raise the speed limits."

After the governor's remarks, Arnie was asked to say a few words about the way it used to be.

"Da MacIntyre family has been in the mining business now for over a hundred years. Elizabeth's great-grandfather, James A. MacIntyre, had a dream about building the best copper mining outfit in the copper country. Da old Tamarack Mine had lived up to that billing. It was certainly not the largest mine in the area; in fact, it paled when compared to da Calumet and Hecla operations that came about a few years later. However, it was one of the more technologically advanced operations. Since it was the deepest mine in the area, it relied on large and efficient steam-powered motors to move and hoist the ore. Later, some of the newest 'lectric haulage trains were introduced at this mine to make it competitive well into the twentieth century.

"But da most important innovation brought to the copper country by J. A. MacIntyre was not a machine; it was da way his employees were treated. From da common laborer to da high-paid miner to my job as mine captain, everyone was paid well, treated well, an' as a direct result, worked well together. I know dis precedent will be followed by the fourth generation MacIntyre management, and dis management style will reinvigorate King Copper once again."

After the speeches, a plaque was presented by the governor to Gary, commemorating the reopening of the mine. The honored guests were to take a quick tour of the mine and mill, and all were invited to a miner's ball that evening at the ballroom of the Calumet Theater. Gary led the party of twenty-one honored guests off the speaker's platform and into the new locker rooms that had been constructed for the mine foremen and engineers. There they all donned proper equipment and coveralls to begin the tour.

CHAPTER 36

The flight from Chicago had arrived at Denver nearly an hour late with the usual delays due to congestion at O'Hare. This meant Pete and Andy were going to have to really hustle to meet with Ray McKinnen at their appointed time.

On the ride over to Ray's office, Andy gave Pete some background on Ray, who was his boss. "Ray is a no-nonsense, hard-hitting, self-made businessman who started North American Metals in 1979 with a single gold mine in Colorado. He was either extremely lucky or smart because a year later, gold soared to over eight hundred dollars an ounce and he made a killing. He quickly reinvested his profits and expanded the company to its current size of five mines. Rather than buy several small mines, which would be mined out in a five-year timespan, Ray focused on acquiring the largest base of gold reserves in North America. The surge in precious metals prices over the past few years has made him wealthier. I think Ray figures gold has made its run during this last recession, and the outlook for a slow recovery has made him receptive to a buyout. Besides, he's got his eye on diamonds in South Africa now."

When they finally made it to Ray's office, Pete was very surprised at the lack of appointments one would normally expect in a president's office. Ray sat behind a single table, which was covered with papers and files. Behind him was a second table in much the same condition. Two unmatched chairs for guests were crowded in amongst boxes of reports, more files, and a bookshelf.

"Glad you could make it," Ray said as he held out his hand for a firm handshake. Dressed in jeans and sporting a handlebar mustache, he could be mistaken for a wildcatter panning for gold up in Clear Creek instead of someone running a company with five gold mines. "It takes forever to get downtown from the airport. I still don't know why they built it almost in Nebraska."

"Delays don't bother us," Pete said. "We came from Chicago, remember?"

"True. I guess we'd better make up for some lost time. Where do you want to start?"

Andy was determined to show Pete that he had charge of the situation. "Why don't we start with the prospectus of North American Metals you sent us?"

"What's there to start with?" Ray asked. "You know as much about North American as the next guy. I'm sure you've appraised Mr. Singer of all our strong points and brushed over the bad ones, haven't you, Andy?" Ray produced a hearty laugh at his own bit of wit. Andy was not amused, but he was stuck. He had helped Ray prepare the information to send to MacIntyre Inc. while Ray had arranged for the board of directors to sell him three times the shares he already owned at considerably less than book value.

Ray continued. "So we don't get bored with trying to impress each other with a sales job, I've arranged for a helicopter tour of two of our operations. On the corner of my desk are our latest financial summaries with production figures. I'll need you to execute this confidentiality agreement, and then we can get down to the nitty-gritty."

CHAPTER 37

At 3:45 p.m., the tour party was about to embark to the sixth level. The party of twenty-one guests accompanied by Gary and Jack rode the cage down to six.

The group was then split into two, with one half heading to the underground dump where the ore was hoisted to the surface in twelve-ton skips and the other going to the number three crosscut to see the solid wall of copper and view a working face. Elizabeth and Jim remained with the governor and followed Jack down to the number three crosscut.

Jim and Elizabeth brought up the rear of the contingent. Elizabeth looked for the rail that she had used as a balance beam the last time they had been there but could not find it.

"Did you lose something?" Jim asked.

"Yeah."

"What? I'll help you look for it."

"My rail."

"Your what?"

"Rail. R-A-I-L," she said in an exasperated state.

"Right," Jim muttered when he finally caught on to what she was up to.

"You remember. You saved my life the last time I was down here. Now I'm forever indebted to you."

"Well, almost correct. We're both in debt as a result of the fateful meeting the last time we walked along here."

"Do you believe in fate?"

Jim did not hesitate to respond. "You better believe I do. Fate governs everything I do. You and me are a product of fate. So is this whole venture. I've wondered more than once how certain circumstances come together, whether it be in a business deal or my personal life. The only conclusion I've ever been able to reach points to fate or destiny."

"That's about as deep a thought as we are underground."

She always had a way of pointing out the tangents that he often found himself going on by teasing him about them. He wasn't sure how much he liked it, but it was effective.

"Okay. You've shut me up. Let's catch up to the rest of the group."

"One more question."

"Shoot."

"What did happen to the tracks that used to be here?"

"Diesel motors, my dear. We abolished all of the old electric trains. You'll see when we get to the face."

"Oh," she mumbled to herself, now a bit embarrassed. She should have known that.

They caught up with the rest of their party just as they arrived at the working face. It had now been three weeks since the development work had ended and mining operations had begun. They climbed single file up the raise into an open stope, which at this point was just large enough for the party of twelve to stand in.

Jack moved to the face, where a pattern of ten blast holes had been drilled. "The ore that you see in the mound on your right was just blasted this morning. If you scrounge around through the pile, you'll be able to find chunks of ore that have large pieces of native copper embedded in them, like this one." He held up a piece of ore for everyone to see that had an irregular-shaped appendage jutting out of one side. He unlatched his geologist's pick from his belt and took a swipe at the side of the rock. A few sparks flew, and the native copper protrusion bent in half, exposing a shiny section that looked like a new penny.

Jack went on to explain how the ore was mined. While he was speaking, a tremor shook the cavern they were standing in, and almost simultaneously, several explosions were heard, including a blast in the stope they were in that sent fragments of rock hurtling through the air like shrapnel. Screams of terror and moans of agony followed in the split seconds that transpired during the cave-in. Then as soon as it had happened, it was over, with nothing but the sounds of loose rock trickling down the walls and the cloud of dust suspended in the now still air, giving evidence of what had just occurred. That is, until the shock wore off and the panic set in.

Arnie was the first to jump into action. He had acquired the legs of a twenty-five-year-old and was now on his feet and taking a quick look around to assess the situation. "Who's able ta get up and lend a hand?"

"Right here," Jack said, dusting himself off.

Cries of pain came from the edge of a pile of rock, where apparently one of the charges had gone off at the face. Bob Grossman was pinned under a slab of rock, and blood was streaming out of a gash across his left shoulder.

"Over here," Jim yelled. "Let's get this off of him."

Arnie, Jack, Jim, and one of the governor's aides braced themselves against the wall and pushed the rock off of Bob. As the rock rolled free, Bob again cried out in pain, for when the pressure was released from his left side, his broken arm slipped against his crushed ribs.

Jim knelt to attend to Bob. Elizabeth crawled over to join him.

"Who's still unaccounted for?" Arnie asked. He took a head count and came up with ten of the twelve that were standing there but three minutes ago.

"The governor!" shrieked his aide.

"Alan!" Jim exclaimed. "They were both standing over by Bob as he was explaining something to the governor while Jack was talking."

"Oh my God!" Elizabeth was horrified. Alan's leg was sticking out from under the pile of rock that had nearly crushed Bob.

They all started frantically digging around his body, and when they had uncovered him to his chest, Jim noticed that the dirt around Alan was moist with blood. There was no movement of the chest cavity, from which part of his rib cage protruded much like the piece of native copper Jack had held up just before the cave-in. *What a repulsive thought!* Jim chastised himself for letting his mind wander. His partner was dead. No time for sorrow now. The governor had to be close by.

"Over here," Jim heard Arnie say. He was working to free the governor. Jim leaped to Arnie's side and began to move rock and dirt away from the governor's head. It was to no avail. His face was almost beyond recognition. He heard choking sounds coming from behind him. When he turned toward the noise, he realized that Elizabeth had become sick to her stomach, having been overwhelmed with the ugliness of such violent deaths.

Jim went over to put his arm around her. She turned to face him, and he could see the streaks of dirt her tears made down her face as the light from his miner's lamp illuminated her face. She let out a moan and whispered to him, "How can something like this happen on a day like today? Any day? Oh, Jim, it's so terrible. I can't stand it."

Meanwhile, Arnie, the veteran miner, had taken charge. He had removed his lamp from his hardhat and was shining it around the cavern like a spotlight. He pointed down the raise they had climbed up and saw the bottom of the raise, an opening that was about four-by-six, was now filled with rubble.

"Folks, it looks as though the number three crosscut has caved in an' blocked our exit out of this stope," Arnie reported to the group. He walked over to the ore pass and saw the same thing. "Our only other means of escape was down the ore pass, but that's filled too."

"That explains why the air flow stopped right after the blast," Jack commented.

"How are we going to get out?" demanded Marty Davidson, the mayor of Calumet, who up until this point had said virtually nothing all day. "We have no air!"

"Not entirely true," Jack explained. "There is a considerable volume of air in this stope and in the raise and ore pass. We'll have to act quickly, but we don't need to panic. We can survive for a long time until somebody can get to us."

"Or we can get out," Arnie said. "Are dose holes all ready to shoot?"

"Yeah," Jack replied. "I believe so."

"Why on earth would ya do a stupid thing like that when ya knew you had visitors coming?"

"I guess it was a last-minute change to bring the tour up here." Jack was starting to get angry with the old man. "Look, you can complain about our mistakes when we get out of here alive. The fact is we're stuck, and yes, the holes are charged."

"Then, Einstein, don't ya see? That's our ticket out of here!"

Already red in the face, Jack stepped forward until he was nose to nose with Arnie. "What, are you crazy? Blast our way out? How do you propose doing that without killing the rest of us? We've got no detonator."

Without backing down, Arnie poked him on the sternum. "Come on, man! Use your head! I guess they don't teach ingenuity in mining schools anymore. You can set off an explosive without a blasting cap or detonating cord. How do you think the loaded holes over there went off and killed the governor and Alan Larsson? Shock, friction, sudden impact—any of those will trigger the rapid chemical reaction you call a blast. Back when I was mining copper, there was more than one way to move the rock."

"Give me a break," Jack retaliated. "I'm a geologist, not a mining engineer."

"Right now you're helpless without me," Arnie shouted. "You and the guys who run this operation are imbeciles, and when I get out of here, I'll see that that fact is proven beyond a doubt at your trial!"

"Settle down, old man! Like I told you, there'll be time to find out what happened later. Now if you've got a way to get us out, let's do it!"

Grossman groaned loudly before he lost consciousness.

At the sound of his suffering, Jim moved back over to Bob's side, only to observe that he had blacked out. He picked up his head and placed it in his lap then felt Grossman's neck for a pulse.

"I don't have a pulse on Bob!" he cried out in horror. "Somebody give me a hand!" Jim didn't know CPR. He had never felt so helpless in all his life.

Jack came over, rechecked Bob's pulse, and immediately set his head back, opened his mouth, and cleared the blood and saliva from around his mouth. He pinched Bob's nose closed and began mouth-to-mouth resuscitation. While he was doing that, Arnie came over to pump Bob's chest to try to restart his heart. They worked feverishly for five minutes as a tandem, with both men performing their tasks in a cadence barked out by Arnie. The rest of the group watched quietly. Elizabeth cried while she prayed for God to spare Bob's life.

Finally, Jack sat back and wiped the sweat off his forehead. "It's no use. We won't get him back. The other injuries he's got have taken their toll."

"I think you're right," Arnie agreed. "He's gone."

With that, they stood up and looked at each other as though sizing the other man up.

"Ya did all right, Jack," Arnie said. "I take back my personal attack, but I still find some of your professional practices questionable."

"If that's the closest you're goin' to come to an apology, I'll accept it." Jack stepped over Bob's body and patted Arnie on the back. "Now, where were we? Oh yeah, the drill holes. We'll need to fashion a long bar to pull the ANFO out of the holes. There's also a nitro capsule in each where we plant the blasting cap. The guys in the stopes usually have a bar around someplace."

Elizabeth was spurned into action. "Now there's something I can help you with. I saw a rod underneath the bench behind that scraper over there."

"Great," Arnie said. "Only that there's a tugger, Liz, and what you saw was a bar."

"As long as it works, it can be a toothpick for all I care," she shot back.

"Sorry, dear." Arnie hugged her. "Jack and I will have us out of here soon."

"Hope so," she answered in a barely audible voice. "God, I hope so."

CHAPTER 38

The other half of the tour party had been listening to Gary expound on the merits of the twelve-ton skips that were employed to move the ore to the surface from where they were standing on the sixth level when suddenly the very ground they were standing on reverberated, and a second later, all electrical power in the mine was cut off. Some members of the group had thought they'd heard the rumble of earth moving in the distance or an explosion or both. Fear rapidly spread throughout the assembly, as now everything had gone completely quiet and all senses were privy to where the movements of the miner's lamps were. People erratically looked around for signs or clues as to what had transpired. Excited whispers became loud questions.

"What happened?"

"Did you hear that?"

"What's going on, Gary?"

"What do we do now?"

Gary picked up the pager phone to reach the dispatcher on the surface, but the system was dead. They had been cut off until backup generators were started to produce a minimum level of power for emergencies or until power was restored. His thoughts turned to Jack Sanders and the other half of the group. There was no way he could contact them, but he could find out if they were all right.

Gary turned to Don Nelson, the mill superintendent, who had been standing next to him when everything shut down. He spoke softly. "Look, Don, I don't know what's goin' on here, but I don't like it. The ground vibration we just felt was just like an end-of-shift shot, 'cept worse. I'm gonna check on Jack and then try to find out what's goin' on. Keep dis under control."

He turned to the group. "Folks, I'm gonna find out why we've got a power outage. Nothin' to worry about. Don here will take care of ya 'til I get back." With that, he was gone from the pocket that housed the rock dump.

Out on the main haulage way, Gary found a shuttle car and drove down to the number three crosscut. He didn't like what he found. Some fifty feet before he reached his destination, his path was blocked by a pile of loose rock. The entire west side of the haulage way had subsided.

He jumped off the shuttle car and ran over to the pile. "Jack! Jack, can you hear me?" There was no answer, just a few trickles of loose dirt running down the wall. "Damn!" he muttered to himself.

Walking back to the shuttle car, he kicked a rock out of his way and then sat on the front of the vehicle. "Now what am I goin' to do?" As soon as he asked himself the question, he knew the answer.

Five minutes later, he arose from his knees. They were wet after having knelt next to the shuttle car to pray. He didn't mind. Gary felt relieved and ready to tackle even this most tragic situation. He paused, trying to decide what his next move should be. He could always ride back to the shaft and climb the nine hundred feet to the surface for help.

He caught something out of the corner of his eye. It was a pager phone mounted next to the bottom of an ore pass. In fact, it was the ore pass that led to the stope in which the remainder of the tour party was apparently trapped.

Trying the pager phone, Gary yelled into the mouthpiece, "Hello. Jack Sanders, can you hear me? Section six-three-one, please respond."

The pager phone next to the tugger crackled at first; then the broken sound of Gary Johnson's voice came through. "Sanders, can you hear… three-one, please respond."

At first the group was startled; then Jack practically dove for the pager phone. He pressed the button on the handset. "Gary, we're here. Where are you?"

"I'm at the bottom of the ore pass. Looks like you've got several feet of rock in there."

"We know."

"Are ya folks all right?"

There was a pause. "The nine of us that survived are. We were just pulling out ANFO to try to blast our way out of here."

"What? What ANFO?"

"There are several loaded holes up here. A couple went off in the cave-in. That's how we lost Bob Grossman, Alan Larsson, and the governor."

Gary thought he'd heard correctly, but the connection was breaking up a bit. "Did ya say lost as in dead?"

"Yes."

"Oh Lord, what's happened?"

"I was just going to ask you that, Gary. We'll have time for that later. Just get us out of here. The air's getting pretty stale."

"Sure thing. I'll need about fifteen minutes to round up some help."

"Yo, Gary. This is Sam." He was the surface operations foreman and had heard the last pager conversation. "We finally got emergency power on here. What has happened down there?"

"A major cave-in, Sam. We need some help. We've got half our party trapped in six-three-one stope. I need a load-haul-dump machine here—a couple of them, pronto! We'll also need some medical help."

"Gotcha. We'll have the cage running in a few minutes."

Gary drove to the rock dump to meet Don and to evacuate the half of the group still there. Upon arrival, he saw that a few of his guests were a bit shaken, but for the most part, everyone was holding up well.

"I caught your conversations on the pager," Don said as he walked away from the group to talk with Gary. "I also informed the group of the deaths and the fact that Jack's group was still trapped but help is on its way. The lady from the Department of Commerce was practically hysterical over the governor's death. All of us were shocked to hear of the three fatalities. The s—- is gonna hit the fan over this."

"I don't care!" Gary shot back. "Right now, I've got nine people trapped in this mine, and I don't need yer analysis nor yer conjectures over what is or isn't goin' to happen."

"Sorry. I'll get these people over to the cage and wait for it."

"Do that. And when the load-haul-dump machine from seven gets up here, have 'em meet me by number three crosscut."

With that, Gary jumped back in the shuttle car and drove around to the other side of the rock dump. He hoped at least one of the load-haul-dump machines, know in mining lingo as LHDs, from section two would be parked there. When he maneuvered past the skip control room, he found that his intuition had proved correct. There was one of his new Toro units. He pulled the shuttle car up next to the LHD and quickly switched equipment. *Great,* he thought to himself. *Now I've at least got a fighting chance.*

When he arrived back at the site of the cave-in, he ran over to the pager phone. "Hello, Jack. I'm back with a LHD. I'm gonna see if I can move some of this dirt from the ore pass. The man raise is another fifty feet away, and it'll take forever to clear that. You got any way of gettin' down the chute?"

"No, I don't think so. Maybe we can rig up somethin.'"

"You do that, and I'll get busy. Let me know if you can get down. Meanwhile, I'll get some more help. Sam, can ya send down the rope ladder we've got up in the dry on the first cage down?"

"Gotcha, Gary. You should have it in a few minutes."

A puff of diesel fumes shot into the haulage way as Gary revved up his machine. He then began the tedious task of scooping up the dirt and rock with the four-cubic-yard bucket on his LHD and depositing the nearly six tons of material some one hundred fifty yards back down the haulage way, where the number two crosscut was.

Moments later, he was joined by a second LHD. Gary and Lucy Watkinson worked skillfully at removing the rock from the bottom of the ore pass as quickly as their LHDs could. They would pass each other along the haulage way at speeds up to fifteen miles per hour, twice as fast as normal use of the machines would dictate.

In the stope, the stark reality of what had transpired was starting to grip the trapped dignitaries. Most of them had never seen death up close before. It was above all a shocking experience, which then turned to a feeling of deep sadness.

Jack and Arnie had given up on extracting the explosives from the boreholes now that rescue efforts were underway. They simply sat in silence with their backs against the face.

What had gone wrong? Jack reflected. He had properly warned Gary about the roof conditions and had carefully planned the blast on seven. What he hadn't counted on was this morning's crew leaving loaded holes on six. It was a last-minute change, and somebody hadn't gotten the instructions right. It was Gary's last-minute change. He was off the hook. Small comfort. This shouldn't have happened.

Elizabeth huddled with Jim away from everyone else. Her usually bright face was now distraught. Her chin quivered, and her voice shook as she spoke. "Never in my wildest dreams did I think a disaster like this could happen. Jim, the governor is dead! Our partners are also gone. All because of this ungodly scheme of ours to bring a mine onstream as soon as possible. Contracts, production, money—that's all that was ever considered. It pales next to the value of those lives." She began to sob.

"You can't blame yourself. Yes, it was an ambitious undertaking, but we don't even know what happened yet. Punishing yourself will not bring them back." Somehow Jim found his own words empty. "However, one thing is for certain. Things will be forever changed. Neither the company nor us will be able to function as in the past."

Those words did have substance. "What do you mean?"

"I mean you should add lust to your list of despicable terms describing our little venture."

Elizabeth was dumbfounded. "What about the other night? Last week?"

"That was another mistake. When we get out of here, we're going to have to reevaluate our whole future."

At first, she appeared shocked. She was silent except for a whimper as she began to softly cry. "You may have to, but I know where mine's going. It's going to the bottom of this hole in the ground without you. Don't give up what we've got. It's not lust. I need you more than ever now."

She hugged him as tightly as she could. He felt a pang of guilt for being so hard on her. Putting his arms around her, he held her while she sobbed on his shoulder.

By now, they could hear the drone of the LHDs working to free them. As the sound grew louder, they took comfort in the prospect that they would finally be able to escape what was almost their burial alive. In fact, for two of them, it had been.

"Hello, Jack," Gary's familiar call over the pager phone.

"Yeah, Gary. How's it goin'?"

"Good, up until now. Looks like we've got a hang-up in the ore pass. I'm gonna shoot it with a couple of sticks. Give me a few minutes; then I'll let you know when I'm ready."

"He's going to set off a charge in the ore pass?" asked a frantic Marty Davidson.

"Don't worry," Jack said. "Gary's an expert. All we'll feel up here is a blast of air. He'll set it so it forces the rock down the pass."

"Hello, Jack." This time it was Sam, the dispatcher. "I've got four EMTs on their way down. Ya need more help than that?"

"Nah. In fact, all we've got down here are some bumps, bruises, and scratches. We do have three bodies though."

"We'll come in for those later. Hang in there; we'll have ya out in no time."

"Thanks, Sam."

Shortly thereafter, the engine noise from the LHDs stopped, and all that could be heard were faint voices coming up the ore pass. That was followed by some pounding and then the loud hammering of an air-driven, hand-held jackhammer.

It wasn't long, and Gary's voice came back over the pager. "Ya ready up there, Jack?"

"Give us two minutes and let it go."

Jack ushered everybody over to the opposite side of the stope. They crouched down and buried their heads in their laps and one another's shoulders. After what seemed like an eternity, a loud, sharp crack occurred, followed immediately by a strong air blast, which drilled small particles of dust and rock fragments into the side of their faces. Then it was over.

"Anybody home?" Gary called up the ore pass.

"You bet," Arnie yelled back through cupped hands. "Ya wanna come up for a visit?"

"Nah, how about you comin' down? I've got a rope ladder for ya to use. Send me a line, and I'll get it up to ya."

The descent down the ladder would have been scary any other day but today. To the rescued, it was one of the easiest things they'd done—climbing out of a stope to freedom. To the rescuers, it was the end of what had been a long afternoon of uncertainty. To all, it was the beginning of a difficult and arduous process of piecing shattered lives and dreams back together.

CHAPTER 39

Andy had just settled into his room at the Brown Palace Hotel in downtown Denver. The Brown was a classic old hotel on the west side of the city. His room was done up with furnishings that reflected turn-of-the-century elegance. It wasn't too different than staying at the Michigan House in Calumet. The décor was to his liking. Despite the fact that he had lived in the area for several years, Andy had only been in the Brown once, and that was in the pub located off the main lobby.

He had switched on the television, kicked off his shoes, and was about to spend a relaxing half hour in his room before meeting Pete and Ray for dinner. The events of the afternoon still swirled in his mind, but he sat straight up in the bed when a just-in news story was read.

"This afternoon, during a mine tour following grand opening ceremonies, a tragic cave-in occurred at a newly-opened copper mine in Michigan's Upper Peninsula. The apparent cave-in occurred on the sixth level of the Wolverine Mine, claiming three lives, including the governor of the state of Michigan and two major investors in the mine. The incident remains under investigation."

"Oh no!" Andy was taken aback by the report, particularly by the loss of life, the governor, at that. Something had gone terribly wrong. He looked at his watch. It was six ten, Rocky Mountain time;

that would translate to eight ten at the mine. Maybe he could reach someone.

Picking up his cell phone, Andy scrolled through the stored phonebook for the phone number of the mine. He decided he'd try to reach Jack first to find out what had happened underground and then talk to his sister to find out what RMS was going to do about it.

"Wolverine Mine," announced the male voice on the other end of the phone.

"Is Jack Sanders around?"

"He is, but he's tied up. Can I take a message?"

"No, tell him this is extremely urgent. Andy MacIntyre needs to talk to him."

Recognizing the voice, the security guard responded quickly. "I guess you've heard about what's happened then, Mr. MacIntyre. I'll see if I can find Mr. Sanders."

"Thanks."

After waiting on hold for five minutes, which seemed like five weeks to Andy, a familiar voice came on the line. "Hello, Andy. I know why you're calling. The story has made all the major wire services by now."

"That's right. What the hell happened?"

"I can't give you all the particulars right now, but someone screwed up when they dropped some fresh ore for the governor to see on six. When the blast went off on seven, some loaded holes in the stope we were in went off. It was pure hell, Andy. Should never have happened—"

"Wait a minute! What do you mean, six? The tour was supposed to be on seven."

"It was, until Gary made a last-minute change this morning. He decided he wanted them to see the high-grade stuff. We had to scramble last minute."

"S—-! So this is the result of a late-inning change of game plan."

"Your analogy sucks! Alan Larsson and Bob Grossman are dead. I watched Grossman die in my hands, Andy. I'm telling you, this ain't good. All hell is going to break loose now. With the governor dead, this place will be crawling with MSHA inspectors and everybody else under the sun. It'll be a long time before we ever open up again, if we ever do. Right now, I don't even give a damn!"

"Get a hold of yourself, Jack. Give it a rest, and I'll talk to you in the morning. I'm sorry for what you've had to go through. It was an accident, remember? Now, is my sister around?"

"She just went back to the house with Jim Thomas and Arnie Tyrronen. You should be able to reach her there in a few minutes."

"Okay. Like I said, get some rest, and I'll call you in the morning. It was an accident. Good night."

CHAPTER 40

It had been the worst day of her life. When Elizabeth had emerged from the mine after spending over three hours trapped in a stope, she was bombarded with questions from reporters waiting behind a barricade.

"Ms. MacIntyre, as the primary stockholder of the mine, can you comment on what happened?"

"Sorry, there's not much to say at this time. This has been a real tragedy, and we will investigate what caused the cave-in. I can't comment beyond that."

There wasn't much to be said. She didn't know what had happened other than correct safety measures might not been taken that morning and three men were dead. The rest of the group was very lucky to be alive with only some minor cuts and bruises. As a matter of fact, it wasn't until she arrived at home did the pain from the cuts on her neck and the side of her face really begin to hurt. She had found small fragments of rock embedded in her face as a result of the blast. They were minor. They would heal. However, it would be a long time before her psyche would be repaired.

The sight of the three bodies being removed from the cage and wheeled on covered stretchers into two waiting ambulances had unnerved her. With her adrenaline levels high, she had not given Alan's and Bob's deaths too much thought once the initial horror of the incident had passed. Sitting in her living room, it was now another matter. Two of her business associates and friends had died in an accident that occurred in a mine she owned. Maybe Jim was right. It was time for a change. Things could not continue along the same path. What to change? She didn't yet know. In time, it would become clearer. Right now, she was too exasperated to think.

Jim caught the empty look in Elizabeth's eyes. She had been staring at nothing for several minutes. He knew her too well to take her reaction to all this lightly. She was undoubtedly distressed.

"Liz." His voice broke her trance, and she turned to look at him. "We've hashed the whole incident out several times over the past hour or so. There's no point sitting here doing it again. We won't know what happened or what is going to happen at the mine for some time. Our plans have gone on indefinite hold. Beginning tomorrow, I'll start to deal with the aftermath personally if you want me to."

"How about if we bury our friends first!" Elizabeth shot back.

"I'm sorry. I didn't mean to be so insensitive. Of course. My only point is that someone will have to make some decisions regarding the project with Alan and Bob gone. They had been calling the shots."

Arnie, sensing this was going nowhere, decided to step in to defuse the situation and calm frazzled nerves. "Look, Jim, like you said, it'll wait until tomorrow. Liz, why don't ya get some sleep?"

"Of course," a frustrated Jim remarked. "It will wait. I'm a bit anxious and in a rush as usual. Good idea. Let's catch some shut-eye. And by the way, Arnie, I just wanted to thank you for your efforts today. Things would have been a lot worse had you not been there."

"Ya woulda made it out. I didn't really do anything. There was nothin' any of us could do."

"Bulls—-! If I recall correctly, you were going to blast us out if need be."

"Well, I'm glad I didn't get a chance to try. That coulda been a little tenuous, ya know."

"So I gather—"

They were interrupted by the phone ringing.

"Want me to get it?" Jim asked.

"No, I've got it," Elizabeth's replied. She arose from the couch and picked up the phone on the phone table next to the dining room.

"Hello, sis," Andy said, showing a note of concern. "You all right up there? I caught the news report on the cave-in."

"Yeah. I'm fine. Just a bit shaken up and I've got a few cuts and bruises. Nothing serious though."

"Sounded pretty serious to me. What happened?"

Elizabeth proceeded to take Andy through the gory details of what had transpired that afternoon. Actually, it did her good to verbalize what had happened. Jim and Arnie sat on the couch and watched the tears well up in her eyes as she described the feelings of helplessness and the despair she felt—that they all felt—when she had been trapped, when she feared for her life, and when she could do nothing to save her friends from a horrid death.

After she had hung up the phone, Jim came over to where she was sitting and put his arm around her. "It's not going to get any easier. Be strong. We'll weather this storm together. Tomorrow, we'll start sorting this whole mess out. Tonight, if you want someone to lean on, I'm here."

"Do you really mean that?"

"Yes."

"Ahem." They both looked up and saw Arnie standing over them. "I think I'll be goin' now. Glad you're feelin' better, Liz. You're in good hands with Jim."

Elizabeth stood up and planted a kiss on Arnie's cheek. She and Jim saw him to the door and thanked him for all that he'd done.

Once Arnie had gone and they had settled back on the couch, Elizabeth asked, "I know this may not be a good time for this, Jim, but what about us?"

Jim did not answer at first. He sat there looking off across the room deep in thought. "You're right. It's not a good time to discuss this. Why don't we leave it at that?"

"I'd like to, but I can't. You've given me a cold shoulder this entire trip. I'm aware of your pressures at home. I'm also aware of your pressures here. You told me you were here for me, and I'm telling you I'm here for you. There are no other strings attached."

Jim just held her for a long time. He savored her presence next to him with all his senses: the warmth of her body next to his, the fresh smell of her shampoo and touch of her hair on his cheek, the softness of her skin and the light sweater she was wearing. It would be so easy to do what he wanted to do next. He had done nothing but thought about the evening they spent together last week. That was the problem. It was haunting him. Now he had much bigger problems. No need to complicate things even more.

"Look, Liz, I don't know what's going to happen next. But whatever it is, it won't happen tonight. Too much has already happened, and I need to go call my wife before she finds out from someone else. No strings attached, right?" With that, he strolled for the door and before closing it said, "I'll give you a call tomorrow. Goodnight."

CHAPTER 41

The dining room at the Brown was a dimly lit place that reminded Andy of an old English hotel. The dark woodwork was plentiful and gave one the feeling that he was dining in downtown London at the turn of the century rather than in the heart of the Wild West. Andy wondered why he had never visited this place before in the years that he'd lived in Denver.

He had relayed the news of the cave-in to Pete and Ray, along with the details he had obtained from Elizabeth. Pete had been horrified when he learned that Alan was among the dead. He and Alan had been pretty close, particularly since they had been working on the Wolverine project together.

"I know how shocking this news must be to both of you," Ray was saying. "It certainly changes the complexion of our discussions tonight. I suppose the best thing to do would be to suspend any further talks until we find out what is going to happen to Wolverine and RMS now that two of the principals in the operation have perished."

"I'm afraid you're correct, Ray," Pete replied. "There's no point in going any further. In fact, an acquisition may even be out of the question now. Who knows what this will do to the company?"

"Well, Pete," Ray said, "it's not out of the question in any event."

"How's that?" Pete looked puzzled.

"I mean that North American Metals may be interested in acquiring Wolverine's holdings if the owners are unable to or do not want to operate the mines any longer."

At first Pete became a bit angry at what seemed to be a ploy to hunt for properties at bargain basement prices; however, he realized that there might not be a choice in the matter. A lot of big contracts hung in the balance, and he knew the investors were already stretched pretty thin with what they had put into the development thus far. He chose simply to not say anything.

The silence was broken by Andy's remarks. "We are to understand that North American is willing to acquire Wolverine given what has just happened?"

"Yes. You see, we've done our homework too. By our estimates, the book value of the company is close to two hundred million dollars. We would be willing to acquire the company for something close to that, say one hundred fifty million dollars."

Pete was still appalled. "I can't address what the company may be worth. My function is more technical than financial, although I can tell you that Wolverine alone has over a billion dollars in contracts lined up and what was formally Kearsarge Mining has sales of over a quarter a billion in copper ingots annually. What you're offering is a small price to pay for such potential; however, I will take this back to Jim Thomas for consideration."

"Better yet," Andy butted in, "I'll relay your offer to Phillip Turner. After all, MacIntyre Inc. does own 80 percent of Wolverine, and as the vice president of mining operations for the majority shareholder, I'd have to say we're pretty interested. No doubt our mode of operation at these mines will be reviewed, and given the loss of the two major managers of our venture in the Copper Country, I feel we should seriously consider your offer." It was apparent that Andy was enjoying flexing his muscle, particularly his senior position over Pete. Nonetheless, it didn't bother Pete since he'd dealt with cocky, rich kids before.

"I'd appreciate that," Ray said. "It would be a shame to see the operations fall apart because of this incident. It's already a tragedy; however, you know firsthand, Andy, that North American is an experienced mining outfit. We've been through cave-ins of our own. It's not pleasant, nor is it easy to rebuild and get things back to any resemblance of normalcy. Rest assured, we'll do whatever we can and would still like to be a part of this venture."

CHAPTER 42

It was almost 10:00 p.m. when Jim opened the door to his hotel room. What a day! He hoped he'd never see another one like it. The thought of a hot shower appealed to him. As he took his shirt and tie off, he noticed the red message light flashing on the phone.

"Front desk. May I help you?"

"Yes. I've got my message light flashing."

"You have an urgent message to call your wife."

"Thank you," Jim said as he slowly hung up the phone. *I've been so caught up in this mess I didn't get around to let my wife know I'm all right. She's probably worried to death. How can I get so wrapped up in myself to ignore my family? This thing has gone too far, Jim!*

He picked up the phone and even had to think twice to remember his home phone number. He'd come close to death that afternoon, and only now did the reality of the situation strike him. Once again, he'd been spared by fate. How often would he continue to ignore happenings and changes in his life that must be more than simply chance? If there was a God, he must be trying to tell Jim Thomas something. It was time to turn his priorities around. No better time than the present and no better place to start than with his relationship with his wife.

"Hello," came Anita's familiar voice on the other end of the line.

"Anita, it's Jim."

"Jim, it's so good to hear from you. I don't know whether to be angry or happy. Why haven't you called? I needed to know you were okay. Oh, God, I'm glad you are."

"Anita?"

"Yes?"

"How fast can you get here?"

CHAPTER 43

The clock on the wall in the Houghton County Memorial Airport read 6:20 a.m. Jim had not slept for almost twenty-four hours, but surprisingly, his lack of sleep had little or no effect on him. Time just simply wore on. With its passing came new realizations. Among them was the fact that an important period in his life was coming to an end. Change was inevitable. Fate had made it so. Or was it fate? Somehow, Jim felt something more powerful than fate taking hold in his life. What it was, he couldn't identify yet. A religious experience? Maybe. How would he know? Or maybe it was just the shock of the disaster. He knew his emotional level was running in high gear. Oh well, he'd talk to Gary about it when he got a chance. After all, Gary had been through the same thing. He respected Gary, now even more so given Gary's heroics. What would he do now?

Jim was not afforded any more time to answer the question because he caught the lights of Wolverine's corporate plane out of the corner of his eye as it roared past the terminal, slowing down from the 140-mile-per-hour speed at which it had landed. Standing up to stretch his legs, Jim suddenly realized that he'd been sitting there for the better part of an hour with his mind racing off in all different directions. Shaking his head to clear any cobwebs, he ran his fingers through his hair as he approached the plate-glass windows facing the runway to watch the plane taxi into the terminal.

As the engines wound down, the door was thrown open, and the pilot emerged and jumped to the tarmac, barely touching the steps. Anita exited the plane with the help of the pilot's outstretched arm.

What a sight for sore eyes! Jim thought. He had sent the plane for Anita just after hanging up the phone some seven hours ago. Mack, their pilot, was just turning in for the night when Jim had made the urgent request to fly to Chicago and back. Fortunately, Mack was used to responding on a moment's notice. It was, after all, part of the job. Private pilots don't fly by the same rules commercial pilots do, so after giving Anita some time to pack and catching a couple hours of sleep, he was off to the airport. Jim had a couple hundred dollars in his pocket as a thank-you to Wolverine Ventures' faithful pilot.

Anita quickened her pace toward the terminal, shivering in the early morning air. As she opened the door, Jim was standing there waiting to embrace her. It was as though he had not held her in his arms for months.

"Oh, baby," Jim mumbled in her ear, "I can't tell you how happy I am to see you. It's been pure hell."

"I know. Come on, let's get out of here and talk about it." She put her arm around his waist and walked with him out to the car. Mack followed with her bags.

By seven fifteen, they were in Jim's room at the Michigan House. Jim hadn't said much on the ride over, just nestled his head in Anita's hair as they watched the sun come up on one of the longest days of the summer. Now he was ready to talk, and talk he did. Anita just sat on the edge of the bed and listened.

"It took losing one of my closest friends to make me realize how out of control things had gotten. I know that you had told me the same thing not long ago, and I was honestly trying to change things. But now, it's as though I've been slapped in the face. Maybe that's what it takes, a wakeup call."

"Whoa, Jim. What's all the guilt about?"

At first he avoided looking at her; then he looked her straight in the eye. He couldn't decide whether or not to tell her about Elizabeth. When he summoned her, he had intended to come clean with everything. Now that he'd had several hours to think about it, he couldn't. Things were bad enough. "Nothing. Let's go get some breakfast. You must be hungry."

They walked down to the dining room hand in hand. "We'll get through this together," she told him.

Jim remembered saying those same words just hours ago. Now he wondered exactly how they all would do this. Words are cheap.

CHAPTER 44

Elizabeth and Tina sat at the kitchen table of the MacIntyre estate rehashing the events of the two days that had transpired since the tragedy. It had been the worst two days Elizabeth had ever had to live through. Not only did she have to discharge some official duties, such as visiting Michelle Grossman, but she had to perform these with Jim. No one should have to be put through all this.

"He brought his wife up here," Elizabeth somberly informed her friend.

"That really sucks."

"Yeah. Makes me doubt if he meant anything he said before. But I did meet her yesterday. She didn't stare me down like I thought she would. Instead, she just looked me over like she was curious."

"You said she was a lawyer?"

"Yeah. She's probably had lots of practice not showing her feelings."

Both of them looked up a little startled as the door that led to the back staircase abruptly opened. Andy walked into the kitchen dressed in a pair of sweats. Noticing their surprise, he chuckled.

"I hope I'm not interrupting anything important. I just came down to see if I could rustle up a cup of coffee."

"Come in and have a seat," Elizabeth said. "I just forgot you were here. Tina was just listening to me feeling sorry for myself."

"You can't do that forever, sis. I came up to help you solve some of those problems and then get you outta here, remember?"

"Yeah, I remember. I hope you're a miracle worker, 'cause that's what it's going to take."

"Leave it to the wizard."

He kissed his sister on the forehead and lumbered over to the coffee maker and poured himself a cup. Taking Elizabeth up on her invitation, he sat down at the kitchen table to drink his coffee. "So what's the pity party all about?"

"Andy!" Tina scolded in a stern voice.

"I'm sorry, Liz."

"Jim brought his wife up to stay with him."

Andy just shrugged. "And that's a problem?"

Elizabeth looked at him incredulously. "I can see you failed sensitivity training."

Her look and commentary didn't faze him. "Have you considered that it's all just for appearances? He has an image to maintain through all of this, and a lot of people are looking… at both of you."

For a brief moment she let her guard down with her brother. "You have a point. I never thought of it that way." She placed her hand on his. "Maybe I have misjudged you."

He held her hand. "Don't worry, sis. We'll get through this together."

CHAPTER 45

The cage slowed to a halt at the surface. The hoist operator gave the signal to let the occupants know that it was safe to lift the gate and step off. Gary disembarked first and turned around to watch the two mine inspectors follow, with Arnie and Jack bringing up the rear.

"Come on over to my office," Gary instructed his visitors. "We can go over da details there."

Without even changing from their mine clothes, the party strolled across the parking lot to Wolverine's office building. Gary found some extra chairs, and they all sat in a semicircle around his desk.

"Let me make sure I understand what I just saw," said Stewart, the chief inspector. "The ten holes that were loaded on six were packed the morning of the blast, but you changed plans and decided to hold the tour on six rather than seven."

"No. I had always planned to hold the tour on six. Unfortunately, dat was not properly communicated to my chief geologist or his foreman. Once they were informed—"

"When was that?"

"Later that mornin.' As I was sayin,' once dey realized where the tour was to be held, dey cleared out the number one section on six and resumed work on the number three section on seven."

"Why on earth would you be blasting when a tour was going on?"

Gary put his head in his hands, and there was silence for a moment. He looked up. His face was strained. "For the life of me, sir, I don't know."

Stewart turned his attention to Jack. "You're in charge of mine planning, aren't you?"

Jack had been deposed before. He knew how to play the game. "Yes."

"Do you also oversee scheduling?"

"Of certain things I do."

Stewart was getting visibly angry now. "Does that include blasting?"

One-word answers whenever possible. Jack remembered the coaching he'd received from his attorneys in the past. "Yes."

"Did you schedule the blast on seven?"

"No."

"Who did? It's not in your records."

"That's correct. Every morning I meet with the shift foremen to go over the production plan for the day. When the plans were changed, I instructed the foreman on seven to drill and load the holes on section three. I did not instruct him to set them off. He apparently misunderstood."

"This misunderstanding took the lives of three men, including the governor of the state of Michigan!"

"I know that."

"Did you also know that you were in violation of several MSHA regulations, some of which I'm convinced, if followed, would have prevented this from happening."

"No, sir. I was not aware of that, nor do I agree with you."

Arnie couldn't hold back any longer. "That, Mr. Sanders, unequivocally demonstrates your ignorance and proves why you should never have held any position of responsibility in this or any mining operation."

Gary held up his hand. "Dat's enough of that kinda talk. I will not tolerate personal attacks on my employees during this investigation. Arnie, I invited ya here today because ya were an eyewitness to what had transpired, and as a former mine captain, ya can lend some much-needed expertise to this discussion. Let's keep it constructive, eh?"

"Okay, Gary. I'm sorry, but arrogant statements like the one Sanders made a minute ago rub me the wrong way, especially when I saw how things were handled."

"How were things mishandled?" Stewart asked.

"Well, sir, I'm having the same problem you are, understanding why there were loaded holes on six in the first place. These should have been reported before any tour was started. In fact, it wouldn't have been a problem to set them off so that a fresh face was exposed for the tour anyway."

"Agreed. Go on."

"After the explosion occurred, it became apparent to me that Sanders didn't know the first thing about mine rescue. Does he or anybody else in this outfit have any training?"

"Yes, Arnie, I do," Gary replied. "However, dat's a valid point. Because we're such a new operation, not all of my foremen have received any special training, nor is it required of dem by MSHA regulations."

"That may be true," Stewart shot back. "Nonetheless, as I was saying earlier, I think this tragedy could have been averted. Your authorization and signoff procedures leave a lot to be desired. As mine manager, I'll have to hold you responsible, Mr. Johnson."

Gary knew this was coming. "I accept responsibility for what happened. However, note dat dis was a result of miscommunication. Dat is not a violation of MSHA requirements. It is a tragic accident."

CHAPTER 46

It had been a long day for Jack Sanders—one of many. He was glad that the meeting with the MSHA inspectors was over and was just now beginning to loosen up with his third beer at Shutes Bar. Andy walked into the bar just after Jack was served his beer, and he nodded to Andy, acknowledging his presence, despite the fact that he was late.

"Sorry about being late," Andy said as he took a seat at Jack's table. "It took me a while to get away from my sister this morning. She's got one bad case of the blues. What a basket case. Should be a piece of cake gettin' her to sell."

"I hope so," Jack said. "That'd be the only thing that's gone right. I just finished a meeting with Gary, Arnie Tyrronen, and the mine inspectors. Fortunately, they blamed it all on Gary, poor son of a b——. I was beginning to wonder though. Tyrronen was spouting off and almost got my balls in a jam. But I'm only the chief geologist. The buck stops with the mine manager."

"That's good. Then nobody suspects that you ordered the charges placed on six."

"Nope. But I gotta tell ya, I was scared. It should have never happened this way."

"I know. I keep telling you, it was an accident. How were we supposed to know that Gary wanted a show-and-tell on six?"

Andy stopped talking as he saw the waitress approach out of the corner of his eye. He ordered a beer to go along with the fourth one that Jack asked for.

"Hey, partner. You better slow down," Andy commented.

"What for?"

"Before you get so soused you spill your guts all over this bar."

"Don't worry, Mr. MacIntyre. I can hold my liquor."

"Yeah, I guess you're right. After what you've accomplished, you deserve a drink. Congratulations, buddy, looks like we pulled this one off."

"Don't count your chickens yet, my friend. It ain't over till the inspectors close the investigation."

"I realize that, Jack. You leave that up to me. Before the dust settles, Gary Johnson will be in jail."

Jack had drunk enough to cause him to be a bit reflective. He thought about how Gary had shown some confidence in him, had gone to bat, gotten him the chief geologist's job, and had even produced some stock options. *What a heel I'd be if Johnson went up to face criminal charges,* he thought. For the first time, he was remorseful for what he had orchestrated in order to set himself up so he wouldn't ever have to bounce from mining camp to mining camp again. It wasn't supposed to happen this way. No one was supposed to get hurt. A small cave-in during the big tour that pointed to a few violations, temporarily shutting down operations, resulting in a default on deliveries; that's the way it was supposed to work. Now, it was complicated.

CHAPTER 47

Jim sat in front of the television in his hotel room at the Michigan House. He rested his chin in his hands as he watched the news commentator review the former governor's accomplishments in his six-year tenure. The clip ended with a live shot of the governor's flag-draped coffin lying in state at the state capital in Lansing.

He felt Anita put her arm across his shoulders and sit down on the end of the bed next to him. They had struggled through the past two days, but ironically, it was the struggling that pulled them back together. Their marriage had been on rocky ground, but they had decided to keep trying. Only time would tell what was in store for the college sweethearts who seemingly had everything going for them a few short months ago.

"Haven't you seen enough?" Anita asked. "There's nothing more to be done here right now. We need to go and pay our respects to Alan's family."

"I've probably seen too much. It turns my stomach every time I think about it, every time I see Alan's crushed body under that pile of rock. I've made so many mistakes, done so many things wrong. Where do I start to undo it? Can I undo it?"

"It's beyond your control, Jim. That's probably why you're so frustrated. Alan is gone, and you should mourn his death, but it's a closed book; nothing you can do or could have done to prevent it. The future of the Wolverine Mine is also out of your hands. The findings of the Mine Safety and Health Administration will determine if and how the mine is to operate, and in fact, when."

"That's what I'm afraid of. So much is riding on this. We've got long-term contracts to fill."

Anita stroked the back of his head as if to relieve a headache. There would be many of them over the next few weeks. She now realized that, given her crash course in the joint venture now known as RMS. "There's still Kearsarge number six."

He looked up and took her hand in his, lining up the diamond on her engagement ring with the pattern on her wedding band. He had forgotten how smart she was. She had articulated the one bright spot all of his latest business deals had produced. "Yes, I know. But it won't cover all the production gaps. I'm going to have to get Pete Singer to look into that. But right now, we've got more important matters to deal with—like burying a good friend."

"Have you got everything wrapped up here that you needed to tend to?"

"Yeah, and I've got a mound of things waiting for me in Chicago, including our major customers wondering if they'll ever see a pound of copper from us."

"You'll come up with something, honey. Now can we get out of here?"

He held up his index finger. "After I do one more thing this afternoon."

"What's that?"

"I want to see Gary Johnson before we fly back. It shouldn't take too long. Hang in there, baby." He gave his wife a hug. As he did, he thought about how lucky he was to have her. Why did he think he needed a young, good-looking girl to fall for him to make his life complete at forty-two? Far from that, it was now only beginning. Changes were inevitable. He respected Gary and wanted to chat with him about what was on the horizon.

CHAPTER 48

"I was hopin' we'd get a chance to chew the rag," Gary said as he took a sip of coffee from the mug on his desk. Jim had called and told him he needed to see him before flying back. It sounded urgent, and they had not really had a chance to talk one on one since the cave-in. He had been surrounded by investigators and reporters, so he'd had little time to ponder what would happen next. Here was his chance.

"From my perspective, it boils down to you and me running the show." Jim was in a mood to take back control of the situation.

"What about Ms. MacIntyre and her brother?" Gary's remarks were on the snide side.

"No doubt they'll have to be consulted, but I'm taking charge here since I'm responsible for holding the line on the orders."

"I hope ya can enforce that. I don't look forward ta working with Andy MacIntyre in any shape or form."

Jim's brow furled at the mention of Andy's name. "I had that feeling. What about him don't you like?"

"Well, I've never been one to bad mouth anyone, but… everything."

"I've always respected your judgment of character, Reverend. Let me deal with him." Jim gave Gary a slight upward nod, a sign of bravado, the kind that means *bring it on*.

Gary put down the mug he had been toying with for the past few minutes and leaned forward, putting his elbows on the desk.

"Just remember, vengeance is the Lord's." Then changing subjects, he asked, "So what's goin' to happen here?"

"I was going to ask you the very same question. I guess that means neither one of us knows, which is probably a fair assessment of the situation. What happened with the inspectors?"

"I think they're goin' to come down hard. In my humble opinion, I think they'll close us down for a while, give us some big fines, and maybe even come after me as mine manager."

"Can they do that?"

Gary stroked his beard. "I don't know, but da buck stops here."

"Well, if they do, count on having the best legal backing you can find."

"Right now, I'd appreciate dat."

With those assurances, their eyes met, and they were silent for a few moments, as if communicating to each other that they were in this together and for that reason they had become close—like blood brothers. Feeling the closeness of the moment, Jim changed the subject.

"Gary," he began, "I've been wanting to talk to you about something personal, if you don't mind."

"Sure. Shoot."

"I'm not sure where to begin. You know, this whole tragedy has changed the way I look at things these days. When the accident happened, I sent for my wife, and she flew up in the middle of the night. We'd been having some marital problems because of all the time I've been spending up here."

Gary held up his hand to stop Jim. "What ya mean is all da time you'd been spending with Elizabeth MacIntyre, right?"

Jim's expression said it all: *ouch*. He had not expected such rough treatment from Gary, especially after promising to stand behind him throughout the investigation. "Yes, it seems that's the underlying problem."

"Speaking of lying, have ya been honest with her?"

"What do you mean?"

Gary shook his head. "Answering a question with a question is usually a sign of guilt or at least avoidance."

Jim was starting to wish he had never brought this up.

"It's not what you think."

"How do ya know what I'm thinkin'?"

After taking the time to carefully weigh his words, Jim responded, "One time, things went too far with Elizabeth. But it wasn't even a one-night stand. I don't want to devastate my marriage over one indiscretion."

"Let me tell ya somethin,' Jim. I'm a rough-and-tumble miner from way back, but even before that, I'd learned about the grace of God. Don't get me wrong. I'm certainly no angel, but I do know one thing. When the good Lord wants ya to know something, he comes right out and tells ya or shows ya. Sometimes, dose of us that's especially stubborn require gettin' hit between the eyes with a two-by-four; however, sooner or later, he gets the message across. In your case, having your life turned upside down is what's finally done it. So, Jim, it ain't circumstances or luck or fate—it's da man upstairs telling you he wants your undivided attention."

"And what is it he wants?"

"Try a commitment, for starters. Now's da time. Turn your life around. Start over if ya have to. Just include Him in your marriage and in your plans. It'll work out a lot better in the long run if you do dat."

"I kind of thought you'd tell me this," Jim said thoughtfully. "In fact, I came here wanting to hear the words. Tell me, how do I go about making the right changes?"

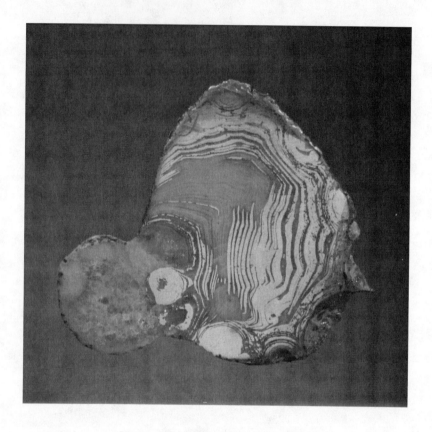

Copper Banding in Quartz (Agate) –
Wolverine Mine

Photo Credit: George Robinson

A. E. Seaman Mineral Museum,
Michigan Technological University

PART III

WAKING UP

CHAPTER 49

The drive down the Eisenhower Expressway was a cinch at 10:00 a.m. *Too bad I can't do this every day,* Jim thought. *Then again, why can't I? Just because I own my own business doesn't mean I have to work my tail off every day.* He liked that thought. When he had more time, he'd have to pursue it.

He parked his car in the underground garage in his building off of Madison Street and took the elevator to the lobby and from there to the twenty-eighth floor. As he entered the glassed-in reception area at the end of the hallway, the Wolverine emblem that he had chosen to represent the company stared at him. He stopped for a moment to place his fingers on the glass and trace the outline of the most ferocious of animals ever found in North America. He thought of how he had argued, rather discussed, with Alan why the animal would represent their newly-formed firm five years ago. That was then. This was now. He was on his way to possibly close out the largest deal they had ever been involved in—the one that looked to put them over the top, which had turned out to be the one that buried them under a mess of debt, federal safety violations, and possible lawsuits. It was also the project that dissolved the partnership and cut Alan's life short. He'd listen seriously to the proposal that Ray would present today.

"There you are!" Jim spun around, startled to see Pete Singer approaching from the reception desk. "I was just going to have Ruth send out the Illinois state troopers to track you down when I spotted you standing there."

Pete had been watching Jim stand at the company entrance deep in thought. "Don't say anything. I know what you're doing. You've got Alan on your brain again, don't you?"

Jim nodded. Pete always had the ability to see right through him. "You're still planning to sell out, aren't you?"

Trying his best to be patient, Pete flashed a smile. "Well, the best thing you can do is turn this thing around and come out smelling like roses. Come on in. I've got some good news for you. It ain't quite roses, but I can smell a tulip or two coming up through a bed of manure."

"Pete, you're a good friend and business associate, but your analogies leave something to be desired." Jim smiled, put his arm around Pete, and let him lead him to the conference room.

Gary got up from his seat at the end of the oak conference table and greeted Jim with a big bear hug. "How ya doin,' boss? It's good to see ya again."

"I'm doing fine, Gary. Just this morning I was thinking about how well things were going, considering this mess we're in."

"Keep your chin up, ol' boy. How's that pretty wife of yours?"

"She's doing well. She has been really supportive through this whole ordeal."

"You're lucky to have her, Jim."

"I know. But it's not luck, or fate, for that matter."

"I stand corrected."

"Ahem," Pete interrupted. "I hate to break up old-home week, but we've got a couple of things to go over before Ray gets here, which by my watch will be any minute now."

"Sorry, Pete," Jim said. "It's just that when you've been through a life-threatening situation with someone, you sort of become blood brothers, or something like that."

"Well, in that case, brother Gary is the bearer of good news this morning."

"I've already been over dis in detail with Pete, so I won't waste your time on da particulars. To make a long story short, we're back to mining copper at Wolverine."

Jim didn't say anything at first. He just sat down at the conference table and rubbed his face with one hand, stroking his chin before replying, "No kidding! Why didn't anyone tell me?" He couldn't decide if he was angry or thrilled.

"Because we started back last Friday, an' I wanted to tell ya in person today."

"That's great. How much are we mining?"

"We got one section up on seven. Da mine inspectors camped out da entire week underground making sure everything was by da book, but we finally got da approval to proceed. Funny thing though…" Gary paused for effect.

"What's that?" Jim asked.

"Dey were a royal pain the first three days they were there. Den, after dey caught their limit of lake trout out on Keweenaw Bay last Thursday, dey were very accommodating and allowed us to blast for da first time in three and a half months on Friday."

"Nothing strange about that," Pete said. "Political Science 101—the best means to move government administrators into action is to prod them with a few perks that don't have to be reported anywhere."

"Now ya tell me. I could have saved three days of heartache if I'd known dat last Monday."

"Then how are we doing on the Chicago Wire order?" Jim asked, trying to gather as much background information as possible before the meeting.

"July and August shipments totaled just over five million pounds from Kearsarge number six. It was da most we could find on short notice. We may get dat number over three million for September, which gets us to around three-fourths of the minimum monthly production requirements for the contract. With one section goin' on seven, we'll add at least one million pounds per month to da total and be on schedule with 'em."

Anxious to slow the stream of bad news, Pete took over the conversation. "So far, they haven't complained about the shortfall in production. If we can get over four million to them next month, we'll be okay there. However, the bigger problem is getting ore out of six to meet the Northern Michigan Refining contract. We're supposed to start shipping this month. That leaves us about a week and a half. There's no way we'll be online on six. Next month, we're in default, and Jack Stallworth at RE Associates is making noises about taking his business elsewhere. We may have to renegotiate the contract with him if we want to hang on to this one."

"Damn!" Jim exclaimed. "That was the most lucrative one of the bunch."

"Which means dere's room to lower the price, hang on to a valued customer, and still make some money," Gary interjected.

"Yeah, you're right. I just don't like cutting margins so much."

Gary became adamant. "Look, Jim. The contract price is for $1.72 per pound. Our original projections for mining da ore were thirty-five to forty cents per pound for the high-grade ore. With everything MSHA has laid on us, it'll increase our costs by at least 30 percent, say to fifty to fifty-five cents per pound. You've got room. Don't get greedy. Anyway, all it does is cut the margin to RMS. Wolverine still gets the dollar per pound from da partnership."

"Again, you're right. What do we need to offer to hang on to Stallworth's business?"

"Let's buy another month's time until November to start shipping and then offer him twelve million pounds per year, three years at the same price we're selling low grade—and I use that term loosely—to Chicago Wire, one dollar and fifty cents per pound. It should fly," Pete responded.

"Fine, what does MacIntyre have to say about all this?"

He shrugged, indicating he didn't know. "They're still letting us handle all the sales and marketing as per our original agreement."

"Good. Keep Andy out of this. With Ray coming in today, I can't help but suspect his motives in all this." Jim was sure Andy was up to no good. He was also sure Andy had a hand in the cave-in. The offer to buy out of Wolverine on the heels of the news of the cave-in had just come too quickly.

"Your suspicions have been confirmed by Lisa in research," Pete answered.

"What do you mean?"

"I mean we've found out that Andy MacIntyre has a 15.5 percent interest in North American Metals. Seems he's been setting himself up to have his cake and eat it too, regardless of who buys who."

"Why, that slimy, good for nothing—"

Gary cut him off. "Now, Jim, don't waste your best superlatives on that guy. It doesn't matter who owns what share of North American. We're in it to get the best deal for Wolverine."

"Which just so happens to be 80 percent owned by J. A. MacIntyre Inc. Mr. MacIntyre just so happens to be the vice president of mining operations for MacIntyre. Isn't that a bit of a conflict of interest?"

Pete held up his hand to stop the train of thought between Gary and Jim. "I would use stronger words than conflict of interest, but since Mr. MacIntyre, as you put it, only has stock holding in one of the two companies, then he only gains if Wolverine sells out to North American."

"True," Jim replied. "However, I thought it was in the best interest of Wolverine to unload this mess on North American."

"Yes," Pete answered. "But only in the short-term interests of the shareholders. Given they'll recover some fraction of their investment and pass on any liabilities, real or contingent, I'd agree; but in the long-term view, particularly if we can get back into operation, then we've only suffered a setback—a severe one, yes. Lawsuits have been threatened, yes. But nothing has come up thus far that we haven't been able to deal with. It may be worth sticking it out in light of Gary's good news."

The intercom buzzed. "Mr. Thomas, Mr. McKinnen is here to see you."

Jim picked up the receiver. "Get him a cup of coffee and tell him I'll see him in five minutes, please."

Without bothering to listen for Ruth's response, Jim set down the phone and resumed the conversation. "That's a good point, Pete. I don't know if I'm prepared to carry that option through, but it's a viable option nonetheless."

Walking around the conference table, Jim stopped to stare out the window at downtown Chicago and Lake Michigan in the background. Without turning to look at Pete and Gary, he asked, "How many sections could we have up by the end of the year?"

"If we can keep MSHA happy, I can put one more on seven and have another going on six by Thanksgivin,'" Gary answered. "How much money do ya want to spend?"

"How much are we over our development budget now?"

"Oh, the shutdown has cost us around eight million dollars so far. We'll spend another two million dollars to get dose sections up to snuff with da extra roof bolting, men, and equipment dat I've got to have on each shift dat I hadn't originally planned on. On six, we've had to put in another drift and to provide adequate escape routes and ventilation."

"Where's the money coming from?" Pete asked.

"Mostly out the monies that were dedicated to the expansion," Jim said. "We've also made about twenty cents per pound on the sales to Chicago Wire that RMS is currently supplying. That's about one million dollars so far based on Gary's shipped-product numbers for July and August. What kind of production do the two sections on seven and one on six get us?"

Gary did a quick mental calculation. "'Bout four thousand tons per day, maybe forty-five hundred."

"What's that in pounds per month?"

"Oh, I'd say around five million pounds per month."

For the first time during the meeting, a big grin came across Jim's face. "That just about covers Chicago Wire and Northern Michigan Refining, right?"

"Yep."

"Can we do it by December?"

Gary was very careful in his answer since he knew he would be held to whatever he said next. "By da end of the year, maybe. At least one. Plan on spending some extra money for overtime and a couple extra haulers."

"How much?"

"Another two to three million over your existing development budget."

"If you can get me at least six million pounds per month by the end of December, I'll see that you get the money."

Gary was all smiles. "Does this mean we're goin' for it, boss?"

"Let's see what Mr. McKinnen has to say. Then we'll decide." Jim picked up the intercom. "Ruth, show Mr. McKinnen in, please."

Ray McKinnen was led in by Jim's secretary. He was a tall, burly man who, like Jim, appeared to be an ex-football player. Recognizing Pete Singer, he moved to Pete's end of the table and offered his hand.

"Good to see ya again, Pete."

"Hope you had a pleasant flight to the Windy City this morning."

"Very."

"Ray," Pete said, "I'd like to introduce you to my boss, Jim Thomas." Ray pumped Jim's hand with enthusiasm that was only outdone by his powerful grip. "And Gary Johnson, our mine manager at Wolverine." Again, Gary's arm was put through a series of violent contortions.

"Have a seat," Jim instructed.

"Where's Andy MacIntyre?" Ray inquired. "I thought he'd be a part of this meeting."

"He was scheduled to be, but I've been authorized by Phillip Turner at J. A. MacIntyre Inc. to negotiate any preliminary terms of sale. You know what they say about too many cooks," Jim added. He had a bit of a twinkle in his eye. He noted that after the meeting he'd have to commend Pete for setting it up this way. Only a few moments ago did he fully understand his reasons—very smooth.

If Ray was at all displeased by the turn of events, he didn't show it. "I guess we should get down to the nitty-gritty. I've brought with me a proposal to buy 100 percent of the stock of the Wolverine Mining Company. If you have the projector I requested handy, I'll give you a quick briefing before lunch."

Pete motioned to the panel in the back of the conference room that held the audio/video equipment. "If you want to give me your memory stick, I'll load them for you."

While Pete set up the software and projector, Ray handed Jim and Gary copies of his proposal. Jim quickly flipped open the executive summary and scanned the section for a price. In the table that summarized the valuation of the company North American Metals had ordered, a fair market value of $190 million was listed. After deductions for contingent liabilities, upgrades to MSHA requirements, and concessions on contracts were taken, an offering of $100 million was made to purchase.

Jim did some quick calculations to determine that he stood to make six million dollars but MacIntyre would probably lose thirty-six million. Jim's thought process was interrupted by Ray. "Now that you've seen the offer, should I proceed?"

"Yes, please do. You've got my attention."

Ray launched into an impressive presentation that focused on the findings of the valuation company he had hired. They had a complete inventory of equipment, good estimates of operating, and capital requirements and had done a fair job at a reserve estimate. He had done his homework. There wasn't much room to argue with his basis for the offer. Naturally, he had deducted large sums for getting the operation back online, and here's where Jim found fault in his analysis. Gary had convinced him he could do it for a lot less. The big unknown was whether they could stave off any legal action and, at the same time, satisfy MSHA.

The presentation wrapped up at twelve thirty. When the lights went on, Jim announced, "We'll hold our questions until after lunch except for one that I'll ask you now."

"Shoot."

"Don't you think one hundred million dollars is peanuts to pay for a company that has one billion dollars in proven reserves?"

Without hesitation, Ray answered, "No."

Jim crossed his arms, his body language saying, *I don't agree.* "Aren't you going to explain your obvious answer?"

"No, it'd take too long, and I'm hungry."

This guy's not too bad either, Jim decided.

CHAPTER 50

As they sat down at their table at the Berghoff, Jim was reminded of the time that he and Alan celebrated their entry into the Wolverine Mining venture. Feeling somewhat nostalgic, he decided to go back to the restaurant today, which had been a favorite of his and Alan's for business lunches.

Over a round of Berghoff dark following the rich German schnitzel, which only the Berghoff could serve, the conversation found its way back to the business at hand. The first barrage of questions came from Gary.

"If ya buy Wolverine, what changes do ya have planned for the management of the operation?"

"Normally, I'd say none in the short term. But given the circumstances, I'd say we'd have to closely review existing management practices and operating procedures and make changes based on our findings."

It was Gary's turn to give Ray a look of disapproval. "In other words, I'm out of a job."

"I didn't say that. What I said was that we'd have to review it." Knowing that his response was not going to be a satisfactory answer, Ray continued. "Let me ask you a question. How is your relationship with MSHA?"

"It's improving. Nobody has suggested that I was at fault. The accident was a matter of directions not being followed and clear-cut procedures not being issued. That has since been rectified."

"Good."

It was now Jim's turn to resume the line of questioning. "How to you propose to meet Wolverine's current production obligations?"

"I'm sure you've got that worked out with RMS in the short term, Jim. In the long term, we'll have to renegotiate and pump some sizable money into the mine to get it anywhere close to the long-term production of twenty thousand tons per day you had planned."

"What if I told you that I'd already done that and that we have made arrangements to be at our original design capacity of ten thousand tons per day by first quarter next year?"

"I certainly wouldn't be surprised. I would have expected you to pull this thing back together as best you could; however, you and I know that there is no way you can cover your long-term obligations, especially those to Northern Michigan Refining. Jack Stallworth will eat you alive. He is brutal, and I suspect he's just buying time, waiting to make his best move. Furthermore, you've got a tremendous liability hanging over your head. Why continue in a business you know nothing about? We are in the mining business. We know MSHA. We can make this work. Can you?"

"Now wait a minute," Gary began. Before he could get out another word, Jim held up his hand to stop him.

"You are probably correct in your assessment. Your analysis as you've presented it today makes a lot of sense. You know mining better than we know mining. In fact, you could cite the cave-in and our lack of safety precautions as an example. You'll get some argument from this gentleman across the table from you, but as his boss, I'd have to say there were some shortcomings—that all brings us back to the offer. If you're serious about taking over this operation, you'll have to raise the ante, or we can't play much longer. As you've correctly stated, we do have options. Granted, keeping the thing would be riskier than turning it over to you, but I'm in the risk business. We've also assessed that."

Ray showed he could be as incredulous as the next guy. "Mr. Thomas, I came here to bail you out of a tough spot. I did not come to negotiate price like a used car salesman. What I have presented to you is a firm quotation for Wolverine Mining. As you can see, we've done our homework. Unless you're prepared to add something to the deal, I cannot go higher than one hundred million dollars."

"Wait just one minute," Pete interrupted. "It wasn't that long ago when I sat in the dining room of the Brown Hotel in Denver with you and Andy MacIntyre when the news of the cave-in broke. You made a ballpark offer on the spot that you'd be prepared to pay one hundred fifty million dollars for a company that had a book value of two hundred million dollars. Why the change? After all, you did your homework."

"Yes, we did. And we concluded that the operation is not worth one hundred fifty million dollars and the risk involved is not worth the extra fifty million dollars."

Pete went on the offensive. "Who's we? Is Andy MacIntyre involved in that determination?"

"Of course not."

It was time to drop the first bombshell into the negotiation. "Why not? Doesn't a significant shareholder in North American Metals share in the decision to make a major acquisition?"

"Yes," replied a noticeably surprised Ray McKinnen. "However, he is no longer part of North American operations. Therefore, he does not set price, only approve deals as any other stockholder would."

Pete ignored the answer and went back on the attack. "Does this mean that Jack Sanders also gets to approve this deal?"

"I don't know who Jack Sanders is!" Ray tried to feign innocence but was starting to get flustered and found other diners looking his way as he raised his voice.

Time to drop the big one. Pete was going for the jugular now. "He's the guy Andy called right after the rescue. You see, I thought you and MacIntyre were a little too close. So I did some investigating of my own. What I've got is circumstantial, but I do have a security man who recognized Andy's voice asking for Jack Sanders. I also have obtained your latest filing of corporate status with the state of Colorado, which shows Andy MacIntyre as a 15 percent stockholder. Now, Mr. McKinnen, I can put two and two together as well as the next guy, or even the Michigan attorney general. What do you say we stick to your original offer of one hundred fifty million dollars?"

Ray opened his mouth and pointed his finger at Pete as though he was going to refute the accusation and the threat but then pursed his lips, dropped his hand to the table, and gave him a slight nod.

CHAPTER 51

Normally, Elizabeth did not make such frequent appearances at the offices of J. A. MacIntyre Inc. In fact, up until a month ago, Phillip Turner could count the number of times she walked in the front door in the last year on one hand. Now she had turned into a regular commuter from Evanston rather than receiving what little information she wanted over the phone or by e-mail.

The door to his office opened. He was expecting her since she had phoned ahead.

"Good afternoon, Phillip."

"Good day, Liz. How's traffic on the way in?"

"Actually, it's pretty light even considering the time of day. Heard from Wolverine yet?"

"No. In fact, your brother was just in here twenty minutes ago asking the same question."

"I guess we're all a little anxious."

He nodded in agreement. "Let me ask you a question."

"Sure."

Phillip paused for a moment for a dramatic effect. "Why didn't Andy attend the meeting with North American Metals today?"

Elizabeth grimaced not liking having to explain an uncomfortable situation. "Pete Singer called me and insisted he not be there. I then called Jim Thomas to ask why. He told me he wanted to handle the negotiations without anybody second guessing him. I told him I didn't really like not being represented at the meeting, but he assured me he would not make any commitments. I agreed, and he agreed to call me as soon as he had something."

"How'd Andy take the whole thing?"

"He was raving mad. I told him I had made the decision at Jim's request, and he went off the deep end. It's the first time I'd seen him that angry in a long time."

"Well, for what it's worth, I think you did the right thing."

They chitchatted a while until the expected call came through. Phillip's secretary put Jim through, and Phillip punched him up on the speaker.

"Good afternoon, Jim," Phillip answered the call. "I've got Elizabeth sitting here in my office."

"Hello, Elizabeth."

Getting right to the point, she replied, "How'd it go with Ray McKinnen today?"

"How does one hundred fifty million dollars strike you?"

Elizabeth let out a shriek. "Did I hear you right? One hundred fifty?"

"You're hearing's okay."

"Congratulations," Phillip said rather dryly. "I never thought you could get that for it. I don't know if Elizabeth told you, but we were looking just to break even."

"No, she didn't, but I figured as much."

"When do we accept and get out of this mess?" Elizabeth asked.

"I suppose you could do it anytime, but I'd like to meet with you first. You may not want to do it after I explain our options."

"Well, they'd better be good ones to keep us from pocketing a seven-million-dollar profit," Phillip proclaimed.

"They'll make you think twice. How about tomorrow morning?"

"Sure, make it ten o'clock over here."

"See you then." The phone went dead without Jim so much as bidding them farewell.

Elizabeth and Phillip just sat for a moment, exchanging puzzled looks.

"What do you think he's got up his sleeve this time?" Elizabeth asked.

"Oh, I don't think he's got anything up his sleeve. The guy is a lot of things, and sound businessman is one of them. Maybe he's discovered gold in the mine too."

"I wouldn't put it past him to surprise us with something like that."

"Well, no use speculating. We'll find out tomorrow."

"I guess you're right."

Not sure of what Andy's role would be in any business decisions, Phillip inquired, "Are you going to involve Andy in this one?"

"Yes, I think I have to, don't you?'

"Yes, that would be the proper thing to do."

"Let me ask you a question this time."

"I owe you one."

"What bothers you about Andy?"

"I don't trust him."

"Fair enough. At least you're honest about it. Give him some time. He'll grow on you."

Phillip may have well have been renamed Doubting Thomas at that point. "He's been here six months and still hasn't."

"Point well taken, Phillip. What do you want me to do about it?"

"If we sell out of the mining business, then get rid of him too."

Elizabeth couldn't argue with his logic. "Let me sleep on that one."

Phillip smiled. "Like you said, fair enough."

CHAPTER 52

The weather that evening was unusually cool for late September. Jim and Anita found themselves at home alone, which was not unusual given that they had a fifteen-year-old high school sophomore at home. They never worried about Julie though. She had proven to be an excellent student, and like most popular high school girls, she was involved in everything under the sun. Tonight, it was a cheerleading practice, after which the squad would meet the star players for whom they cheered at Bertinelli's Pizza Parlor.

Thus, Jim found himself in the midst of domestic bliss as he rummaged through the pile of wood on the back wall of his garage, looking for an armload of small pieces to use as kindling in the fireplace so he wouldn't have to dig out his axe from wherever he had stowed it for safekeeping last spring. Alas, there in the far corner, protected by two rather large, furry, mean-looking spiders, was the dry kindling. Now to battle the beasts for their home, which in five minutes would be the start of a roaring fire.

Although it might have actually taken six or seven minutes, Jim soon had a fire going in the family room that was indeed a work of art. Once satisfied that another masterpiece had been created, he left the room to summon Anita.

It had been a long time since the two of them had sat in front of a roaring fire and contemplated life over a fine glass of chardonnay. After the accident, Jim had drastically reduced his work schedule and was trying hard to spend less and less of his time on his business. That was not an easy task since Alan had left behind a plethora of unfinished projects on his desk. The only solution that Jim had found one frustrating afternoon was to toss half of them in the circular file and forget about them. The others, in which Wolverine was invested or had some sort of a stake in, he delegated as best he could. Pete had really stepped up to pick up the slack.

"Oh, this feels nice," Jim told Anita as she settled into his arms.

"Yes, it does. It's been too long."

"You know, I'm working on changing that."

"I know. I've seen what you've been trying to do, and I'm proud of how you've handled all of the problems since the mine disaster."

"You know, Anita, I've made some poor choices. I can only hope to make things better someday."

"A few more evenings like this wouldn't hurt."

"You're right. Maybe we should plan some time away." He had been looking into a Caribbean cruise. It had been a long time since he'd taken a vacation, and he couldn't remember when he and Anita had gotten away together.

"That would be nice. But…" She rolled her eyes.

"But tomorrow I have to decide whether to take what looks like a sixteen-million-dollar profit for Wolverine Ventures and sell out or to stick this out, make it work again for a much larger return. Selling the mining company and then the firm makes a lot of sense. If we stay in it, there's probably no way we're selling this for a few years until we're back up and operating with a good track record. What should I do?"

"I'm afraid I can't advise you on that, dear. Besides, doesn't MacIntyre make the final decision?"

"True, but I'm the one who will essentially make the decision for them tomorrow when I present them their options. It's all in what I choose to tell them or how I present it."

"Probably so. Then I guess it's up to you."

"No, it's up to us. Should I retire now?"

"What would we do with all this time on our hands? Or even worse yet, what would *you* do with all that time on *your* hands?"

"Travel, get involved in a few select projects. Who knows, maybe even write a book?"

"Who are you kidding? You're forty-three years old. You couldn't sit still for a minute. This is the longest you've sat since—I can't remember when."

They both stared into the fire. Jim had his arm around her shoulders. He pulled her a little closer. He had wanted her to reinforce his innate belief that he should keep this thing going. For all the times he had wanted to just close down the business he and Alan had built since Alan met his untimely death, there were many more when he wondered if he could ever be happy doing anything else.

After a long silence, Jim unloaded the big question they both knew he wanted to ask. "But what about us? Where does it leave us if I become immersed in the mine operations and sales?"

"It leaves us where we were before." Anita turned to look Jim in the eye so he could not mistake what she was about to say. "You are a dreamer and a workaholic. You will stop at nothing until you have fulfilled your ambition. This is the biggest project of your life. You just told me you could net sixteen million dollars for the company if you sold out. More than half of that would come to us. Who couldn't live on that? I don't need to tell you because you believe you can parley that into ten times that sum or more. Nothing I can say will change your mind. I don't want to be the one standing between you and the fulfillment of your dreams."

She got up and kissed him on the cheek. "I'm going to bed."

CHAPTER 53

Jim had never felt better when he pulled his Jaguar XJ-S out of the garage and pointed it toward the Windy City. The sun was out, the air was warm, and it was a beautiful fall day. He was going to make the best of it. What was it Gary had told him to remember? *Put it in God's hands, not yours.* For the first time in a long time, well, maybe ever, Jim prayed on his way in to the office.

His watch showed 8:17 when he stepped off the elevator and headed for his office.

"Pete and Gary are waiting for you in your office," Ruth informed him as he turned the corner.

"I kind of thought they would be," Jim answered without breaking his stride. Then he stopped, turned around, and addressed his secretary. "By the way, good morning."

"Good morning to you." Usually, Jim didn't say two words when he entered the office in the morning.

Gary's hearty greeting met him at his office door. "Good mornin,' boss."

"Good morning, gentlemen."

"We wanted to know what your final decision was, so we camped out in your office, and we refuse to leave until you give us the answer we want," Pete demanded.

"We're going to operate the place if MacIntyre agrees."

"That's what we wanted to hear." Pete grinned from ear to ear then turned to Gary. "Let's go. That's all we needed to know."

They got up and headed to the door without so much as looking back.

"Don't you want to know the particulars?" Jim wanted to justify his decision to someone since his wife wouldn't let him do that last night.

"Nope. You've got to convince Phillip Turner that this is the right thing to do. If you need us, you'll know where to find us. Gary's got an afternoon plane back today. Let him know if he can get working on the new section we discussed yesterday."

At first Jim found it hard to believe they had waited for him just to have the brief exchange. But the more he thought about it, the more he came to realize that it was their way of showing him their support. How could he let these guys down?

After spending an hour putting together some notes for his meeting with MacIntyre, he caught a cab over to their LaSalle Street offices. It was located near the top of one of the bank buildings on the street, which represented the financial district of Chicago. *How appropriate,* Jim thought. *Even their choice of an office location reflects the basic business of managing an enormous estate.* J. A. MacIntyre Inc. had occupied the Lasalle Street address for many years since the Chicago office was established by Elizabeth's great-grandfather in the 1920s.

As was his habit, Jim glanced at his watch when he stepped off the elevator and headed for the double wooden doors with the name "J. A. MacIntyre Inc." inscribed across the door on the right in old English script. *That's probably the way it looked ninety years ago.*

Upon entering, he reached into the inside pocket of his suit coat and pulled out a brass card case and handed the receptionist his card. They had gotten a new girl at the front desk since the last time he visited, and she obviously did not know who he was. "I'm here to see Phillip Turner and Elizabeth MacIntyre," he said.

"Are they expecting you?"

"Yes, I have a ten o'clock appointment with them, and I'm four minutes early."

Without so much as acknowledging his reply, she picked up the phone and announced his arrival to Phillip Turner. When she placed the receiver back into its cradle, she said, "Please follow me to the conference room. Mr. Turner, Ms. MacIntyre, and Mr. MacIntyre will meet you there."

He followed her like an obedient puppy, and when they arrived, she offered to get him some coffee, which he graciously accepted.

Before she made it back with his coffee, Phillip entered the conference room, followed by Andy. Not a particularly welcoming sight, but Jim forced a smile anyway. "Good morning, Phillip, Andy," he said as he extended a hand to each of them.

With the niceties out of the way, they sat down, and Jim pulled out copies of Ray McKinnen's proposal along with the latest status report on the mine, which Gary had prepared yesterday afternoon. His coffee arrived, along with Elizabeth. He took a long look at her as the receptionist set the coffee down in front of him. My, she was as striking as ever. The black business suit that she wore accentuated her figure nicely. Jim couldn't help himself as he undressed her in his mind, knowing full well what a soft yet firm body resided under the clothes. *No, Jim, you can't think like that. It will get you into trouble,* said the little voice in his head. His marriage was just now starting to get better.

"Mr. Thomas," the receptionist repeated, "would you like cream or sugar with your coffee?"

"Uh, no thanks," he muttered. "Elizabeth, how are you these days? It's good to see you again."

"Likewise. You're looking good."

The moment was awkward. It had been three months since they had seen each other, and a lot of things had changed. Jim was trying to keep this on a professional level. "So are you."

"Now what's this you tell me about a better deal than selling out Wolverine Mining for one hundred fifty million dollars and both of us pocketing a nice little return on our investment?" she said, tactfully changing the subject to avoid further uneasiness.

"Since I know you like the direct approach, let me get right to the point. First of all, it's not really a better deal. What I came here this morning to discuss with you are a couple of options that we now have, which is certainly a far cry from where we were three and a half months ago."

He paused. Remembering what he had started to do before Elizabeth made her grand entrance, he handed everyone a copy of North American Mining's proposal and the status report on Wolverine. "What I'd like to do is review each of these documents with you and then give you some projections that Pete Singer and Gary Johnson have worked up on future production out of the mine."

Jim then proceeded to spend the next forty-five minutes highlighting the proposal and reviewing the conversations that he had had with Ray McKinnen the previous day. Finally, he got around to the facts that Pete had uncovered. Jim decided to call it as he saw it.

"As you can see by the figures in the executive summary of North American's proposal, the fair market value of Wolverine Mining is conservatively estimated to be $190 million. That, in my opinion, makes the negotiated sale price a fair offer; however, we were only able to get to that point with McKinnen after we pointed out some possible problems with his attempt to acquire Wolverine at bargain basement prices."

"Here's where it gets interesting." Jim took a moment to look at his audience, particularly Andy. He had hoped his prelude would have started Andy sweating bullets, but it hadn't. At least not yet. He continued.

"Our research indicates that within the past year, Andy MacIntyre has acquired a 15.5 percent holding in North American Metals. Of course, he did it through a dummy corporation, Western Commodities, but it wasn't too hard to trace. In fact, McKinnen never even tried to sidestep the issue by claiming that there was no shareholder named MacIntyre. Obviously, the two have a close working relationship given that McKinnen was Andy's boss before he came to work for MacIntyre Inc. The fact is, he never quit working for North American Metals, including orchestrating this whole deal."

He waited. Andy said nothing. Elizabeth and Phillip had turned to stare at him. They too awaited a response.

"What can I say that Mr. Thomas hasn't already said?" Andy was not defensive; rather, he went on to explain his position quite matter-of-factly. "I don't deny my shareholding in North American. I've been a shareholder for a long time now."

"True," Jim interrupted. "But until recently, your shareholdings were well under 5 percent."

"That's correct. I simply invested when I saw a good deal. What's wrong with that, Mr. Venture Capitalist? Wouldn't you do the same?"

"Not when such a blatant conflict of interest is involved! Tell me, what did you give North American in exchange for 10 percent of the company?"

"That, my friend, is none of your business."

"I beg to differ. It is all of our business. It is the key issue on the table today. It escalated the price of our investment because therein lies the reasons why Ray McKinnen would just as soon pay much more for the company than he planned just to keep the Michigan attorney general's office out of the picture."

Now Andy was angry. Jim had pushed the right buttons. He stood up and shouted across the table at Jim. "Just what are you accusing me of?"

"Criminal behavior. Suspicious circumstantial evidence behind the *accident* that took the life of my partner, a business colleague, and the governor of the state of Michigan."

"Why, you SOB. You're just sitting here throwing out libelous statements like you're some detective setting the final scene of a murder mystery."

"That's not too far from the truth. It may well be a murder, and I intend to pursue it to determine precisely how you did it."

"Whoa, hold on!" Phillip jumped in. "This is getting out of hand. I'm not going to stand by and let you two get into fisticuffs over a mining accident. Jim, I'll have to ask you to leave the room, if you would, to cool down while I have a little chat with Andy here."

As Jim exited the room, he could here Andy ranting and raving. "First he screws up my sister's life, and now he wants to mess up mine. What's with the guy? He got some vendetta against the MacIntyres?"

Jim shook his head and headed for the break room to refill his coffee cup. He hoped that he had made the kind of impact he had planned for the confrontation in there. The break was welcome. It would give him a few minutes to plan how to proceed. The element of surprise had worked well in this instance. Now he would go in and finish what had turned in to an explosive presentation by giving them all the reasons they should not let North American Metals and Andy anywhere near the Wolverine Mine in rapid fire.

He took his coffee and moved out into the reception area to make himself comfortable while he waited. A check of his watch told him that it was 11:22 a.m. The review and subsequent confrontation with Andy had taken more time than he thought. *No good. I want to get this thing over before lunch. If it drags on, the emotional factor will no longer play my way.*

Minutes passed by ever so slowly. Eleven thirty, then eleven forty-five. It was almost noon before Phillip Turner strolled out to get him.

"Sorry about taking so long. As I'm sure you expected, we had a little bit of dirty laundry to hang out, and it took a while before I was satisfied that I had all the facts. I find we owe you a debt of gratitude for bringing this to our attention, although I would appreciate your being a bit more discreet next time."

"Yes, I too must apologize. It was a premeditated move; however, I'm sure you can imagine my anger when I learned of Andy's behind-the-scenes involvement in this thing."

"Oh, Mr. Thomas, I do not have to imagine your anger. I experienced the same sentiment when I fired him five minutes ago."

This time it was Jim's turn to be shocked. Never in a million years would he have expected Elizabeth's brother to be dismissed at the drop of a hat. Not after all she went through to bring him into the family business.

"You let him go?" Jim exclaimed, still astounded. "Just like that?"

"Sure. You don't think we're going to tolerate that type of behavior in our organization, do you? As you intimated, it smirks of criminal behavior."

"I agree. You did the right thing. I was just a bit surprised."

"Well, you're not the only one capable of dramatic action."

"I guess not." Jim had just gained a great deal of respect for Phillip. He wondered how much convincing Elizabeth needed to make that move, or maybe this was just an easy out.

CHAPTER 54

The rain beat hard against the window. It had come out of nowhere. What had started out as a cool but clear Halloween night was now a terrific storm. In fact, Jim thought he could hear sleet bouncing off the copper sheeting that trimmed the old MacIntyre estate. It was a night suited only for ghosts and goblins.

This was the first time Jim had been here since last June. Elizabeth had invited him to come over and watch the trick-or-treaters instead of sitting over at the Michigan House by himself. The MacIntyre house was a perfect house for Halloween festivities. It loomed three-and-a-half stories off the street behind enormous one-hundred-year-old oak trees. The streetlight on the corner cast eerie shadows against the large windows on the front of the house. Adding to the effect were the dim lights that Elizabeth had turned on in the front entrance hall that made the stained glass glow with a spooky hue, as though the light came from the bowels of the house itself. Any child that braved the walk up the front steps past the large cedar bushes where who-knows-what awaited him deserved to be treated.

On this particular Halloween, Jim was wrestling with his own ghosts. He had convinced himself that he had to see his dream of building a new copper mining empire in northern Michigan to its rightful conclusion, no matter what the costs. That did not include letting Wolverine Mining fall into the hands of Andy MacIntyre or Ray McKinnen. He owed that to Alan. He owed it to himself not to turn his back on the biggest moneymaker that Wolverine Ventures had put together in six years.

So he made the commitment. He would personally oversee the rebuilding process, including the production targets from the number six and seven levels by Christmas. He would restructure the sales and operating agreements.

This had challenged all his negotiating skills. There was nothing easy about soothing irate customers over lower-than-expected deliveries.

Furthermore, a new very personal challenge had presented itself. He was going to get Andy. Since he first postulated Andy's involvement in the "accident," he was not going to leave one stone unturned. They may have pacified MSHA, but MSHA was not aware of the circumstances surrounding the cave-in. It would take some doing, but he was going to nail the guy.

Elizabeth returned from answering the door. "It's ten o'clock. That's supposed to be the last of them. I turned out the front light. We'll hang around down here to catch the last of the stragglers. But just long enough to finish this wine."

She poured him another glass. Jim couldn't remember if it was his fourth or fifth one. It didn't matter. His head was beginning to swim with the benign thoughts of impending intoxication. The flickering light from the fire caused him to lapse into a trance as he watched its reflection on the ceiling. He had spent most of October in the Copper Country just working to get the mine back up to full production. Elizabeth had originally wanted to sell out, but he had convinced her and Phillip that the operation could be turned around by the end of the year and profitable the first quarter of next year. They had agreed to leave their money in the operation if he would agree to manage the turnaround. This meant that Jim would again be spending the majority of his time up here working with Elizabeth.

"I'd offer you a penny for your thoughts, but I know you venture capitalists would want a buyback clause in case I turned them into a bestseller." Elizabeth laughed at her own joke. Even Jim saw fit to smile at this attack of his persona.

"Why so quiet?" she inquired.

"Not sure. Guess I'm just reminiscing about our time spent here like this almost one year ago."

"Any regrets?"

He paused. This one he had to think about. "No, I don't think so."

He felt the warmth of her body above even the heat of the fire as she snuggled next to him and leaned her head on his shoulder. The scent of her hair was better than the nose of the wine. She lifted her head and smiled, her naturally intense blue eyes matching the rare, natural blue diamond earrings catching his attention. "Despite the tragedy and all we've endured, I don't have any regrets about becoming your partner. We will make this work, and we will find out what happened back in June."

The wine had caused Jim to lose any inhibitions he may have normally relied upon. Instead of resisting temptation, he pulled her close and kissed her. He watched her eyes close as her lips parted and the taste of her mouth became part of the overwhelming sensual experience. When he came up for air, he watched her open those incredibly blue eyes. "You certainly kiss better than Alan did."

The repulsive look on her face said it all.

He laughed. "Alan and I had become very close over the six years we worked together. Well, not quite that close." He bobbed his head and waved his hand in jest. "But he really helped me by believing in my decisions and always backing me up. He understood where we needed to go and what we needed to do to get there. This venture was his discovery, and I want to make it succeed and bring to justice those behind his murder. Even if that includes Andy."

She held his face in her hands. "I want those things as much as you do. Don't worry about Andy; he's out of the picture. He's not a player; he's a pawn in all this."

Jim didn't say anything. He hated Andy but didn't want his feelings to get in the way. Before he had a chance to worry about it, she kissed him again. She was now in full control, and Jim found himself defenseless in combating her advances. Once again she skillfully played her hand, saying all the right things, making all the right promises, and using every weapon in her arsenal to capture Jim's loyalty and devotion to their relationship. He reached for the lamp by the sofa and turned it off to prevent any late trick-or-treaters from seeing what came next.

CHAPTER 55

Joe Maki had been the Keweenaw County prosecuting attorney for the past six years. Most of that time had been spent prosecuting drunks, drug addicts, and the occasional sex offender. Rarely had he handled a murder case. Thus, he immediately became acutely interested when he received a phone call from Chicago businessman Jim Thomas outlining what he believed to be the murder of three men in the Wolverine Mine last June. *No,* Thomas had thought. *It was no accident. This was a planned event. At the very least, second degree or manslaughter.*

Maki knew quite a bit about the incident. He had followed it quite closely last summer; however, when MSHA concluded that it indeed was an accident, he forgot about it and gave it no further thought, until Thomas called with what he said would prove to be damning evidence that showed that his partner, a prominent local businessman, and the governor, no less, were killed under some very suspicious circumstances. On the basis of a single phone conversation, Joe could not decide whether this guy was out for vengeance or whether he actually had something. Well, there was only one way to find out, so he showed up at Wolverine's offices at 9:00 a.m. sharp.

He was shown down the long corridor in the mine office building to the conference room across the hall from Gary Johnson's office. Joe had not been on the Wolverine site since the mine had reopened and was amazed at the flurry of activity that was taking place.

In the conference room were assembled a couple of familiar faces. Gary got up to shake his hand and made the introductions. Arne Tyrronen and Elizabeth MacIntyre he recognized. Joe was introduced to "Tiny," a big, burly security guard. Sizing up the man as he stood to shake Joe's hand, he saw that the guys who worked the mines never lost their sense of humor. Tiny was around six feet seven inches tall and was every bit of three hundred pounds. Obviously, nobody got on the property without his permission.

Jim Thomas was introduced last. The Chicago businessman wore an expensive tailored suit and was well groomed. He was a handsome man with a slight tinge of gray on the sides of his head, giving away his forty-three years of age that his physique would never have belied.

Joe took a seat at the end of the conference table. Jim began by saying, "As I told you over the phone, we have reason to believe that the tragic accident that took place here almost four months ago was no accident. The evidence that I'm going to present to you may be circumstantial, but there may be enough of it to make a case. Too many coincidences occurred, which have led me to believe that event was planned."

"So you've already told me. Now tell me something I can sink my teeth in to."

"All right. First, there's a meeting in Denver, during which North American Metals is entertaining an offer for a buyout by Wolverine Mining. By coincidence, the accident occurs the same day the meeting takes place, and that night the president of North American proposes to buy Wolverine."

"So what?"

"It's all too convenient. Even if you were that lucky to find a turn of events that would change the course of a business deal one hundred and eighty degrees, I know of few chief executives who could unilaterally make those decisions on the spot."

"So you think the cave-in was staged to ruin Wolverine Mining and make it a target for a takeover?"

"Yes. This is further substantiated by Tiny answering a phone call from Andy MacIntyre, who orchestrated the deal to Jack Sanders, who was responsible for underground operations."

"What do ya mean?" Joe gave Jim a puzzled look.

"I mean that Andy was on the phone immediately after Jack arrived back on surface after being rescued by Gary here."

"Another coincidence. Oh, see what ya mean," Joe caught himself. "Go on."

"Well, Tiny also overheard Jack on the phone."

Joe wheeled around in his chair to face Tiny. "And what did he say to Andy MacIntyre?"

"He said, 'It should never have happened.' Jack was all shook up. Andy musta tried to calm 'em down but couldn't. He told Andy, 'This ain't any good—all hell's gonna break loose, and there'll be inspectors to answer to.'"

"Interesting, but nothing worth pursuing yet." Joe stroked his chin in thought. "What else ya got?"

"Secondly," Jim continued, "we have a copy of the latest filing of an annual corporate status report with the state of Colorado that shows Andy MacIntyre is a stockholder owning 15 percent of that company. It's a pretty clear case of setting up one company in which you're a part of the senior management team in order to profit from another company in which you're a shareholder."

"You've done a good job of exposing unethical business practices, but you told me we'd be discussing murder." Joe's tone became harsh.

"It goes back to the so-called accident. The cave-in was to be a staged event for the governor's entourage. It ended up killing three people because the location of the underground tour was not communicated."

"Then the deaths were indeed an accident."

Jim was fast becoming furious. He leapt up from his chair, toppling it on its back. Pointing a finger at Joe Maki, he yelled, "Damn it! My partner was killed because of a scheme that Andy MacIntyre dreamed up with Ray McKinnen to make a fast buck off of this operation. There has got to be a crime that fits the bill!"

The room was silent for a moment. Finally, Joe calmly replied. "Yes, Mr. Thomas, there are several things Andy MacIntyre could be charged with that range from racketeering to manslaughter. Whether any of them would stick or not is another issue entirely; however, since this was such a highly visible incident and the governor of our fair state was killed, then I believe the next step is to inform the state attorney general's office. The issues here are complex. One thing I can tell you is that we're not dealing with murder. White-collar crime? I suppose."

With that, Joe got up and headed for the door. He turned back before he stepped into the hall. "I'll be in touch, Mr. Thomas."

CHAPTER 60

Jim had just been introduced to the new president of Kearsarge Mining, Jack Stallworth. He couldn't believe his ears! Jim had not met Jack before today. Alan had handled all the communications with North American Refining. Jim was so taken aback that he spilled part of his beer on the bar when he reached for the bottle to fill his glass.

"Why, Jack, I honestly don't know what to say."

"That's apparent," Stallworth responded as he eyed the bartender mopping up Jim's mess. He was obviously enjoying the moment. "It's a small world, Jim. You must understand. There was an opportunity created, and we jumped on it."

"We, meaning Northern Michigan Refining?"

"Oh no. That's just one of our operating companies. We is RE Associates."

"That's right." *How stupid can you get?* Jim was mentally chastising himself.

"Mr. Thomas," the manager interrupted, "you have a phone call." She handed him a cordless phone.

"Who is it?"

"Your wife."

"Excuse me," Jim said to Jack Stallworth.

"Certainly, we'll talk some more over lunch."

Jim walked around the corner and headed for the manager's office for some privacy. He had a deep, sinking feeling in the pit of his stomach. When it rains, it pours.

"Hello, Anita," he began, and then before she could get a word in, he continued, "I know you're calling because I didn't get in touch with you last night."

"Now that you've figured that much out, let's hear it." Her voice on the other end was very strained. She was doing her best to keep her composure. "It's pretty bad, Jim, when I have to track you down at a business lunch. Or are you lying about that too?"

"Now hold on a minute. I'm not lying about anything—"

"I hope she was worth it!"

"What are you… no, it's not that."

"Then what? What is it? Am I not important anymore? Was I just an anchor when Alan was killed? Disposable?"

Jim took a deep breath. He didn't need this now. How was he going to diffuse this one?

"Hold on. Which of the questions would you like me to answer?"

"*All* of them, damn it!"

"Anita, I plain and simply didn't have a chance to call you earlier. I met with Elizabeth for a while last evening—"

"I knew it!"

"…*just* to make sure what I was going to tell the prosecuting attorney this morning was not going to upset her. After all, it is her brother I'm accusing of murder. It was a common courtesy. Nothing more. I got back to the hotel, and after a couple of drinks, I just collapsed. I should have called you no matter what the hour, but I didn't. I'm sorry. There's nothing more to say. I've been in meetings all morning, and I'm in the middle of a meeting and need to get back."

"What did the PA have to say?" She was curious now that her temper had subsided.

"He said murder was out of the question. We couldn't prove anything of the sort on the circumstantial evidence that we have;

however, he was going to bring it up with the state attorney general's office."

"Just make sure that happens." She was offering him professional advice now. "Maybe you need yourself a real good, big-city lawyer instead of the country bumpkins they have up there."

"Maybe. Do you know of any?" He was really pushing his luck now.

"Why, you son of a—nah, that's not worth getting even more upset over."

"Look, Anita, I've really got to get back. Call you tonight?"

"You better, or don't bother coming home!"

"I will, promise. Talk to you then."

The phone went dead. Such an abrupt end to the conversation meant that he only had a temporary respite. He looked at the phone in his hand, breathed a sigh of relief, and headed back to the bar, only to find that his party had adjourned to the dining room and had already ordered lunch.

When he entered the dining room, he found that a seat had been reserved for him located strategically between Jack Stallworth and Elizabeth MacIntyre. His day was getting more interesting by the minute.

Jim apologized to Jack. "Sorry about the interruption."

Before Jack could say anything, Elizabeth asked, "What's wrong Jim? Forgot to check in last night?"

Jim rolled his eyes. *So this is how it's going to be,* he thought.

Jack saved him from having to answer. "Hey, Jim, I've got a yacht moored at the marina. It's a beautiful day. Why don't we finish lunch and go for a cruise and discuss where to go once we get on the boat."

CHAPTER 57

Opportunity is defined by Webster to be "a combination of circumstances favorable for the purpose." There was no denying that opportunity had presented itself front and center to one Jim Thomas. The question that remained was: for what purpose?

Jim racked his brain trying to come up with an answer other than the obvious, which was empire building. He had gone beyond accumulating money. He was well off by most measures of wealth already. What he was after was a legacy. He wanted to make his mark—to create something that he would be remembered by, much like Elizabeth's great-grandfather, James Andrew MacIntyre, had done here in Calumet. Jim would take his great-granddaughter and use ol' MacIntyre's money to renew a legacy. A mining baron recreated a century later. Why not? It seemed like a worthwhile endeavor.

So it was in the stateroom of Jack Stallworth's yacht that Jim pondered the opportunity before him that afternoon. Jack had excused himself to take an urgent phone call from his office in the main salon, leaving Jim behind with his second cognac rolling around his brandy snifter, with the waves created by a brisk wind that first day of November. What a smooth operator Jack was. After surprising Jim by being introduced as the new president of Kearsarge Mining at lunch, Jack had made arrangements to spend the afternoon with Jim and Elizabeth on his boat. Thus, just off of Eagle River, Jim was feeling the invigorating effects of good company, good liquor, and a good deal. Elizabeth had excused herself to climb up to the fly bridge for a better view. Jim had declined to join her but now was having second thoughts.

Oh, what the hell! he thought as he put the snifter down to pull his jacket on, picked up the glass, and made his way to the stern. As he passed through the main salon, he found Jack still on the phone and pointed up to indicate that he was headed up top to join Elizabeth on the bridge. Jack nodded an acknowledgment and resumed what appeared to be a fervent discussion over copper prices.

It was never as easy as it looked in the ads—climbing the ladder to the fly bridge on a yacht while holding a drink in one hand as the vessel cruised over two-to-three-foot waves at fifteen knots; however, after only having spilled once on his jacket, Jim successfully navigated his way to the bridge.

"Quite the view." He greeted Elizabeth as he crossed the bridge to the front rail, where she was looking out over the bow.

She turned abruptly, obviously startled. "It's one I've always enjoyed. There is nothing more spectacular than the Keweenaw Peninsula when viewed from the greatest of the Great Lakes."

"Yes," Jim agreed. "There's also nothing like the raw beauty and power of nature to put one in a philosophical, if not poetic, mood."

The expression on her face suggested that she questioned the sincerity of his comment. "Are you being sarcastic?"

"No, not at all." He couldn't believe his luck with women today. He should just give up. Everything he said was misinterpreted. "In fact, I'm enjoying myself immensely. Your reflection a moment ago struck me as poetic. It also showed how much pride, or maybe love, you have for this area."

"I do. Many years ago, my daddy used to take me out on his boat. I guess I was reminiscing a bit when you came up."

They paused to take in the scenery. Jim put his hand on her shoulder, and she removed it.

"Not the time or the place," she said. "Look over there." She pointed to the starboard side. "You can see where Eagle River empties in to Lake Superior, and on top of the hill, you can see the top of the courthouse."

"Is that the one we're going to try your brother in?"

Oops! He blew it *again! Keep your mouth shut, Jim,* he scolded himself.

Before he could apologize, she responded calmly to his surprise. "Yes, I suppose it is where Joe Maki could bring Andy and McKinnen to trial if he decided to."

"Don't forget Jack Sanders. He was the actual killer."

"Maybe so, but I think he can be persuaded to testify on our behalf."

"How so? I thought he worked for North American with those other crooks."

"He did. You should have taken some time to know the people we've got working up here, Jim."

"That may be true, but what has it got to do with Jack Sanders turning in his partners in crime?"

"Arnie and I had a long talk with Gary after Tiny came forward with his information on the phone conversation he overheard."

"Yes?" Jim turned to look her in the eyes.

"It seems that Gary had gotten to know Jack pretty well in the time Jack worked for him. Gary believes that Jack's only real motivator is money. In fact, Gary was trying to motivate him in other ways by taking him to church and befriending the guy. But I guess he was never successful. The guy's a real loner. A selfish one at that."

"You're suggesting we bribe Sanders?"

"*Bribe* is such an ugly word. Besides, we could never bribe a witness; however, we do have money…"

"That's what I like to hear," Jack Stallworth bellowed as he stepped off the ladder.

Elizabeth spun around. "Just what did you hear, Jack?"

"Nothing, my dear." He put his arm around her waist. "I was not eavesdropping. I am not that kind of a person. I only heard that you have money, and that's good news because we can put it to good use."

"I'm sure you can," said Jim, who was a little upset looking at Stallworth standing there with his arm around Elizabeth when he had been rebuffed. "But I thought you venture capitalists were the guys with the money."

"That, my friend, is a much exaggerated impression that we try to put forth. Not true, Mr. Wolverine Ventures?"

"I'm afraid I'll have to agree with you."

"Then that won't be the first thing we'll be agreeing on today. You and I have much to talk about with the beautiful Ms. MacIntyre here. After all, the one thing we venture capitalists like to do is make money—fast. Then we can get the investors off our backs and really start to enjoy the fruits of our labors."

"That's one short-term view I guess."

"Come now. It's the only view you can take and call yourself a venture capitalist."

Jim was getting a bit red in the face. "Well, no. I can't agree with that. The situation is just the opposite of what you describe. The venture capitalist is the one that wants the quick out with the high rate of return, and the entrepreneur is the one who's in for the long term. Here you are, actually running one of RE Associates' investments, and you call yourself a venture capitalist? No, it is you who have crossed over the line and have become the entrepreneur. I believe my involvement with Wolverine Mining puts me in the same boat. Elizabeth has always been at least a passive investor, but I think all along she has been rather active and becoming more so. Therefore, let's call a spade a spade and get on with the business at hand. How do we grow Kearsarge Mining, Wolverine Mining, Northern Michigan Refining, and RMS?"

"Nice speech. It has some good points, but not enough to warm me up to the point of not shivering in this cold air. Let's go down and discuss a strategy. I guess old habits do die hard."

"Yes, they do." Jim and Elizabeth spoke simultaneously then looked at each other wondering what the other might be referring to. With that, they adjourned to the stateroom.

After several minutes of discussion and having poured over the balance sheets from all the respective companies, they were rapidly coming to the point where they would have to decide how the empire would be structured.

"I believe," Jim began, "that RE Associates has the most to gain out of any deal we put together."

"How so?"

"You already own Northern Michigan Refining and the largest copper mine and mill up here. Now you want to secure the only source of high-grade copper in the United States by owning Wolverine Mining, which you already have access to through the partnership of RMS. Even with the reduced price of one dollar and fifty cents per pound that we renegotiated back in September, you still make somewhere around twenty cents per pound sold to your refining company. The profit you're making on the high-purity, high-conductivity copper alloy you sell to Ford is at least one dollar per pound by your own projections. Why buy Wolverine?"

Jack had been waiting for that question. "Quite simple. It appears that your profit on the ore is forty cents by selling to RMS. Then add your twenty cents net from the partnership's profits. That's sixty cents per pound. So on twelve million pounds per year, I make one dollar and twenty cents, and you make sixty cents per pound. Both are respectable profit margins, but only for twelve million pounds per year. If the market for hybrids and electric cars takes off, and many project they'll make up 20 percent of the new car fleet by 2020, I'll need a lot more than that, and I'd like to know I've got it at a price I can afford."

Looking over the top of her glass of wine, Elizabeth offered one of her few comments. "So, Jack, are you saying we've got you by the… ahem… proverbial gonads?"

Jack Stallworth may have been a polished and experienced businessman, but he was totally unprepared to deal with such off-the-wall remarks made by the beautiful woman sitting next to him, especially since she reached down and demonstrated what she meant. He couldn't help but stutter.

"We… well, yes, I guess I am."

"Now that you mention it," she continued, "I believe you may be right. After all, we are sitting on the perfect raw material that you need without having to buy precious metals on the open market."

She had Jack's and Jim's undivided attention. Elizabeth was a listener. She did not engage in lengthy oratory, particularly on a subject she was not well versed in. Obviously, this was a different situation.

"As you may or may not know, we were offered one hundred and fifty million dollars for Wolverine six weeks ago when things looked a lot more grim than they do now. Rather than take the money and run, we decided to ride this one out. I know that was the right decision. With the planned expansion, we will be as large as Kearsarge but with one big advantage: our ore reserves are twice as rich. Therefore, from everything I've seen, given your patented technology and our reserves, I'd suggest a fifty-fifty partnership for this empire, which will include Wolverine and Kearsarge Mining, RMS, and Northern Michigan Refining. If we're going to all bet on the future of the native copper reserves still in the ground up here, let's do it in a big way. Consolidate everything and split the ownership."

He just stared at her. "What makes you think your mine is worth as much as Kearsarge and Northern Michigan Refining put together?"

Elizabeth said nothing. She just set down her wine glass, raised her hand, and made a slow and purposeful squeezing motion. She didn't even smile. All Jack could see was Lake Superior reflected in her blue eyes. All Jack could hear was the drone of the yacht's engines and the vessel slicing through Superior's waves. As a stone would slowly come to rest on Superior's bottom, so the conversation had been put to rest by the one whose very soul was a part of these north woods and waters. It turned out she was much better than either of these seasoned veterans at negotiating a deal. Jim couldn't help but marvel at what he had just witnessed.

CHAPTER 58

It was 1:20 a.m., Thursday, November 2. The phone had been ringing several times.

"Hello?" she said while clearing her throat.

"Anita, sorry about calling so late."

"Jim? What time is it?"

"Late. I just got in to the hotel, and I promised to call you tonight. Or rather this morning."

"Did Elizabeth finally crash on you and you slipped away to call me?" Her voice strained with cynicism.

There was a long pause, during which Jim could faintly hear another conversation on the line, something about Richard and Susan's wedding plans. He wanted to tell them not to do it.

"Yes, you're very perceptive. We've had a wonderful time and are both exhausted from wild sex like you and I have never known. What a difference a younger woman makes." Jim was angry. He was also lying. He was, in fact, alone in his room at the Michigan House after having bid Jack and Elizabeth good night just minutes ago. Jack had offered to take Elizabeth home since Jim was feeling a bit tipsy from the food and drink following the agreement to consolidate the companies they all owned into a massive partnership.

"You a———."

"Will you be defending yourself, or will you need a good lawyer?"

"You son of a b———."

"Just send my things to the MacIntyre estate up here. Ruth has the address."

"You…"

Jim set the phone down hard. He looked up at the ceiling then down at the floor. The alcohol made him dizzy. He felt sick. What had he done? He fell back on the bed. That was the last thing he remembered.

CHAPTER 59

Elizabeth drove her mother's old Mercedes into the carriage house. Jack came around and opened her door. He motioned for her to exit with a wide sweep of his arm. "After you, milady."

"Why, thank you, kind sir."

They strolled arm in arm down the ramp to the back door of the MacIntyre estate. Taking the back stairs up to the master bedroom, Elizabeth asked, "Did you bring a change of clothes?"

Jack shook his head. "No, I wasn't sure what was happening."

Walking into the master closet, she selected a black lace negligee. "Boy, I'd say you didn't. I had to take over and close the deal." She came out of the closet looking like a model for Victoria's Secret. "I moved your clothes to the guest closet down the hall. Having men's clothing in my closet is too hard to explain."

"To whom?"

"I didn't think full disclosure was part of our arrangement. Now, are you going to fulfill your part of the bargain?"

"Speaking of which, you drive a hard one."

Elizabeth put her hands on her hips. "Hey, there's nothing wrong with a fifty-fifty split, and don't forget, I still have to buy out Jim at some point."

Jack wasn't listening. He couldn't help but stare at this incredible woman wearing only enough to accentuate the curves of her body. It would be foolish to stand there and argue with her. He opted to stroll down the hall, returning a couple of minutes later with a couple of champagne flutes and a cold bottle of French bubbly. "This complements French lace teddies very well."

She peeled back the comforter. "Compliments will get you nowhere. Are you planning on takin' care of business?"

CHAPTER 60

The morning after: it was not just a song by Maureen McGovern. It was an experience that was best forgotten quickly.

With his head pounding and his stomach reminding him of what he had consumed the night before, Jim staggered out of bed and found the bathroom before he became violently ill. Was this any way to feel after closing probably the biggest deal of his life? Jim had plenty of time to think as he stared into the toilet bowl. *Is God punishing me? What would Reverend Johnson say about this?*

There was no time to find out. He had to act fast. Fumbling through his briefcase on the dresser, he found his black book with key phone numbers in it. Aha! There it was. Filed away under "P" for pilot was Mack Dennison's name and home number. Jim dialed then glanced at the clock. It read 7:30 a.m. That was 6:30 a.m. Central time. *Oh well, that's what I pay him for,* Jim thought.

After seven or eight rings, Jim heard another groggy hello on the other end.

"Mack?"

"Yeah. Who's calling?"

"It's Jim Thomas. Sorry to bother you so early, but I've got a bit of an emergency. I need to be in Chicago right away. Can you get the plane up here pronto?"

"Sure. I'll need some time to file a flight plan. Give me about three to three and a half hours."

Looking at his watch and doing a little arithmetic in his head, Jim figured he'd be home by around noon Central time. "No problem, Mack. I'll see you at Houghton County about ten o'clock. I appreciate it. See ya then."

Hanging up the phone, he walked over to the window of the suite he had rented on the southeast corner of the building. Drawing back the curtain to get an unobstructed view of the city, Jim saw the sun just beginning to rise over the east end of Sixth Street. The longer, red wavelengths of the morning sun cast a pink hue on all the buildings in town. Over to the south, the old shafts from the Osceola Mine reflected the sunlight so brilliantly that it looked like the east side of the shafts was aglow from a fire inside.

We'll have the ol' mines up here heated up, Jim thought. *Now, if only I can heat up my marriage and cool down this romance… or do I want to? Well, you'd better decide, ol' boy, 'cause you're on your way to try to resolve the mess you made in anger a few hours ago. There's only going to be one way to solve the problem too. You have to make a choice.*

Why is it I'm always making these choices? Anita isn't being reasonable. She tells me to pursue my dream and but then doesn't like the consequences. She doesn't understand what it takes. She gets jealous and jumps to conclusions. Like I need this headache. Maybe I should just leave and quit worrying about it.

Heading into the bathroom to shower and shave, Jim decided he would call Elizabeth, no… make that Jack, to let him know that he would be out of commission today… no, make that indefinitely. *Yeah, I'll tell him an emergency came up that I needed to attend to back in Chicago and that I'm leaving immediately. No further explanation required. Boy, working for yourself does have its advantages.* As for Elizabeth, he'd cross that bridge when he came to it. *One crisis at a time, please.*

CHAPTER 61

The Wolverine corporate plane touched down on the runway at 11:14 a.m. as Jim watched from the lounge in the private aircraft hangar. Mack pulled the aircraft up to the hanger three minutes later and swung the tail with the wolverine on it toward the hanger so the nose of the plane pointed out to the airfield.

Jim had made arrangements for immediate refueling while he awaited the plane's arrival. A serviceman headed out to the plane with a hose over his shoulder as soon as Mack shut down the twin engines on the Beechcraft King.

When we make our first one hundred million dollars on Red Metal Enterprises, we'll have to spend seven on a new Gulfstream, Jim thought as he studied the plane that had served Wolverine Ventures since 2006.

"How's the flight?" Jim greeted Mack as he came into the lounge.

"It's a little choppy up there today. Hope you didn't have a big breakfast."

"No breakfast." That was because he was too sick to eat this morning.

Mack poured himself a large Styrofoam cup of coffee, placed a lid on it, and turned to see if Jim was ready to board. "Go ahead and get on the plane. I'll grab your luggage as soon as I visit the little boy's room."

Jim didn't reply. He simply strolled to the plane, ascended the steps, taking care not to bang his head on the door, and settled into the leather chair with the work center next to it.

Once airborne, he reclined his seat to gaze out the window for a moment. The plane was being tossed around pretty good as they cleared the treetops on the south end of the runway. Jim studied the topography to keep his mind off his queasy stomach.

As the plane gained altitude over Portage Lake, Jim looked down on the summer homes and cabins that had been shut down for the winter. He recalled the howling winds last December that blew with such ferocity down the shipping canal. Now, exposed by the defoliation process, the homesteads were at the mercy of the elements. The houses dotted the shoreline, each a small fortress against the wintry winds from the west and the north—much like the one he experienced on the fly bridge of Jack Stallworth's yacht yesterday. The seasons were again rapidly changing. How he used to love change. In and of itself, it was a motivating force in his life. It was the reason he set out on his own six years ago after working ten years as an economic analyst for McKenzie Management Consultants in their Chicago office. And yes, he was still a big believer in fate and the role that it played in changing one's life. So once again, here he was at a crossroads, only this one was the most bittersweet one he'd ever encountered. What would he do when he landed? Jim picked up the phone on the counsel of the business center and placed a call.

After giving Mack the rest of the week off, Jim found his car in the Avis lot at O'Hare. He knew the owner of the franchise, who let him keep his car on the lot under good security. Turning left out of the lot, he accelerated quickly down the access road, passing two rental car buses along the way and enjoying the sound of the twelve cylinders moving the car to a speed of over eighty miles an hour before he had to brake to catch his exit to Irving Park Road.

The clock on his dash read 12:38 p.m. He had left a message with Anita's secretary to meet him at one o'clock. Provided traffic was not too heavy, he should be at Giovanni's Restaurant on Roosevelt Road in twenty minutes. The only question was: would she be there?

The answer to the question was found in the form of Anita's BMW parked next to the handicapped spaces near the front door of the restaurant. The workday lunch crowd had already dissipated, and parking spaces were plentiful.

Pulling into a space opposite her BMW, Jim collected himself with a deep breath. He closed the door of his Jaguar and strolled for the front door of the restaurant. He paused for a minute to let his eyes adjust to the dim light, having just walked in from bright sunlight, and scanned the tables in the main dining room for his wife. She had spotted him first and was signaling him with her hand from the corner booth. Jim nodded and made his way over to the table.

He could tell she was tense as he sat down. Both neglected any greetings or pleasantries; Jim just slid in the booth opposite Anita. She was looking down and fidgeting with her napkin. Before Jim had a chance to break the ice, the waiter was standing at the table asking if he'd like anything to drink. With the way he had felt all day, Jim declined anything from the bar and settled for a glass of ice water.

After the waiter departed with their orders, Jim opened the conversation with the monologue he had mentally prepared all the way down to Chicago that morning.

"First of all, Anita, I have to apologize for the way I talked to you last night. I know it's not a good excuse, but I was drunk. I let my emotions get away from me. I had had a difficult time keeping people from jumping to conclusions on me all day, and when you did last night, I simply lost my temper. Please forgive me for that. I was out of line."

She looked up at him with glistening eyes. He could tell she was fighting back tears. "Apology accepted."

Jim continued. "I also must tell you I lied to you last night. I did not spend the night with Elizabeth. I was by myself. Jack Stallworth took her home after dinner. I had too much to drink and retired to my room. It was late because we were up late celebrating the formation of RMS, which combines Wolverine and Kearsarge Mining, Northern Michigan Refining, and Red Metal Sales. Elizabeth negotiated a great deal for us as a 50 percent partner in the whole shebang. It marked the culmination of the development work I've been doing up there for more than two years. I guess it was worth celebrating."

"I won't deny that, but why couldn't you call me earlier? Before dinner maybe?"

"One thing led to another."

"That's what I was afraid of. Couldn't you tell how upset I was when I tracked you down at the Miscowaubik Club? You don't even answer you cell phone when I call. Do you know how embarrassing it is to call your secretary to find out where you are?"

"Yes, I knew you were upset. You made that clear in no uncertain terms, remember? However, I called, and I'm here!" His voice was rising. He had to catch himself to prevent other diners from enjoying their conversation.

She said nothing. She did not want to antagonize him any further at this point.

Jim just looked at her as he took a sip of water. The waiter showed up during the lull in the conversation, almost as though on cue, to deliver their salads.

It was time to get to the nitty-gritty. Despite his rehearsals on the plane, he wasn't quite ready to deliver the next lines.

"Look, Anita, I'm beyond trying to lie to you or cover things up. We've been together too long for that. I flew down this morning to try to set things straight. It's time we did that. There's too much mistrust here."

She cut him off. "With good reason!"

"Yes, I'll give you that much. Let me finish, please. The truth is, our marriage is doomed. I now realize that, and I think you know that too. I've been trying to pull back together the biggest investment we've ever made. I'm going to do that. I've already lost my partner and my friend. The stakes are high. You say you're in this with me, but you really aren't. I'm going to finish this no matter what it takes. No distractions. No excuses. No more marriage problems."

"You're leaving me?" She was surprisingly composed.

"Yes." Jim had prepared a much more eloquent expression of his feelings, but even his polished presentation skills failed him at this moment.

Silence. The sounds of silverware against china, of muffled conversation from across the room, of dishes in the kitchen, of the easy-listening music over the sound system became most annoying, even unbearable. Jim struggled to keep his composure. Anita cried softly and openly, with tears falling from her cheeks onto her napkin still folded next to her plate, making damp circles on the cloth.

Jim started to say something, but Anita looked up at him and shook her head no.

"Just leave, please."

He did.

CHAPTER 62

December 24 brought with it a light snowfall in Laurium that made the streetscape on Tamarack Street in front of the MacIntyre estate picture-postcard perfect. The white powder had fallen so softly in the absence of wind that it was piled several inches high on the branches of the massive maple trees in front of the house. Now and then one of the piles would overflow and create a stream of fine white mist to the sidewalk below.

Elizabeth had invited Jim over so he wasn't alone at Christmas. Jim had moved into a suite at the Michigan House and had not had much contact with Anita and Julie since leaving Barrington last month. Only John had maintained any contact with him, calling him on a regular basis to report on life at Northwestern.

Making for a perfect setting, the chimes from the nearby church on the corner could be heard. With favorite Christmas carols reverberating through the icy air, Jim proposed a toast to their first Christmas together.

"This is to the first of many enjoyable Christmases together." He raised his glass of champagne, and they encircled their arms as they sipped.

Elizabeth whispered in his ear. "You don't know how I've longed for this moment or how lonely last Christmas was."

"I know how lonely Christmas without family is. I am so glad to be here. It wasn't easy breaking away like that, but I knew I had to do it sooner or later if I was ever going to be truly happy."

"And did it work?"

"Did what work?"

"Did leaving Chicago make you happy?"

"Do I look happy?"

She set her champagne glass down and placed her hands on the sides of his face. Turning his head, she looked him in the eye. "Yes, at least you look quite contented."

"So much so I could purr."

"Then let me make you a happy cat." She grinned slyly. His puzzled look told her he didn't understand why she was leaving. "Don't worry, pussycat." This time, she giggled as she planted a kiss on his nose with her finger. "I'll be right back."

Aha, Jim thought, *present time.* He reached into his pants pocket. Carefully extracting a small gift box, he hid it behind the bottle of champagne. No sooner had he finished his maneuver when Elizabeth reentered the room, dressed in a fur coat. He loved the way she looked in the full-length sable coat. Her long, blonde hair was highlighted by the darker brown tones in the coat, and as in the brochures put out by the furrier, all he could see beneath the coat was her long, slender legs, suggesting that the fur was all she had on. He knew that to be true and found the thought very sensual.

Watching his eyes, she posed for him at the edge of the Jacuzzi, placing her foot on the side and showing her bare leg and thigh. "Like it?"

"The coat?" he asked as innocently as he could.

"No, the model!" With that, she let the coat fall to the floor. Straddling him, she grabbed the back of his head and pulled his face to hers. Planting a big kiss on his lips, she bit his lower lip.

"Ouch!" Jim yelled as he flung his head back. "What did ya do that for?"

"That's for your comment about the coat, and you might want to check your shirt pocket for your Christmas present."

He slid his hand into his pocket and extracted an envelope. "What's this? A love note?"

"You might say that."

He removed the paper from the envelope, noting that it felt almost like parchment. Unfolding it, he was stunned. It was a stock certificate with his name on it. One hundred thousand shares of the Ford Motor Company. With a book value of about fifteen dollars per share, it was worth some one point five million dollars.

"What do you think?" she asked.

"Wow."

She never ceased to amaze him, but this had to be the ultimate surprise. Knowing she was waiting for more of a response, he asked, "Why?"

"Because I'm falling in love with you, and now that we have everything up and running again, we're going to help make Ford the leader in electric cars. A year from now these shares will be worth ten times what they are today. You can cash in and do whatever you want then. I want to help you achieve your dream."

Tears trickled down his face. Jim was touched. He was speechless. What can you say when you've just received a fortune for a Christmas present? He pulled her close to him and held her tight.

When he had finally come out of shock, he remembered he had something for her too. "I also wanted to make this Christmas special for you." He reached for the box and handed it to her.

She tugged at the bow and purposefully unwrapped the gift. Opening the box, she gasped. It was a diamond ring with matching earrings. Elizabeth recognized them immediately as being natural pink diamonds, a rarity among rare gemstones.

Smiling ear to ear, Jim explained, "If you're going to wear a fur coat around the house, you must have the proper accessories. These are from the Argyle diamond mine in west Australia. A friend of mine who is a diamantaire managed to get his hands on these. The gold in the settings is from the Caribou mine in Canada, where your family business still has a minority interest—quite international. What else does a well-dressed girl need?"

"Nothing," she exclaimed. "Nothing at all. I've got everything I've ever wanted right here."

"Oh, I almost forgot something." Jim reached into his pants pocket and pulled out two tickets. "Since RMS is closed for the holidays, I thought you might want to go skiing with me."

"Are those lift tickets?"

"They sure are."

"Can I have a lift upstairs?"

"You sure can."

CHAPTER 63

Christmas Day and Boxing Day were spent by Jim and Elizabeth skiing in the Porcupine Mountains at the Indianhead Ski Resort. Having tired of the hills in the western Upper Peninsula, they decided to try the riskier terrain of Pike's Peak and the surrounding ski resorts.

The morning of December 27, Jim and Elizabeth boarded the Wolverine Ventures' plane, now in a hanger at the Houghton County Airport, and flew to Colorado Springs. At lunchtime, they were checking in to the Penrose suite at the Broadmoor overlooking Mount Baldy.

Jim and Elizabeth entered the suite by strolling under a pair of marble columns in a private corridor that connected the three bedrooms with the private dining room, kitchen, and sitting room. Original artwork decorated the walls.

Elizabeth peeked into the dining room. "No problem finding a place to eat here." The oak table had ten chairs set around it, with a large chandelier hanging over the table. A fresh floral bouquet decorated the table. She then noticed the silver tray of appetizers set on the serving table. Smoked salmon on thin slices of rye bread, caviar, and fresh strawberries awaited her along with a bottle of Don Perrier. "Oh, Jim, you think of everything, you little devil." She threw her arms around his neck and gave him a sultry kiss. "Thanks!"

"Later." Jim motioned for the door. "Our luggage will be here any time. You don't want to embarrass the bell captain, do you?"

"He's probably seen two lovebirds up here before."

"I suppose, my little chick-a-dee," came the reply in Jim's best W. C. Fields's impersonation. "Come on, I'll show you the rest of the place."

Jim unlocked the door that led into the sitting room. The plush surroundings and the fireplace made for an eloquent yet cozy setting. A fire had already been lit in the fireplace. Stepping up from the sitting room, they walked through the parlor onto an enclosed veranda. The view from the top of the main building was magnificent. Of course, for three thousand dollars per night, it should have been.

A knock on the door told them their luggage had arrived. Elizabeth showed the bell captain where to put their suitcases and skis, and he showed her how to operate the jets in the sunken tub off the master bedroom.

"What a great idea," Elizabeth proclaimed after the bell captain had left. She opened the drapes in the sitting room to look out over Broadmoor Lake. "Oh look, Jim. There's a couple of black swans swimming on the end where there's no ice. How unique!"

"Yeah. They are different. Just like the observer." He put his arms around her waist as he stood looking over her shoulder out the window. "This is a wonderful way to finish off the year."

"You want to stay until New Year's?"

"I don't know. Just a thought. Seemed like a good one a moment ago."

"But I didn't bring enough clothes. I thought we'd ski a couple of days and then leave."

"There are some very nice shops in the Springs. I'm sure you'll find something. Let's see what happens."

"Another good idea. Let's play it by ear. We're on no schedule." She took him in an embrace that nearly knocked the wind out of him. He returned the gesture and then just held her while he looked over her shoulder out the window at the majestic peaks of the Rockies as they rose over the plain. He would never tire of the smell of her hair, the warmth of her body, the softness of her sweaters, and her smooth skin as her cheek rested against his neck.

After a while in that position, she lowered her head back to look at him. "Can I ask you something?"

"Sure. Why do ask permission?"

"Because I want you to promise you won't get mad."

"How ridiculous. I won't get upset. Promise."

"Okay." She paused. "Can we go up to Denver to see Andy?"

"What?" Jim didn't see that one coming.

"You promised," she reminded him quickly.

He placed his hands on her shoulders and pushed her back to look into her eyes. By now, he could read her emotions in her eyes. When he did this time, he realized that they were sincere, even pained. The look softened Jim's initial response.

"Now can I ask you one question?"

"Yes. Anything."

"Why?"

"He's my brother. The next time I see him, I don't want it to be in a court of law."

"He belongs behind bars!"

"Maybe so, but he's the only family I've really got. Do it for me. Please." This time her eyes were begging him.

"All right. I'll accompany you because I promised. I don't like it, but I'll do it anyway. And I don't guarantee my behavior."

She responded with a big smile. "I don't ask for anything more, and furthermore, your behavior has never been guaranteed."

They embraced one more time, simply enjoying each other as only two people falling in love can do.

CHAPTER 64

Jim hadn't realized how wrapped up in RMS he had become until he had taken the time to get away. It felt so good to be away from it all and to simply enjoy the marvelous woman he had come to know and love.

They made the most of their time the first two days they were in Colorado. Using their private plane to hop from one ski area to another, they had skied at Telluride, Copper Mountain, and Purgatory. When they ran low on clothes because of their extended stay, they took a break and did some after-Christmas shopping in Colorado Springs. Light snowfall each night had made for perfect skiing conditions the following two days.

By December 30, they had finally tired of skiing. Jim was thankful for the sunken tub and the massages his roommate so expertly provided. At forty-three, he was starting to feel his age after so much physical activity.

He stepped down from the hot-tub platform into the bedroom to find Elizabeth hanging up the phone.

"Who was that?"

"It was Andy. I gave him a call to let him know we'd be coming up tomorrow. He invited us over to his chalet. I accepted, but on one condition."

Jim's eyebrows rose, producing an inquisitive look, which was far better than the grimace he had first showed her at the mention of her brother's name.

"No more skiing—you're far too old for that!" She laughed and then got up to give him a hug to ease the pain of the joke; however, it wasn't the remark that pained him—it was the thought of seeing her conniving brother that bothered Jim. Nonetheless, he had promised, and at least it would give him a chance to finally confront the jerk. He'd had a few days to prepare. Ever since he found out that there was little he could do legally, he often wondered what he would do if given the chance. He'd soon find out. One thing he had learned. There is no justice in the justice system.

So the next morning, their plane took them up to Vail, where they found Andy waiting for them right on time at the terminal. He greeted Elizabeth with a hug and a kiss as though they were being reunited after having been separated by birth. Jim found the whole scene repulsive but did manage to smile when he shook Andy's hand rather than break his nose, which was his natural impulse.

"Do you have any bags?" Andy asked. "I can load them into my car before we head on up to the chalet."

"No. We weren't planning on staying *that* long." His comment brought about a sharp tug on his sleeve from Elizabeth.

"Fine," Andy said. "We'll just have to make the most of the time we do have then." He was doing a wonderful job of keeping his cool.

The ride up Route 9 to Breckenridge was spectacular. The Colorado sunshine on this last day of the year made the snow glisten. The contrast of the white peaks against a blue sky with only a few small clouds was striking. It was enough to raise anyone's spirits, even Jim's.

They turned off the paved road onto a gravel road lined with jack pine. At the higher elevation, there was considerably more snow accumulation. It was apparent that Andy used this chalet frequently since the road had been kept open all winter and was well traveled. Two-foot snow banks bordered the road for the quarter-mile drive to the chalet. On the last turn, the pines parted to expose a large A-frame built into the mountainside with a picturesque view surrounding the structure on three sides.

"Nice place," Jim complimented Andy from the backseat.

"Thanks. I've always dreamed of owning my own place up in the mountains like this. It took a while, but I finally made enough money to afford this little getaway." He shot a quick look at Elizabeth to make sure the keeper of the family fortune was listening. Even Jim didn't miss picking up the tone of bitterness in his voice.

Andy didn't stop there. "You're a self-made millionaire, Jim. You of all people surely understand the satisfaction in having made something out of nothing."

Getting tired of Andy's carrying on, Jim decided to end the conversation in a hard-handed manner. "True, but only if you've done it with honesty and integrity does it mean anything."

Stopping the car abruptly in the parking place next to the stairs up to the chalet entrance, Andy turned around to face Jim and retaliate then thought better of it. "I agree. Welcome to my hideout." Then, turning to his sister, he said, "Come on up. I'll rustle up some lunch."

Forty-five minutes later, they were sitting down to a meal of Rocky Mountain rainbow trout almandine trimmed with herbed rice. The table was set next to a pair of sliding glass doors, and they could gaze over a couple miles of wilderness as they ate.

"I didn't know you could cook this well," Elizabeth said. "You were afraid of the kitchen when you lived at home."

"That was so long ago, sis. Many things have changed since then."

"Yes, Andy, that's true. In fact, you're the thing that's probably changed the most."

"Is that good or bad?"

She contemplated her answer. "I haven't decided yet. You came back into my life this past year after being gone so long, and then you disappeared again just as quick as you appeared—and under questionable circumstances, I might add. You forced Phillip Turner into firing you. I guess that's why I came to see you today. I wanted to find out for myself what has happened and why."

"I guess I owe you that much. Where do I start?"

"I would suggest you start with why you weaseled your way into the family business through me and then tried to pull away the one piece that means a great deal to me and our family heritage."

Andy studied his sister's face before he replied. He could see the hurt expression. "I wanted to claim what was rightfully mine. I've had to fight and scratch for everything I've got. I also think I've done a respectable job at it. When I found out you were getting back in to the mining business in the Copper Country, I knew I wanted a piece of that action."

Elizabeth shot him a look of disbelief. "Why? You turned your back on it a long time ago. You told Dad you didn't need him or his money and left."

"I didn't have a choice. He ran my life far too long. If I wanted anything, it was always under his terms. The money always had strings attached. Maybe you could live with that and be his good little girl. I couldn't. So I left."

Elizabeth's face softened a bit. "I understand all that. But why after all these years come back and then deceive me into thinking you wanted to be a part of the business when all you were really after was the mining company?"

"Because I knew you wouldn't give me any part of it. Your response was exactly as I expected it to be. Earn your way back into my good graces, brother. Here's a few crumbs. Prove that you can be a good boy and then maybe, just maybe, I'll let you have a little piece of the pie."

"Can you blame me?"

"Yes, I can! Maybe I expected too much to be welcomed back with open arms, and when that didn't happen, I decided to go along with your little game. Now instead of Dad running my life, Sis will do it. Make me a vice president. Give me a bit of responsibility and let me *earn* my share of my family business. What a bunch of bull! I'll learn about Wolverine and then take it with me."

Elizabeth was silent. Tears welled up in her eyes. Instead of being angry, she found herself feeling ashamed of herself for treating her brother exactly the way he described. That, however, did not excuse his actions, and Jim was determined to let Andy know that.

"You and that SOB Ray McKinnen made a valiant attempt to do just that, but fortunately, your sister had the vision to see right through that little plan. And now, rather than having sold out for a 10 percent profit, MacIntyre and Wolverine are poised to make enormous profits next year."

"That doesn't surprise me," Andy added.

It was now Jim's turn to resume the inquisition. "If all you were after was your share of the MacIntyre business, why try to acquire it in the way you tried?"

"It was the only way that had any likelihood of succeeding. Do you think Elizabeth would have given me 40 percent of Wolverine Mining if I asked her for it?"

"No, but what you did was so underhanded, even criminal."

Andy was beginning to get upset. His response was noticeably louder. "What is so criminal about making a bona fide offer for a mining company that faced a tremendous liability at the time the offer was made?"

"Your involvement in the liability, for starters."

Now Andy was red in the face. "What are you implying? That I had something to do with the cave-in?"

"Absolutely!" It was Jim who was on the verge of yelling back at Andy. "The so-called accident that took the lives of three people, including my partner!"

"Well, you couldn't be more wrong. I was not involved in any shape, manner, or form. I might have had aspirations to own the operation, but I would never go to those extremes for personal gain."

"Not intentionally, but as usual, you were in over your head," Jim nearly screamed at him. "However, I'll be pleased to quote you in court on your *aspirations*. That at least gives us motive."

Turning his attention from Jim to Elizabeth, Andy's expression changed from an angry one to a hurt one. "So is that the reason for the visit? To try to obtain evidence for some trumped-up charge you plan to bring against me?"

"No, that's not why we came. I wanted to hear your side of the story. I even forced Jim to come up here against his will. But I did come for some answers. You owe me that much after what you did."

"I gave you those."

"Yes, you did precisely that—gave me some answers."

"They are *the* answers. They are *the* truth. They may not be the ones you came to find, but they're all I've got to offer. If I say any more to you, I'll only incriminate myself in this lawsuit that Mr. Revenge over there wants to slap on me."

"No, you're both wrong about that. There won't be any lawsuits."

They both stared at her. Jim had seen her assert herself before and knew she meant business. Andy wasn't sure what to think.

"You heard correctly. I'm telling you both right now. There will be no lawsuits. Is that clear, Jim?"

What a test for their relationship. He was on the spot. There was nothing more Jim would like to see than Andy MacIntyre facing at least a manslaughter rap. Now he was being asked by Elizabeth, Andy's sister, to give it all up. Blood is definitely thicker than water. But none of that mattered because Joe Maki had refused to prosecute for murder and Jim wasn't interested in a civil white-collar suit about business practices.

Standing up from the table, Jim realized they had been watching him for some time. Both of them appeared anxious as they awaited his reply. He walked over to where Andy sat. "Andy, I really didn't mean to threaten you with a lawsuit. That would accomplish nothing. It certainly wouldn't bring Alan back, and I certainly don't need any monetary retribution." Jim lowered his head to stare at the table as though the weight of his shame was too great to hold his head up. When he looked up, he brought the 9mm Kahr subcompact pistol up to the side of Andy's head and pulled off the safety. "I hope that you can live with what you've done because the rest of us will have to; however, I am giving you one last chance to come clean. It really is good for the soul."

"What kind of..." Elizabeth grabbed her brother's arm and stopped him in mid-sentence then turning to Jim demanded, "What are you doing?"

"Getting the answers we came for. You're right. There will be no legal action; this way is much more effective and less expensive. Do you know that I can get 9mm rounds for only thirty-five cents apiece?"

"You wouldn't pull the trigger, you coward," Andy sputtered. "You've got too much to lose, including my sister."

They stared at each other for what seemed like an eternity. Finally, Jim lowered the Kahr and stepped back, smiled, and fired, putting a round through Andy's left arm.

Andy cried out in pain, "You a———!"

Elizabeth screamed, not knowing what to do or say.

Jim calmly said to Andy, "You were wrong on both counts. I *will* pull the trigger, and I *will not* lose your sister. You, however, have just experienced an unfortunate gun-cleaning accident, which will remind you to always pull the slide and check the chamber before handling a weapon. Consider this very nice PM9 a gift. Next time I won't be so kind, so you'd better hope there is no next time."

He reached into Andy's pocket, extracted his car keys, and said, "You can pick your vehicle up from the airport. Maybe the paramedics will give you a lift from the hospital. By the way, in case you're entertaining thoughts of using the gun right away, the magazine in the gun is empty. I didn't want to waste any ammo. After all, it does cost thirty-five cents a round."

"Now if you'll excuse us," Jim said as he headed for the door. He stopped to see if Elizabeth would follow.

As Jim drove the Highlander off the mountain and descended toward the airport, he thought he'd test the water with Elizabeth. "You know, I did say I couldn't guarantee my behavior."

"Yes, but where did the gun come from?"

"It's an unregistered piece I picked up in Colorado Springs."

"When did you do that?"

"After you decided you wanted to see Andy. We did do some shopping the other day. I decided I needed to accessorize my purchases."

"And you thought that was really necessary?"

"If I didn't, I wouldn't have done it."

"Even with a gun to his head, he didn't tell us anything we didn't know."

"He's really good at that," Jim said.

"Yes, he always was a little weasel."

"Well, now he's a wounded weasel with a couple of decisions to make."

"Do you think he'll keep his mouth shut?"

"He has so far."

"Yeah, I guess you're right."

"I wouldn't worry about Andy anymore."

Elizabeth thought for a moment before replying. "I don't know why I ever did. He obviously has ever only worried about himself."

Something inside Jim told him he had made the right decision in how to handle this situation. It just plain felt good. He knew this was his only chance to extract some revenge for Andy's involvement in the so-called mining accident. So Andy had a little accident of his own.

CHAPTER 65

January.

New Year's resolutions, year-end financials, below-zero weather, business plans, mid-winter carnivals, and board meetings.

It was a busy time. The winter days in the Keweenaw were short. Daylight gave way to darkness near 5:00 p.m., and working long hours became a habit during this time of year. So it was in the Houghton mining district.

Jim stood in the corner of the conference room. It was part of a large suite of rooms on the fifth floor of Kearsarge Mining, now RMS, that occupied the west side of the building. Jack Stallworth's office entrance was to his back on the north wall of the room. It was snowing heavily outside, with the wind blowing off of Lake Superior.

He remembered the first time he had been to these offices just over a year ago. Grossman was a towering man—lean in stature but bold and direct in his actions. Stallworth had some of those qualities—he was bold, but his stocky frame brought to mind a wrestler. That he was. He would grapple fearlessly with any issue or obstacle that confronted him. Grossman was direct yet delicate. His approach was always from the background. Stallworth took things head on. My, how Jim missed Bob. He had become a real friend. His instantaneous rapport with Alan Larsson was characteristic of the man. Now both of them had been gone for more than six months, their lives given up hundreds of feet below the surface where the storm outside raged.

What a loss, Jim thought. *Worse yet, what a crime. And Andy MacIntyre has the gall to deny any responsibility for the tragedy. He even believes he had a justifiable reason for his underhanded tactics. Wonder how his arm is doing.*

"Why the scowl?"

Jim spun around to see Elizabeth staring at him with her hands on her hips.

"Oh, sorry," she said. "Didn't mean to startle you."

"That's okay," he said, smiling back at her.

"You still didn't answer my question."

"Uh, I was just thinking,"—he hesitated—"about Alan and Bob Grossman." He lied, or actually chose to emphasize only a part of his thoughts. "How tragic their deaths were." Pausing once more, he decided to explain further then hope she'd drop the subject. "Coming back to this room jars my memory. I can't help but think of how things may have been different if they were still alive."

"How so?"

Oops! That's not what he wanted to say. "Well, for starters, we wouldn't be having this meeting with Jack Stallworth. We'd be planning our strategy to sell him more high-grade concentrate at inflated prices."

"I suppose that's true. We might even own a couple of gold mines out west too."

"That's true as well." Jim scratched his chin as he contemplated what might have been.

"But we don't," Elizabeth added matter-of-factly. "Is that so bad?"

"No, we've recovered quite nicely."

"Very well, I'd say. So tell me, Jim, do you still believe it's fate?"

He didn't have to think that one after New Year's Eve. "No, I believe it's a matter of choices more than fate."

"So much for philosophy," she commented as she touched his shoulder. "Come on. Let's hunt up Jack, get this show on the road, and make a few right choices."

Going through the connecting door into his office without knocking, they found Jack on the phone. He held up his index finger to indicate that he'd be off in one minute and motioned for them to have a seat.

Covering up the receiver with his hand, he said, "Gary's on his way up. Once he gets here, we'll get started."

Jim and Elizabeth acknowledged with a nod.

Ten minutes later, they entered the conference room, where Gary was patiently waiting for them. After exchanging greetings, it was time to get right to the production report since it was getting rather late.

Gary began by reviewing the monthly production figures for the last quarter: five million pounds in October, six million in November, and eight million in December. Kearsarge was supplying two to three million pounds of the monthly totals, but the ever-increasing numbers were coming from Wolverine as two more sections on level six and seven came online, and the next two sections that Jim had approved bringing online at an additional cost of five million had just kicked in last week. That was two weeks behind schedule but close enough to meet the contractual commitments to Chicago Wire and Northern Michigan Refining.

He ended his production report with his projections for this quarter. "So far dis month, we've exceeded last month's production, an' we should see another four million pounds processed in the next week. As far as February and March go, I see us gettin' to the ten-million-pound mark from Wolverine and holding steady there. I recommend we hold 'ere for a while an' take a breather. It's been a real push to get this far. Although we could get another two million pounds from Kearsarge an' start to stockpile."

"Thanks, Gary," Jack said. "I appreciate the job you've done in meeting these excruciating production requirements."

"Dat's the good news." Gary's wry smile meant that he had a bombshell to drop. Jim at least had come to know him that well by now.

"And the rest of the story," Jack spoke dramatically, imitating Paul Harvey, the famous radio commentator.

"Da rest of da story is dat we've been growing too fast." Gary's Upper Peninsula accent came out particularly strong. "Ya see, I've added forty guys in the last two months. None of dese guys have been properly trained. Some have mining experience, but not many. If we don't take da time to hold production, bring on another ten individuals, and institute proper training procedures, we're setting ourselves up for another disaster waiting to happen."

"That is a problem," Jack said.

"Why?" Gary demanded.

"Because Ford informed me last week that they want more bullion for the electric car project."

"You got ta be kidding." He glared back at Jack. "We can only perform so many miracles."

"Just one thing, Gary—before we renegotiated, Northern Michigan Refining's contract was for thirty-six million pounds this year. We settled for twelve. Now we need at least our original order to lock up this deal with Ford; plus, they may want options on more."

"Sorry, Jack, no can do!"

"I didn't ask you. I'm telling you what we need to do."

Most men would have exploded or simply stood up and walked out. Not Gary. He was too cool. He turned his attention to Jim and awaited his response.

Jim held up his hand as if to signal a truce. "Whoa, guys, there's no need to get excited." Turning to Gary, he asked, "What about the two million additional tons that Kearsarge can supply, which you were going to stockpile?"

"Now, Mr. Stallworth, you wanna have your cake an' eat it too. Three months after gettin' a lower price for reduced shipments, ya want the level of shipments restored to their original value. I told ya after the cave-in and I'm tellin' ya now—no can do!"

Jack shot out of his seat, and firmly placing both hands on the conference table in front of him, he leaned across the table until he was nose-to-nose with Gary. "I'll say it one more time. You will find a way to do it, or I will find someone else who will!"

"Be my guest!" Gary shouted back and turned to leave.

"Hold on, boys." This time it was Elizabeth who decided to act as mediator. "You two are acting like a couple of spoiled brats who can't have their own way. Look at this scene. This is supposed to be a board meeting."

"You're right," Gary answered sheepishly. "I'm sorry for lettin' my temper get da best of me."

"Jack?" She raised her voice as she said his name.

"Okay, okay. Just don't make us shake hands and make up."

"No, that would be asking too much from you two bullheads; however, it's my turn to deliver an ultimatum." Jim had seen her do this before less than three months ago with Stallworth.

She stood up to look them in the eye. "Jack, I will not have you threatening my mine manager's job. As developers of Wolverine, we do not tell Jon Johansson how to operate Kearsarge. Neither will you make operating decisions for Wolverine. You own 50 percent of RMS, not 51 percent."

Jack stood motionless. Elizabeth continued. "Gary, you will not treat Jack with such disrespect and not come in here making demands like this is some union bargaining table. We are the owners and directors of this company. You have been asked for your recommendations, and they will be considered. You will execute the directives of this board to the best of your abilities. Is that clear?"

"Yes," he said and sat down dejected. Jack followed suit.

Remaining on her feet, she added, "I will propose that we stockpile excess Kearsarge capacity to ship to Chicago Wire and move as much high-grade ore as possible to Northern Michigan Refining. By the end of March, we will add one more section to accommodate three million pounds per month going to Northern Michigan Refining. Can we do that, Gary?"

"I believe we can open up our first section on eight by then."

"Good, then get us a cost estimate and get the equipment ordered. Is there agreement?"

"Aye," answered the other two board members.

"There's your directive, Gary. Now how about a break in the action."

Jim stood up. He had been the only one who hadn't gotten his morning exercise. "One last thing. I want to make sure everyone realizes this. These problems are good problems, ones that I'm only too glad to deal with. As of the end of this month, with the kinds of production figures Gary has reported, RMS will be the one of the largest producers of copper in the United States, with a total of twenty-three million pounds of copper processed this month. That's ten from Wolverine and thirteen from Kearsarge. Not bad, huh?"

Jack nodded his head in agreement. "Now that you mention it, not bad at all. By the end of March, that number will be more like twenty-seven. Multiply by roughly one point five and that's forty million dollars per month of copper sales, not to mention the added revenues from Northern Michigan Refining. Over half a *billion* a year! Not bad!"

CHAPTER 66

The house on Eighth Street in Calumet had been a mine captain's house when it was built by the Osceola Mining Company one hundred years ago. With history repeating itself, it was once again a mine captain's house; however, this time around, there were many differences. Whereas Thomas McCormick had been a hard-drinking, callous Cornish miner known for his iron-handed rule of the Osceola Mine, Gary Johnson was the antithesis in character.

The Reverend Johnson, as he was known to the locals, was local pastor of the Methodist church. He had served the tiny Mohawk Church because nobody else had wanted to. The large churches of Calumet and Laurium were a handful for any minister; thus, the Reverend King was more than happy to relinquish the forty-five-member congregation when Gary offered to serve (without taking any salary) thirteen years ago.

During the next two years, nothing short of a miracle transpired at the tiny little church on US Highway 41. Partly because of his tireless efforts and partly because of his inspired preaching, the reverend tripled the size of the congregation in just twenty-four months. This was in the face of declining membership in almost all of the mainline denominations at that time. Such an achievement rarely goes unnoticed (even in the Methodist bureaucracy). The district superintendent was soon asking Gary to take one of the larger churches in the area and do it again. What he didn't realize was that Gary was as independent then as now. Furthermore, Gary was torn between his two loves: his desire to serve his LORD and his love of mining and the Copper Country where he was born and raised. Ultimately, he felt he could do both and decided to remain a part-time pastor of the Mohawk Church.

Up until now, this task had been manageable. Now it was becoming formidable. When he had decided to sell out his little piece of Copper Country mining history to two young entrepreneurs from Chicago, never did he dream it would explode into what RMS had become. He was now being forced into a position where he had to make a choice. At present, he was performing neither job to his satisfaction. In many ways, he blamed himself for the tragedy that had happened last summer. After all, the mine inspectors had cited his lax safety and mine management programs as primary reasons for the accident, despite the fact that there were never any criminal charges filed. For that, he thanked God every day.

When the doorbell rang, Gary found himself in front of his computer completing his usual twelve-hour workday. He knew he was getting too old to be putting in sixty-hour weeks, but that's what one and a half jobs required of him. He looked at his watch. It was 8:00 p.m.

Opening the front door, he found Jim standing there, shuffling from one foot to the other to stay warm while he waited.

"Well, Jim, what a nice surprise! Come in out of da cold. You Chicago guys aren't cut out for our Copper Country winters."

"I'm not a Chicagoan anymore, Gary. I've been living up here for a couple of months."

"So I hear. Like I said, let me know how ya survive your first winter, an' if you come through, I'll buy ya an adopted Yooper shirt next summer."

"Ya, sure, that'd be great." Jim tried his best to put on his Upper Peninsula, or Yooper, accent.

"So ta what do I owe the honor of this visit?"

"I've never been to your house."

"Then let me take your coat and show ya around. After dat, you can tell me the real reason ya paid me a visit, not that I mind."

The old Thomas McCormick house was filled with late nineteenth-century eloquence that had been well preserved. The foyer opened up into a large hallway graced by a winding staircase. Polished woodwork was abundant. This carried over into the oak-paneled study at the end of the hall that Gary led Jim into. So far, all Jim had seen was the hall and the bathroom adjacent to Gary's study, which had been redone in an 1890 motif, including a freestanding, brass toilet paper holder.

Jim sank into one of the overstuffed leather high-backed chairs that set against one wall in the study. Gary decided to end the tour and sat opposite Jim.

"So, boss, what can I do ya fer?"

"I came to talk to you about Jack Sanders."

"I was kinda wonderin' how long it was gonna take ya."

Leaning forward in his chair, Jim addressed Gary. "Help me out here, Gary. I need to know what Jack's role in the accident was. I know what happened—what I'm trying to find out is what's behind the events."

"I really wish I knew that too. Then maybe I could stop blamin' myself. Sure wish I could have that day back. But wishin' ain't doin' either of us any good."

"Do you at least know his whereabouts?"

"Sorry. Can't help ya there either. Let me tell ya what I do know, which ain't much."

Gary sat back in his chair and took a moment to collect his thoughts. "As ya may or may not know, Jack Sanders hung around long enough for da mine inspectors to talk to him, and den, I had his two weeks' notice. He was one of da best if not da best man I had workin' for me. His geostatistical predictions of ore quality and reserve quantity have proven to be right on. As a professional, he left nothin' ta be desired."

Looking directly at Jim and raising his right hand to act out his next thoughts, Gary continued. "However, on da other hand, as a person, Jack was a different breed. Or actually, among miners, he was not uncommon. He was definitely a loner, a drifter. He was also searching. He was not happy with his life and was looking for change, not unlike someone else I counseled last summer." He cast an accusing eye Jim's way. Jim was squirming.

Wanting to change the subject quickly, Jim tried to redirect the dialogue. "So Sanders was unstable. Does that mean he'd commit murder?"

"Dat's too big of a jump. Jack's search may not have included God, but he was not capable of killing anyone."

"How do you know that?"

"He was motivated by money, but he was not greedy. I know what you're thinkin.' Ya think Andy MacIntyre paid Sanders to cause the accident. Well, dat could be true, but Jack didn't even plan to have an accident, even if he was paid to."

"I think I follow what you're saying, but how could that be? There were unauthorized blasts on both levels six and seven. He was covered no matter where the tour took place."

"Tink about it. He was with the party that was trapped. He wasn't goin' to endanger himself unnecessarily. Furthermore, he thought the tour was goin' to take place on seven until only a couple of hours before the tour. He only had enough time to drill and blast that small pile of ore you saw on six. Another point, he was concerned about possible roof failure, and he was obviously concerned about taking the tour to seven after blasting a fifteen-hole pattern to expose some fresh ore. This man was not out to hurt anybody. He wasn't even out to scare anybody. Let me ask ya somethin.' What happened with that blast on seven?"

Scratching his chin, Jim answered, "Nothing."

"Exactly. If he was paid to make an accident happen, he would have had to report that absolutely nothin' happened if the tour had taken place on seven as it originally had been planned. Wanna know one more thing?"

"I know you're going to tell me."

"Arnie Tyrronen says he panicked after the cave-in. Arnie was ready to hang dis guy. Is that your observation? You were there."

"Yes, now that you mention it, I thought Arnie was going to have his hide right on the spot. Jack did little for the rescue effort. Arnie did everything."

"Dat's not like the competent chief geologist I described a few minutes ago. It's also not like a murderer. Jack was just as surprised as the rest of ya. He's innocent."

Jim shook his head to indicate disbelief, but he was convinced. Everything Gary had lain before him made sense. "But if that's the case, why has he disappeared?"

"He knows something that he doesn't want any of us to find out. I tried, but he wouldn't talk to me at all after the accident. He avoided me at all costs. When he left, all he said was, 'I hope ya don't blame me.'"

"You think someone has paid him to keep his mouth shut?"

"Yep."

"Andy MacIntyre?"

"Yep."

"Thought so."

CHAPTER 67

Jack Stallworth posed next to the prototype plug-in hybrid electric vehicle (PHEV) on the Ford Motor Company's test track just north of Ann Arbor, Michigan. It was a crisp but sunny day. For the last day of January, it was unseasonably warm. This had made for a large crowd to have gathered for the carefully orchestrated media event. Jim and Elizabeth watched Jack and Harold Peterman, chairman of Ford, preside over the occasion from their seats on the speaker's platform.

The occasion was the formal announcement by Ford that they were to begin the production of the plug-in hybrid electric car scheduled for introduction in the next model year. This was indeed a momentous occasion! Jack savored every moment. His dreams of taking a little start-up company that possessed the technology to manufacture the highly-conductive alloy necessary to make the car economical to drive over a reasonable range before recharging had formally come to fruition.

By sharing in his success and owning half of the group of companies that did everything from mine to refine this native copper resource found only in Michigan's Upper Peninsula, Jim and Elizabeth were also forced to bask in the limelight. In a matter of two weeks following the board meeting where Jack announced Ford's desire to expand orders for the high-grade stock, they had become celebrities on both a state and national level. In fact, the Alumni Association at the University of Michigan was hosting a luncheon in Jim's honor—the most famous Michigan Wolverine at the moment.

The major television networks were all present, as was *Time* magazine, who heralded the three entrepreneurs as "The Three Mining Yoopers." Since only Elizabeth had any roots in the Upper Peninsula, the other two directors of RMS had donned "Adopted Yooper" sweatshirts for their picture session for the cover of the magazine. Her natural beauty had made for great cover material. Good looking and rich; what more could you want?

Down on the track, Jack and Peterman were bidding the driver of the car good-bye in a fanfare that included a marching band. One of Ford's best engineers was to drive the car west to Los Angeles in a ride sure to draw more publicity to the car.

"Are your cheeks getting sore from smiling so much?" Elizabeth whispered in Jim's ear.

"No, those cheeks aren't sore, but the other set is from sitting around so much listening to all the BS being delivered around here," he wistfully replied.

"Hey, Dad," said a voice behind them.

Jim turned to see his son, John, jogging in their direction across the test track. "Why, John, I didn't expect to see you here." Jim hadn't seen John since he moved to Calumet over two months ago. At that time he had stopped by to let John know he was leaving. John had said little then because he was shocked. He did stay in contact by phone on occasion. Jim did send him some spending money, some of which he must have spent on Northwestern wear because that was what he was wearing in this Michigan crowd. That didn't even bother Jim. He was just glad to see his son.

"Hey, I just came to see my famous dad. You don't think I was going to miss this, did you? It's not a bad drive over here from Evanston. I left early this morning."

Elizabeth, feeling a bit left out, chimed in. "How is school going for you, John?"

He glanced her way long enough to give her an irritated look for just being there. "I'm doin' all right. Nailed a three point two last semester."

Then, not waiting for a reply, he turned to his dad. "Look, Dad, the reason I came over here is that we've got to talk—*alone*."

"Now?"

"No, of course not."

"Well, I've got an alumni luncheon, but how about I find you after that?"

"Sure."

"Where?" Jim asked.

"Don't worry, I'll find you after the luncheon outside the Union building."

"About two o'clock?"

"Okay." John shook his head in agreement. "See ya later," he said to his dad and, ignoring Elizabeth, turned and jogged back across the track.

"That was a warm reception!" Elizabeth said, hands on her hips.

"Yeah, nice surprise," Jim agreed until he looked back at her and saw how upset she was.

"You might say that!" she shot him a puzzled look.

"Oh, I didn't realize you were being sarcastic."

"He at least was polite enough to answer my question. It's obvious he wants nothing to do with me, but at least he's still talking to you. I guess I'm just the home-wrecker. Do you think your kids will ever see me as anything else?"

"Like anything else, you'll need to give it some time for them to accept what has happened," Jim replied halfheartedly. His mind was on his son, and he was trying to figure out what could be so urgent.

The luncheon had been another drawn-out affair. Jim wasn't sure if he liked or despised being honored at his alma mater. Regardless, he was getting used to the limelight. Success did feel good. His accomplishments were being recognized nationally! It was a mountaintop experience, as the Reverend Johnson would have said.

As he strolled from the Union building, he spotted John waiting for him by the steps. "Hi, John. Sorry I'm a bit late. I had some trouble getting away in there."

"That's okay. Your celebrity status is rubbing off. The backfield coach even stopped me to ask how you were doing today."

"Oh yeah? That's nice. Who is that?"

"Jerry Mueller."

"That right. Now I remember. He played tailback a couple of years before I made the team."

"Let's duck in here so we can talk."

They walked thirty yards to a little coffee shop across the street. After sitting down, John opened the conversation. "You know, I had a hard time answering Coach Mueller's inquiry about you today."

Jim was puzzled. "What do you mean?"

"Well, I really didn't know how you were. I haven't heard much from you."

Somehow, Jim knew this was coming. Storm clouds were forming over his little parade. There was a moment of silence in which Jim began to feel the pangs of guilt he had pushed to the back of his mind for so long.

"I know I've not stayed in touch the way I should. I do apologize for that. Believe it or not, it wasn't intentional."

"Yeah, I know. You're just too busy with your conglomerate these days, and when you're not working, you're shacked up with that woman who…" John was so furious he couldn't go on.

Jim didn't know whether to stand up and slap the kid for being so disrespectful or thank him for being so truthful. "Go ahead, son, let me have it both barrels. I've got no excuse for my behavior. All I can tell you is that I am ashamed at the way I've treated you and Julie, and I am sorry."

"What about Mom?"

Jim tried not to think about Anita and the pain he had caused. Their last meeting still haunted him. He never got to tell her how sorry he was or why he had to do this. "What about her?"

"You just left her high and dry."

"She got what she asked for."

"She didn't ask for a separation."

"She asked me to leave; what's the difference? It'll be better to end it. I know I hurt her. I just need out—fast."

"Why?"

"Things had changed for me. Life in Chicago was no longer the life I knew before the accident."

Jim's last comment was greeted with a look of disbelief from his son. "Don't give me that crap, Dad. It started long before the accident."

"Yes, it did. In fact, the accident forced me to try to start over again in Chicago. It didn't work. I couldn't do it. I could never be happy there again or with your mother."

"Just like that!"

"No, not just like that. I agonized over this for many months. I had to pursue this dream and bring it to a successful conclusion. I could not have been happy otherwise."

"So, Dad, are you happy now?"

For a college freshman, John was asking very probing questions. Jim was trying his best to be honest with his son, but he was unsure of the answers to such questions himself. "Yes, son, I think I am. What I mean is that in many ways, I'm very happy, but when I think of all the pain, I'm also very sad. Does that make any sense?"

"Yeah, it does. Money doesn't buy happiness, does it?"

"No, it doesn't. But I didn't do it for the money. I had a discovery to make. I had to discover myself. I had to know if I could take a little mining company and make a real difference. You saw the excitement this venture has generated. Plug-in electric cars will make a big difference in our environment for years to come."

"You're right. They will. You did make a difference. You've found fame and fortune. By God, you're on the cover of *Time* this week. But now what?"

"I've got some unfinished business to tend to."

John just sat there deep in thought. "Do you know that this whole thing has become an obsession with you?"

Jim wasn't fazed by John's line of questioning. "I wouldn't call it that. I would say it's been a passion of mine. Without this commitment, I could not have succeeded like this."

"It's more than commitment or passion. You have a single-mindedness about this venture that is consuming you. Maybe you are happy, but at what cost?"

Jim was trying to remain calm so as not to ruin the only family relationship he had left. "Are you being judgmental?"

"No, not at all. This past year I became a Christian. Meeting Melissa was the best thing that could have happened to me. She has shown me that there are more important things in life than winning. That's why I enjoy playing for a football team with a losing record. All I'm trying to tell you is that you've changed. I don't think it's for the better. Look at what you've achieved. Be happy with that. Let all the rest of it go. Leave vengeance to the LORD. What else could be unfinished? Why don't you just come home?"

Jim started to respond, but John stopped him by holding up his hand. "I have been very angry with you, but I'm here because I have learned to forgive you and I love you. You know it says in the Bible that love covers a multitude of sins."

Jim wasn't looking for a sermon, especially from his son. "So you are being judgmental. Now you're forgiving me for my sins?"

"Well… yes. I mean, no, I'm not judging you. But you have to admit you have sinned. Besides, it's not me you need to ask for forgiveness."

"I've tried to talk to your mother. She's not listening."

John stood up. "Look, Dad, I've got to go. I don't want to argue with you. Try talking to God instead. He is listening." With that, John gave his father a hug and left him standing in the coffee shop stunned.

CHAPTER 68

The first week of February was traditionally winter carnival week in Houghton. Michigan Technological University was renowned for the ice sculptures carved by student organizations. The largest sculptures often towered thirty feet or more. The carnival was the main event of the winter season. Tourists from around the Midwest converged on Houghton for the weekend to see the ice statues and take part in the many winter sports and activities that constitute a winter carnival.

One of the off-campus activities this year was a ball hosted by Elizabeth MacIntyre in the ballroom of her estate. With oak floors and a corner set up for a band, she had decorated the room to look like a winter wonderland. Dancers this evening would float around the room through snowflakes and around an ice sculpture that a local artist had made—a replica of the Wolverine Mining Company's shaft.

As guests arrived at the front door, Elizabeth greeted each one of them, asking personal questions that evoked a smile or short story of a loved one or a career. She was the perfect hostess. When one is raised as an heiress, one becomes proficient at social functions.

Jim, on the other hand, felt very awkward. He was at home in corporate offices or boardrooms, but this situation was foreign to him. It was much like the press conference and ceremonies in Ann Arbor a few days ago. He wasn't sure whether or not he liked or hated the attention.

Much of the RMS senior staff was present, as were a few select customers. Many of Elizabeth's friends had also come for the occasion, including Mary from Chicago and Tina, her childhood friend.

In fact, Jim specifically remembered Tina's entrance tonight. Usually, she was distant and cold toward him. She had rarely stuck around whenever he was present. However, tonight had been different. She entered with a much different air about her, one of confidence, not shyness, which she typically projected. Riding proudly on her husband Eric's arm, she seemed to fit right in to the aura of affluence that surrounded an event such as this. At first Jim had been pleasantly surprised. Now he began to wonder why the change in attitude.

A hard slap on his back put an abrupt end to his thought process. "How ya doin,' Jim ol' boy?" Gary bellowed. Without waiting for a reply, he added, "Ya looked great on TV the other day. Even better on the cover of *Time*. How does celebrity status suit ya?"

"Well, Gary, I don't know. It feels kind of strange."

"I thought that's what ya were strivin' for. Guess it's a bit different when ya finally catch what ya been chasin' all these years, huh?"

Not knowing where this was going, Jim muttered a bewildered reply. "Yeah, guess so." He did not want another soul-searching session at the moment.

Neither did he get one. Gary was just doing a little gentle probing as always—enough to awaken a guilty conscience. After all, isn't that what ministers are trained to do?

"Good for you," Gary replied. "Hey, I've got to go. I need to catch up with Arnie Tyrronen over there. Gotta a couple of shop questions for 'em. It's good to pick his brain once in a while. He knows what he's talking about. Ya ought to try it sometime." And again, without waiting for a reply, he bid Jim farewell.

By nine o'clock, all of the guests had arrived, and Elizabeth and Jim made their way up to the ballroom to mingle with the crowd of some sixty people. As always, Elizabeth looked like a model out of a page of a fashion magazine. Jim never did get over the thrill he felt every time he looked at her. There was not a physical flaw about her. Her complexion was peaches and cream. Her figure, hourglass. Besides that, she was intelligent and witty. What more could he ask for? He wasn't sure. Apparently, the reverend's remarks had gotten to him once again.

The band struck up a slow tune. Jim took Elizabeth's hand and led her to the center of the room without so much as saying a word. A few of the guests joined them. Pulling her close, he could smell her French perfume ever so faintly. The silkiness of her evening gown and the warmth of her body underneath were exhilarating. He found himself aroused and leaned forward to nestle his face in her hair. She responded by pulling herself a bit closer, and they drifted across the winter wonderland, oblivious to anything or anyone else in the room.

"Mmm," he murmured quite contentedly.

She raised her head to look into his eyes, as though searching for a further explanation for the moan. He recognized the look and appropriately whispered, "I love you," into her ear.

She mouthed her reply, and they both smiled.

"You sure know how to throw a party."

"You sure know how to build a successful venture."

They drifted around the room a few times, thoroughly enjoying the moment and each other. Their mood was apparent to their guests as well. Many stopped to watch and smile. The music, the ballroom, and the mood had magically transformed the midwinter ball to a thing of beauty. Those in attendance soon forgot about social appearances and began to be themselves—the key to a successful party.

Jim and Elizabeth mingled with their guests as a good host and hostess should do. Stopping at the table where Tina and Eric sat, they pulled up a couple of vacant chairs to talk.

"You're looking very good tonight." Jim smiled as he ran his eyes down Tina's fitted gown. "It looks like horseback riding agrees with you."

"Yeah, although it's kind of tough to do much riding this time of year. Must be the skiing."

"Oh, I didn't know you where a skier," Elizabeth said with a hint of surprise in her voice.

"Well, not much of one yet. Just took it up this winter. Found out it's a lot of fun."

Tina laughed. "Yeah, you rich folks have certainly know how to do that."

It was supposed to be a joke, but it didn't come off that way.

Elizabeth, a bit offended by her longtime friend's longstanding habit of shooting a few barbs her way about her family's money, couldn't help herself. "What's that, Tina? Skiing or fun?"

Realizing her social blunder, Tina simply answered, "Both."

Having won the little skirmish and quite pleased with herself for doing so, Elizabeth decided to warm up the conversation. "You know, Jim and I love to ski. Now that I know you're a skier, we'll have to hit the slopes together sometime."

"Sure," Tina and Eric both agreed, nodding their heads as confirmation, although they and their friends both knew the skiing weekend would never materialize.

With the social obligation now met, Elizabeth and Jim bid them good evening and moved on to the next table.

About 12:30 a.m., the party was starting to fizzle out. Most of the guests had left. Jim found Elizabeth at the bar getting herself a glass of champagne. He sat down on the stool next to where she was standing and motioned for her to take the vacant stool next to his.

"How are ya doing?" he asked.

"That's not a very good line for picking up a girl."

"So you're in one of those moods, huh?"

"Whatever that is, yeah, I guess I'm in one of those moods."

"Well, as long as I'm picking you up, does that mood include wild, unrestrained lovemaking?"

"A couple more glasses of this stuff and it will."

They both laughed. Jim turned toward the bartender and yelled, "Bartender, the hostess needs two more glasses of champagne."

The bartender returned a puzzled look since he had just poured her one. From behind him, a voice said, "I'll take one of them. She can't drink two at a time."

Jim turned around to find Arnie Tyrronen standing behind him. "Well, hello, Arnie. Haven't seen ya for a long time."

"That's true," Arnie said. "I thought I'd at least say hi before I took off tonight. I wanted ta see how my little girl's doin.'"

"Just fine, Arnie," Elizabeth answered.

"Ya know, girl, you'd made your granddad mighty proud with the way you've restored the mining business around here."

"Thanks, but I didn't do it myself."

"Don't sell yourself short. *You* did it. *You* financed this guy here." He gave Jim a friendly wink and then continued. "*You* didn't back away when the goin' got tough and anyone else would've sold. *You* put together partnership that got ya into Ford's pocket. All in less than a couple of years. *You* should pat yourself on the back."

Jim did it for her.

"However," Arnie hesitated with a dramatic pause, "there's one more thing that you need to do."

"What's that?" She raised her eyebrows with curiosity.

"Let me tell you a little story," he began. "A century ago, when mines like the ol' Wolverine Mine that you're now working were first developed, the Cornish miners used to bring these little Yorkshire Terriers to work with them. Do you have any idea why?"

Elizabeth and Jim both shook their heads no.

"Back then, yes, even before my time, the mines were a lot closer to the surface. Many of them had problems with rats. The Yorkies are fearless little dogs. They're also very persistent. They'd go after every last rat in the mine and chase it out. They made working conditions a lot more tolerable and safer."

"So you think I ought to get a Yorkie?" Elizabeth asked, her face showing that she obviously did not make the connection.

"Exactly. You've got yourself a couple of rats in your organization that need ir-rat-dicating." He grinned at his pun. "In this envelope is the name of a pet store owner who can supply you with a Yorkie."

He handed her a sealed envelope and bid them good night. They looked at each other, then at the envelope, then at Arnie as he left the room.

"Should I?" Elizabeth inquired, as though asking for permission to open a birthday present.

"Well, yes, you should. I can't stand it much longer."

In the envelope was an index card.

Jack Sanders
(602) 555-4378

CHAPTER 69

Globe, Arizona, was a very pleasant place to be in early February. The weather was temperate, with daytime temperatures often in the mid to high seventies. The blue skies framing the mountains, in which copper mining was prevalent, made for a perfect day to be outdoors.

Jack Sanders was taking full advantage of his semi-retirement on this particular Saturday by basking in the sunlight on his boat along with several other fellow boaters on top of the Theodore Roosevelt Lake behind the Roosevelt dam. Today, however, he was by himself, leaning back in the captain's chair of his Fountain 47-foot cigarette-type speedboat. Underneath him were two 465 hp MerCruisers that could bring the boat to a top speed of over seventy miles per hour. Normally, such a speed was fast enough to scare the girl he quite often had in the seat next to his into sitting in his lap. Not today though. The only thing in his lap was a cold Coors beer.

His tenure on the water was meant to be a time of introspective reflection. Last Sunday, he had made a decision. For the first time since moving out here from Michigan, he had decided to go to church. The closest he had come to church before that time was when he had been invited by Reverend Gary Johnson (and accepted, believe it or not) to attend the little Mohawk Methodist Church.

In six months of living in Arizona with a new house, a new four-by-four truck, a new boat, and the occasional consulting job with a couple of the copper producers in the area, he had not found a way to enjoy his new lifestyle. He had once remarked to Reverend Johnson that all he ever wanted was to get a piece of the pie so he could quit chasing around the mining fields. Now that he had acquired enough money to only work when it suited him, he was being chased. By what, he was not quite sure. Whatever it was, it was relentless.

A more spiritual person might call it conviction. A humanist might call it the pangs of a guilty conscience. Semantics did not matter. It was now a matter of getting rid of the beast that concerned Jack. So as a first effort to do just that, he had found a nearby church and had showed up on Sunday morning at the appointed time for worship as listed in the phonebook.

He could not recall what it said over the door, not that it mattered either. It was Christian something or maybe just Christian. Regardless, the pulpit-pounding preacher had spoken directly to him that morning. How? He wasn't sure. Again, what did it matter? The guy acted as though he had Jack's life history before him and then proceeded to tell him how he could go about making a few changes. Starting over—what was it he called it? A new life? No—a new creation. Yes, that was it! If any man is in Christ, he is a new creation; the old has passed away and the new has come.

Those words had rung in his ears for most of a week now. At first he didn't know how to respond. The preacher had issued an invitation to come forward during the service to accept Christ into his life. Well, Jack was to have no part of that. He had enough trouble living with himself rather than getting somebody else involved. That was it! He had practically bolted for the door as soon as the last hymn was over. Fortunately for him, he had been able to sneak past the preacher at the door when he was shaking hands with a young couple who obviously had wanted his ear for something. Jack had simply shuffled around them, catching the preacher's eye, but that was all.

Then it started. He couldn't sleep. He couldn't eat. All he could think about was the cave-in last summer. The details of what had happened raced through his mind over and over again. Twice during the past week, he had woken up in a cold sweat, reliving the horror of death. He kept seeing the governor's face as they moved the pile of dirt and rocks from on top of him. It was nearly beyond recognition. Bone and flesh had hung off of one side of his head while a myriad of color intermingled with the dirt on which he lay. Even the recollection of the scene was enough to make Jack sick.

He had been scared. Actually, scared did not adequately describe how he had felt during those three weeks after the accident. Fear had been living so deeply within him he could taste it. Those three weeks when the mine inspectors were crawling all over the mine along with every branch of law enforcement agency imaginable had been the longest three weeks of his life.

However, the investigation was over almost as quickly as it had started. At first he had been puzzled by the brevity of the whole ordeal. Nonetheless, he was relieved. He was relieved to know that nobody had made the connection between Andy MacIntyre and himself. He was relieved to know that nobody accused him of murder. He was relieved to discover that Gary Johnson had stepped forward as mine manager to take all the heat for what had transpired. He was relieved most of all when the county sheriff had told him he didn't need him any longer and that he was free to go. Nobody had to repeat those words to him. He was gone!

He knew he had left Gary holding the bag. He knew he should have been more open with Gary about the details of what had happened underground. But Gary didn't ask, and he didn't volunteer any additional information. Fortunately for him, Gary wasn't a good manager. Gary was a good miner, but in overseeing the operation, he was in over his head. Jack believed Gary knew that but was afraid to admit it, even to himself. That was Jack's one saving grace. Gary was so anxious to take the blame because he knew things were out of control that Jack was able to slip right out the back door unscathed. He hoped that by now Gary would have learned to put his foot down when pushed by the owners of the operation so that he didn't find himself in the same predicament.

The only problem was that when he tried to sneak out the door last Sunday, he didn't completely escape. Thus, the phone call to Arnie Tyrronen. It had taken him nearly a day to dial the number, and he hung up when it started ringing the first time. But finally, he'd mustered the courage to make the connection.

Why Arnie? Well, Arnie was there. Arnie was not stupid. Arnie knew those charges were there and didn't hesitate to point them out. He probably suspected that this was something more than negligence or poor management as the mine inspectors concluded, but he elected to keep his mouth shut. Why? Probably because Gary was a good friend, and he knew that the only thing that would come of pursuing the issue further would be hardship for the good Reverend Johnson.

So now it was time. Time to come forward with the truth. Time to face the consequences, whatever they may be. He wasn't sure what would happen, but it had to be better than living like this. You see, Jack did believe in ghosts. It was time to get rid of them.

With that conviction, he put his feet back on the deck of the boat and sat up. Taking stock of his beloved lake one last time, he fired up the engines and plunged the throttle on both forward. They both responded with a roar and a forward jolt that lifted the front end out of the water at a sharp angle, as though the craft was going to take off at the end of a runway. When the needles on both of his tachometers rose past 3,300 revolutions per minute, he reached for the toggles that controlled the trim tabs and dropped the bow. Within three seconds, the boat leveled out, the engines churned over four thousand revolutions per minute, and he was skimming across the water at a tremendous rate of speed.

Jack felt better. He was now ready for anything. Time would tell.

CHAPTER 70

Monday evening brought with it a horrific February snowstorm in Laurium. Mother Nature was intent on displaying her artwork on anything left outside. The north wall of the carriage house on the MacIntyre estate was white from the gale force winds pounding snow against the brick. Large wafts of snow hung from the eves and seemed ready to break loose as an avalanche any moment to some unsuspecting passerby.

Today, that passerby was Jack Sanders, still in shock from the extreme change in climate from Globe, Arizona, to Laurium, Michigan. Fortunately for him, the snow tumbled off the porch of the house after he had slammed the front door. Looking back, he decided that he must be doing the right thing because normally he'd have been underneath that pile.

"Nice weather," Jack remarked as he entered past Elizabeth. "You really didn't have to."

"This'll just make ya appreciate Arizona all that much more," said Arnie, who had also come to the front door to greet Jack.

"Maybe so, but actually, I kind of missed this place."

"Let me take your coat and let you warm up by the fireplace," suggested his hostess.

"Thanks," Jack mumbled as he looked into the front parlor to see who else was present for dinner tonight. Stepping through the door, he acknowledged with simply a nod Jim Thomas and Gary Johnson seated on the sofa in front of the fireplace.

They both stood to shake Jack's hand as he approached the roaring fire. Jim motioned Jack to a chair opposite the sofa facing the fire. After being subjected to the winter storm, the warmth of the fire was welcome.

Elizabeth rejoined the group and broke the awkward silence by asking Jack if he'd like something warm to drink. She suggested an Irish coffee or her latest concoction, a chocolate-covered cherry. Her description of the drink was so intriguing that Jack decided he'd at least have to give it a try.

Almost instantly, kitchen help appeared through the swinging door that connected the dining room to the butler's serving pantry and the kitchen. Nearly as quickly, Jack's drink was set on a table next to him. He picked up the crystal clear mug and took a sip. Elizabeth was right. This was fantastic! The sensation of chocolate with a bit of Amaretto added some kick to the drink. Setting down the drink, he waited for the show to begin.

As hostess and emcee, Elizabeth began. "Thanks for coming, Jack. I know it must be tough for you, but I can't tell you what a relief it is that you've decided to come forward with the truth."

"I don't know how relieved you'll be when ya hear it."

"It doesn't matter, Jack. We've lived for several months with this tragedy. Any light you can shed on it will be most welcome."

"I understand," Jack said, aware that the introduction had been made and now he was in the spotlight, center stage. It was time to let it all hang out. He looked at Arnie and received a reassuring nod. He still couldn't bring himself to look Gary in the eye, given that he'd left him in a bit of a lurch.

He took a breath. Wondering whatever made him do this, he spoke slowly and deliberately. "I know of no other place better to begin than at the beginning. As you may or may not know, I'm a drifter. I've worked at more mines in more countries than I care to remember. Ten years ago, I joined an up-and-coming outfit in Lakewood, Colorado, called North American Metals. A couple of months after I signed on, a young engineer with a name that sounded like it came right out of some family archives in Newport, Rhode Island, was hired: James A. MacIntyre IV."

This first revelation brought about a couple of surprised looks from his audience. Jack used the moment to pause and take a sip from his drink. "I thought to myself, *This guy isn't for real—he must be lost or running or something.* Curiosity got the best of me. I made an effort to get to know him. Well, lo and behold, he hails from this rich family from Chicago who made a fortune in the mining business and then disowned him. Talk about bitter! Wow!

"As time would have it, I came to find out how this kid was a lot like myself. Ya see, he was always trying to prove his worth. Probably more to himself than to anyone in particular. Anyway, it really struck home. I found him to be a mirror in a lot of ways. He worked night and day to become the best mine designer and economist in the gold business. Andy knew how to make a buck. Ray McKinnen recognized that early on. That's why he took him under his wing."

Noticing that he now had them a bit puzzled by relating Andy's life story to them, he brought the monologue back to himself. "I also had something to prove. I was going to be the best damn geologist in the business. Thus, I set out to learn the emerging science of geostatistics. I couldn't find any programs that would estimate grade in small blocks using sporadically-placed drill hole data, so I got myself a laptop computer, devised a way to weigh the reliability of the lab data, and spent nights writing software. A year later, it wasn't very fancy, but my little computer and program could take most core hole information you had to feed it and spit back an amazing amount of information. Accurate information."

"I'll vouch for that," Gary interrupted. "The predictions you did on six and seven have proven to be right on what we've mined so far."

Undaunted, Jack continued. "That's what I mean. I figured out how to show anyone what's in the ground in a very unpredictable ore body such as gold or native copper where the valuable mineral appears as nuggets or veins that occur sporadically across all three dimensions in the field."

At this point, Jack drank down the last of his chocolate-covered cherry and made a twisted face. "Here's the kicker. Nobody pays any attention to reserve estimates and quality predictions that show a high-grade ore, well beyond management's wildest dreams. They always factor the estimate and call it a best-case scenario; that is, everyone but Andy MacIntyre. He took the time to look into my numbers for the Eagle's Nest Mine and believed them. He then took the information, devised a mine plan to high grade the mine, and told Ray McKinnen he'd make him rich in two years. It worked; Ray made a few million dollars, Andy won himself a chunk of the company, and I wound up empty-handed."

Jack stood up and paced in front of the fireplace. "To show you what a fool I was, I went through the whole exercise again not once but twice. I came away with the requisite pats on the back and salary raises but nothing more. I also came away angry. I'd had it! I told Andy that if this was the way it was going to be, I was packing."

"When was that?" Jim asked.

"About two years ago."

"Ya mean when I hired ya?" Gary added.

"You got it!"

"So you did tell Andy you were leaving." Jim was phrasing a question as a statement.

"No."

"Wait a minute," Gary piped up. "Are ya tellin' me you were working for Andy and for me while you were at Wolverine?"

"I guess that's a correct statement."

Gary was really perplexed now. "How? Why?"

"Andy had just come back from the reading of his mother's will. He was pissed but not so much so that he didn't have a plan."

"For what?" Elizabeth inquired. She had until this point almost felt sorry for her brother's predicament.

"To take over the mining business of J. A. MacIntyre Inc."

This was really no surprise to Jim, Gary, Arnie, or to Elizabeth, for that matter.

Elizabeth thought she should clear the air. "What you're telling us, Jack, is no earth-shattering news. Andy told me that himself just after Christmas when Jim and I paid him a visit last year."

It was Jack's turn to be taken off guard. Almost inadvertently, he blurted out, "What else did he tell you?"

"Well, nothing really," Jim said. "I was hoping you were going to shed some light on that."

"There I may be able to help you, but first, I need to know what Andy said."

"Why?" Jim asked.

"It's important. He's a born liar. I want to know if he implicated me."

"And if he did?"

"Then I'm not so sure I should be sitting here without an attorney present. In fact, I'm not even sure why I'm sitting here confessing to you folks right now. I might have to be saying the same things from the witness chair destroying my own defense one of these days."

At first it looked like they had come to a roadblock. Things were not about to move any further until Gary piped up. "Then, Jack, why did ya come here? Was the voice inside your head gettin' too loud for you?"

"Yes, Reverend, it was."

Gary couldn't remember the last time Jack had addressed him that way.

"You see, this was all triggered by a sermon I heard the Sunday before last. It was as though the minister was speaking directly to me—as though nobody else was sitting in the pews. He asked me if I had a burden that was getting too great. He told me I could relieve that load by coming forward to the altar. I didn't want to do that. I mean, I did want to leave this load there, but I didn't feel comfortable doing it."

Moving forward on his chair, Gary looked Jack right in the eyes. "So tell me, are you comfortable now?"

"Absolutely not!"

"Then do somethin' about it."

"What, convict myself?"

"No," Gary assured him. "Ya don't have to do that. You've already been convicted by the Holy Spirit. No court of law would be that relentless. What you're feelin' is the hand of God upon your conscience."

"Well, I don't like it."

"Of course not, but you're only one step away from entering God's kingdom and finding peace with yourself."

"What do I have to do?"

"You've already told us."

"I don't follow," Jack said.

"*Confess*—not to us or to a civil court but to God. Tell 'em what's on your mind and ask forgiveness. Ask him to replace the burden on your heart with the Spirit of Jesus Christ."

"Will you help me, Reverend?"

Gary began by praying for Jack. Everyone bowed their heads and listened intently to what was going on. When Gary got around to praying with Jack, Jack began to fill in some of the blanks. There were tears flowing from Jack's eyes. His voice quaked. But finally—finally—Jack Sanders had done something in his life he could be proud of and live with. In fact, he would live forever because of what he had done in MacIntyres' parlor.

What a moment. The rest of them present couldn't help but feel the power of God, his Spirit as it moved in Jack that evening. The emotion was overpowering, and to witness the hand of God was more moving than the confession itself.

CHAPTER 71

Much to everyone's delight, spring had come early to the Copper Country. The past eleven weeks had proven to be very hectic, and Jim was looking forward to a tradition he'd just discovered: opening day of trout season.

The last Saturday in April was the first day of the brook trout fishing season in Michigan. It was a well-kept secret that the brookie fishing in the Keweenaw Peninsula was the best this side of the Rockies. Many an angler would arise at sun-up this day to pursue the elusive little but tasty fish native to many of the streams that emptied into Lake Superior.

As he rose from the bed in the master suite of the MacIntyre house, he firmly planted his feet on the floor and sat on the edge of the waterbed, watching the first rays of sunlight illuminate the sky. The large maple trees outside the window took on a reddish hue from the long rays of sunlight, which made the newly-budding leaves look orange.

Looking at the clock to see what time it was, Jim saw the first quarter report lying on the nightstand. He had fallen asleep last night studying the balance sheet of RMS. It was their first full quarter of consolidated operations.

Picking up the report, he remembered the stormy board meeting that was held in Jack Stallworth's office in late January. Turning to the profit and loss statement, he found that once again Gary Johnson had been right on with his production figures and shipping schedules.

Jim looked over the production figures. Shipments from Wolverine totaled thirty million pounds; those from Kearsarge also totaled thirty million, including ten million required to fill orders that he had brought in for Wolverine. He was amazed! Wolverine was only at 60 percent of design capacity, and it was producing as much copper as Kearsarge, which was double the capacity in terms of raw ore-handling capabilities. The beauty of such a rich ore deposit.

Of course, this wasn't the only advantage gained. Sales of copper alone had brought in revenues of some $102 million. Even with added sections in the mine, operating costs for Wolverine were only $24 million, as opposed to $42 million for Kearsarge. Nonetheless, the $36 million in gross margin and $22 million in net before taxes was something Jim would be happy to live with. This didn't include the additional $5 million in net profit that Northern Michigan Refining had added to the total by sales of four million pounds of high-grade alloy to Ford Motor. His share of first-quarter earnings was 10 percent of $27 million, a cool 2.7 million dollars. He'd never made that kind of money or even dreamed of it before.

He must have been mumbling to himself because Elizabeth stirred and rolled over to the spot he had vacated. Realizing he wasn't there, she opened her eyes to find him sitting on the edge of the bed drooling over the financials.

"Wha—what are you doing?"

"I was admiring our earnings one more time," he sheepishly admitted. "The results are incredible."

"Yeah, I know. I thought you were going fishing."

Jim glanced at the clock. He had been sitting there for more than a half an hour. It was already after seven. He was late again, and Gary was going to be pissed. "Oh s—-! I lost track of time. I was supposed to meet Gary ten minutes ago." He reached for the phone to call.

"Men," Elizabeth muttered and rolled back over to escape the sunlight so she could go back to sleep.

Forty-five minutes later, Jim and Gary had reached Gary's favorite hole on the Traprock River. As usual this time of year, the water level was high and the current brisk. So was the conversation.

"Did ya get your report from that private eye ya hired?" Gary asked.

"Sure did," Jim answered. After unsatisfying answers, or rather lack of them from Andy and Jack Sanders, he decided it was time to enlist some help. "He was very prompt in delivering it to me last Tuesday."

"I suppose you've got every detail memorized by now."

"Well, not quite, but it did make for interesting reading."

"How so?"

"It's tough to know where to start."

Laughing, Gary replied, "I've got all morning, and so do you. Now let's hear it."

Knowing that Gary was aware of the investigation and the basis for it, Jim narrowed the discussion to only include the sordid details of Jack Stallworth's rise to fame.

"A graduate of Harvard's business school, Jack was born and raised in Massachusetts. He had found his way into investment banking right out of college by becoming a strategic planner for the Bank of Boston. He later helped them set up a venture capital subsidiary, the Boston Capital Corporation, before being lured away four years ago as a managing partner in RE Associates. He was very successful in specializing in mining and precious metals operations. His buyout of Northern Michigan Refining was a bit peculiar since he had not invested in a start-up operation before. Even more unusual was his leaving Boston to accept a line management role when they acquired Kearsarge Mining. There ended up being a twenty-eighty split between Jack and RE Associates. This we were aware of. In other words, he ended up owning 10 percent of RMS at the time we did the deal for the fifty-fifty partnership.

"Shortly after our board meeting in January, Jack exercised his stock options with RE. With an inside stock swap that was permissible under a loophole in the security holder's management agreement, Jack was able to buy out RE's 40 percent of RMS. Now he is the single largest shareholder of RMS Enterprises, holding a full 50 percent of the company personally. With our first-quarter earnings and increasing net worth, that makes him a very wealthy man."

Gary didn't say anything at first. He just watched his fishing line cut the surface of the stream as the water flowed by, creating a wake that was ever so small. "So Jack has finagled 50 percent of RMS right out from under your nose."

"That's one way of putting it," Jim answered. "In some ways, it doesn't affect us at all, but one very large question remains."

"I believe even a backwoodsman like myself knows that." Gary laughed. "How did he get RE to relinquish their share of a profitable company like RMS?"

The mystery had become so intriguing that Gary almost missed the tug on the end of his ultra-light pole. A bit startled, the expert fisherman set the hook and then proceeded to try to bring a twelve-inch brook trout upstream to his net. This was not an easy task with submerged logs, overhanging tree branches, and only four-pound test fishing line. Nonetheless, he succeeded after five minutes of bringing the fish back and forth across the stream.

After extracting the trout from his net and removing the hook, he carefully placed it into the pouch he had slung over his shoulder. With the distraction out of the way, he returned to the question at hand. "Well? Do ya know the answer?"

"Not exactly," Jim said as he scratched his chin. "Here's where it becomes more difficult to find out what went on. The information including detailed financial statements obtained from an RE staffer didn't reveal how the shares were valued or how they were originally paid for. I think Stallworth, being the smart cookie that he is, managed to use RE's money to get himself into this deal. It was undoubtedly well planned since he had negotiated a buyout position before the deal was finalized. I would guess that the money to RE probably hasn't even been paid. You realize we have another quarterly board meeting coming up Monday, and I would wager that Mr. Stallworth is going to ask that RMS make its first dividend payment to shareholders of record post January thirty-first, which is when he transferred the shares. That is how he'll pay off RE Associates."

"All that's fine and dandy, but what has it got to do with what Jack Sanders told us back in February?"

"Absolutely nothing! Don't you see? Stallworth is better than we've ever given him credit for. Once we found out about Andy's and Jack Sanders's botched attempt to cause the cave-in on six when the governor was there, we finally decided to look elsewhere."

Jim could see the bulb in the back of Gary's head light up. "That would put ya on seven where a blast could cause roof failure an' set off the loaded charges on six."

Jim smiled. "Keep talking, my friend."

"The only person who would have known about the possibility of roof failure would have been the foreman on seven who was told to hold off until additional roof boltin' had been completed."

"That's right. But he didn't. Hold off, that is. Instead, he went ahead and set off a mighty big round on seven, the repercussions of which would definitely be felt on six."

Gary was in such deep thought that he didn't even notice that his rod tip was bouncing crazily with another fish on the other end. Jim did notice and waded over to the point in the traprock where Gary was standing. Taking the pole from his hand, Jim proceeded to reel in another nice trout. All the while, Gary just stood there, staring into space with a blank look on his face.

Watching Jim open up his pouch and drop the second fish in, Gary finally responded. "All this while I blamed myself for the lack of communication. It wasn't that at all! It was premeditated murder! I didn't order that blast. Jack didn't order that blast. The mine inspectors wrote it off as a stupid mistake because nottin' was ever written down in da operatin' log. There never was any time. Things needed to happen fast if the tour was to stay on schedule. The foreman on seven set off the blast. He claimed Sanders had never told 'em not to."

"Do you remember who that was?"

"Sure do! I've gone over this thing day after day. I can visualize all the details."

"Who was the foreman?"

Without hesitation, Gary answered, "Eric Kramer."

"You're right."

"What's this got to do with Stallworth?"

"The private investigator I hired said he was successful because he had only one rule, which he always followed: no exceptions."

"What's that?"

"Follow the money."

Again, Gary's brow lowered in deep thought. "Now dat I think about it, Eric and Tina were floatin' around dat little party of yours like they had done it all their life. She was wearing a dress that probably cost as much as one of her horses."

"Right again."

"Are you tellin' me Stallworth paid Kramer to…" He didn't finish the sentence. It was too painful.

Jim nodded his head up and down vigorously. "We're going to find that out by Monday when we have the next board of directors meeting."

"You're going to confront Stallworth with what exactly?"

"With the investigator's report."

"An' you'll think he'll just 'fess up once he reads it?"

"There's some pretty damning evidence."

"Speaking of damnation," Gary said.

Oh no, here comes the sermon, Jim thought.

"How about you leave that to a higher power."

"You mean bypass the local yokels, like Joe Maki, and go straight to the state attorney general's office." Jim smirked.

"Damn it! Ya know what I mean." Gary shot him a scowl. "You're enough ta make a preacher curse."

"I am particularly proud of that."

"You're also incorrigible."

"Please. Enough with the compliments. You're going to give me a fat head."

Another trout on Gary's line ended the conversation. *Hmm,* Jim thought, *three on his line to none on mine. I must be doing something wrong.*

CHAPTER 72

Nearly three months had transpired since Elizabeth had been handed an envelope by Arnie that had begun an extensive investigation. Jim had asked Elizabeth if he could handle the fact-finding effort with the proviso that she be kept informed of major developments. This was done with the intent of keeping her at arm's length from anything that involved her brother. Over the past year, she had been subjected to an emotional roller coaster that was beginning to take its toll.

Now, Jim had no choice but to drop her down one more gut-wrenching hill. This one led straight down from Laurium and into the Traprock Valley via Bootjack Road right to Tina Kramer's front door.

So it was on Sunday morning that Elizabeth backed her mother's Mercedes out of the drive and drove the six miles from the MacIntyre estate to the Sutter (Tina's maiden name) farm.

As she drove past the budding trees and came to the crest of the steepest part of the hill that brought the road into the village of Lake Linden on the shores of Torch Lake, she was reminded of the many times she had ridden her bike down this very same road almost twenty years prior to go horseback riding with Tina. The differences in social standing meant nothing to the girls, whose only real concerns were a horse that might have been favoring one leg or a boy in school who might have been favoring one of them.

Elizabeth pulled into the driveway and wondered if this really was a good idea, just dropping in without notice. Opening the door, Tina acted rather surprised. "Why, Elizabeth, what brings you down here today?"

"I came down because I needed to talk to you," she replied, getting right to the point.

"Well, come on in. I've always got time to talk with an old friend."

Tina had a pot of coffee still warm on the kitchen counter. Pouring a cup for each of them, she initiated the conversation. "What's wrong? Trouble in paradise? Is Mr. Right turning out to be Mr. Wrong once he's had a taste of success and MacIntyre money?"

Elizabeth couldn't believe her ears. She thought back to the last time they had spent some time together alone outside of the Snow Ball. It was last year. Wow! Maybe that explained this treatment. It was anger for being ignored—no, couldn't be. Whenever she'd been too wrapped up to look up Tina in the past, Tina had always sought her out. It definitely was something else.

"Whoa, Tina. When did you get a bug up your a—?"

"I beg your pardon?"

"I didn't come here to seek counseling on my relationships. I came here to talk to you. It's been too long. Is that why you're upset?"

Realizing that she had gone too far, Tina backed off. "Yeah, I guess it is. We lost touch for a long time, and I didn't want to see it happening again."

"No, let's not," Elizabeth said, smiling as though proclaiming a truce. "We've been friends for so long. I came down here to talk about something that's come up."

"I take it it's not Jim."

"That's right."

"Then what is it that prompted you to hop in your car and drive down to see me after such a long time?"

Setting down her cup of coffee, Elizabeth looked her friend straight in the eye. "I'm afraid Jim has discovered Eric's involvement in the Wolverine Mine cave-in."

Despite Tina's attempt to remain composed, Elizabeth knew her friend well enough to see that she was flustered. Tina did not turn white or anything that drastic; just a little color on her cheeks gave away her nervousness.

Elizabeth continued, "He knows Eric set off the blast that caused the cave-in last year."

Quick to defend her husband, Tina added, "Because he was never told not to. The tour was taking place on seven."

"Although that may be true, he also loaded the holes in crosscut number three on six. He was, after all, the foreman in charge of blasting that day."

"Elizabeth, it was an accident! He couldn't be or wasn't held responsible for last-minute changes in the plan for the tour."

"There's a major flaw in that argument. The tour plans were never changed. Jack Sanders just simply forgot. Eric didn't know that. Jack had always planned to have the blast go off on seven to create a little panic, maybe a cave-in, but not murder. He's confessed, Tina; I suggest Eric do the same."

Tina's chair fell over backward as she shoved it out to stand up. She was yelling now. "How dare you come down here to accuse my husband of murder! He was a pawn in the whole scheme."

Rising to leave, Elizabeth got in the last word. "It was no accident that Eric got hired on. I saw to that when you planted the idea in my head. It was no accident that Eric was working that day. I made sure the tour date fit his work schedule. And finally, it was no accident that you've been flaunting money you never had before. Jack Stallworth made the deposit. Be careful, Tina. Jim is on to you and Eric. He will bring on some heat. I saw him shoot my brother in the arm when he couldn't get the answers he wanted when he had a gun pointed at his head. He's gone a little crazy with his own investigation and become a vigilante. There's no telling what he would do next. I just came to warn you."

CHAPTER 73

Sunday evening brought with it a sense of purposefulness that Jim had not known before. It had been exactly ten months and twenty-four days since the tragedy at the Wolverine Mine. Finally he had pieced together the events of that fateful day and the affairs that preceded it.

Now they were in a position to act. The quarterly board meeting was to be held in fifteen hours. They were poised for the confrontation.

Rather than go out for dinner as Jim had suggested, Elizabeth offered to cook them something at home. Every now and then she liked to surprise Jim with her culinary skills. Tonight, it was brook trout *meunière* garnished with parsley and lemon wedges. Served with asparagus and red potatoes, the meal was as good as anything one could find in a restaurant.

Jim had just returned from the wine cellar with a bottle of chardonnay that would complement his fresh catch of yesterday perfectly. After removing the cork, he placed the bottle in a crystal ice bucket that Elizabeth had filled with ice water and proceeded to cool off the wine by rotating the bottle back and forth in the frigid water. *Almost as cold as the stream I was standing in yesterday,* he thought.

In a few minutes, they sat down on the end of the long dining room table in the MacIntyre dining room to enjoy the collation they had carefully prepared for themselves. They had transformed the necessity of eating into a regal occasion. Both seemed to thoroughly savor the ambiance.

"A little dinner music—that's what we're missing," Jim said as he headed through the pocket doors into the adjacent parlor to turn on the home theater system they had recently installed. Frank Sinatra's "I Only Have Eyes for You" came over the speakers.

"That's nice," Elizabeth said. "Is it true?"

"Absolutely. I would hope you'd know that by now."

"Yes, but a girl can never hear that enough."

"How long has it been since we've taken the time to enjoy a moment like this?" Jim asked.

"I'm not sure, but I know it hasn't been since the visit Jack Sanders made."

"Yeah, you're right. Seems I've become so caught up in playing detective that I've forgotten to take the time to smell the roses."

Taking a sip of her wine, Elizabeth nodded in agreement. "Coming back from Tina's house this afternoon, I thought of the same thing. You've been so obsessed with getting to the bottom of this thing that you've ignored just about everything and everybody."

"Unfortunately, that's true. But now I'm at the end of the road."

"Are we really?" He returned a puzzled look. "What I mean is, are we really at the end of this horrible thing? So we finger Stallworth. Then what?"

"Then we get rid of that sneaking, conniving son of a b——."

Elizabeth laughed. Her reaction visibly annoyed Jim. "Are you going to shoot him too, like you did with my brother?"

"Can I? I've been practicing."

"No, you can't! Since when did you become a vigilante?"

"Since the local prosecutor, Joe Maki, told me I had nothing to pursue regarding a murder conviction."

"But now we have evidence and even confessions from all parties involved."

"With the exception of Stallworth."

"Do you really think you can go in there like on television, confront him with undeniable evidence, and get a confession or explanation? You've been watching too many episodes of *Monk* or *Castle* or something."

Jim was now beyond annoyed. He was getting angry. "Are you mocking me?"

"Well, maybe having a little fun at your expense. I'm sorry. I know how hard this is for you." She puckered her lips and blew him a little kiss, which brought a smile. By now, she was learning how to pierce all of his defenses.

Pushing back her chair, she got up, moved around the end of the table, and sat on his lap. Putting her arms around his neck, she reiterated her question as a statement. "Okay. Let's say you pull this off. You never told me what happens after we get rid of Stallworth."

Once again, Jim was in a quandary. He hadn't really thought that far ahead. Trying to do so now was becoming difficult. Sitting on his lap was a thirty-two-year-old beauty. Her aura surrounded him completely. Before dinner, she had changed her clothes. Her soft angora sweater and the perfume she had splashed on before sitting down to eat overwhelmed his senses. What was a man to do? At forty-three, he had everything he had ever dreamed of. Why argue with the one who had made it possible? *Just give up, Jim,* he told himself.

"I don't know. Let's hear your idea."

"Nothing, because we won't get rid of him."

Although he suspected she had something like this up her sleeve, hearing the words still astonished him. "What?"

She had positioned herself so she was nose-to-nose to him now. "You heard me. I think we should do absolutely nothing."

"But why?"

"What good would it do to push Jack out? He's the best promoter we've got. This deal with Ford is the best thing that ever happened to us. He and Harold Peterman have established a rapport. Who else could we ever get that would have a direct line to the chairman of the Ford Motor Company?"

"Yeah, you've got a point there. But you're forgetting Mr. Stallworth's reprehensible behavior."

"And you're forgetting that he managed to make us thirteen point five million last quarter, and we're just getting started. You and I will probably make sixty million dollars this year. I'll be smiling all the way to the bank." She paused and shook her head. "No, Jim, I'll never forget, especially now that I've learned the truth. I'm satisfied to let it go at that. You need to do the same. Let Alan's death go. Nothing you do will change that or even make you feel better. Putting Stallworth in a federal penitentiary won't help. Let it go. You just need to decide to look ahead, not behind you."

He pulled her close. "You're mostly right; however, just for the record, shooting your brother did make me feel a lot better." She smiled and then nestled her head next to him as they embraced. Yes, he was a romantic. Yes, she had him spellbound. And yes, she was right! He had always considered fate to be a factor in his life because he never really planned things out well enough. He was a dreamer, not a planner. Thus, he had always accepted the unexpected as fate.

"If that's what you want, then that's what I'll do," he said. "I'm glad we didn't sell out. I can live with a criminal for a partner if Wolverine Ventures is getting a 20 percent share of a sixty million profit this year."

"Great. How about I warm up the hot tub in the master sitting room and we'll have dessert up there?"

"Mmm. What are we having?"

"You'll find out soon enough."

"I can hardly wait."

"You'll need to wait a few minutes. Why don't you put the dishes in the dishwasher? It'll pass the time for you."

Elizabeth kissed him and then headed upstairs. Jim got up and began to clear the table. The phone rang while he was loading the dishwasher, but Elizabeth didn't pick it up. *She must be busy with preparing dessert,* Jim thought. It went to voice mail. The base unit was in the kitchen, so Jim could hear the message.

"Hey, Liz, it's Mary. Got your call, but I've been gone all weekend. Sounds like the Wolverine Mine is doing well. Wish you'd let me have a piece of the action when Jim first came to Continental. What are you and Jack going to do with all the money? I know. Buy your best friend a condo in Grand Cayman. Call me. I've got one picked out."

Minong Mine – Isle Royale

Photo Credit: Nina Asunto

PART IV

A NEW DAY

CHAPTER 74

It was a sunny, warm day in early July, just over one year since the cave-in at the Wolverine Mine. Jim rose early to prepare breakfast for Gary on his new Rampage forty-five-foot convertible yacht. Suspended in a slip at the Ripley Marina, the yacht had become Jim's home in the Copper Country. Since taking delivery of it a couple months ago, he was enjoying his summer place on the lake. He had grown tired of the Michigan House and wanted a place of his own. This was perfect. He could even move it to Chicago if he wanted to.

Right now, Jim just wanted to bring some closure to this year-long nightmare that had consumed most of his waking moments and much of his sleep. So it was with the PI's final report in hand that he would seek Gary's counsel as to what to do with the information he now possessed. As he watched the sun come up over the Portage Canal, its rays sparkling off the small ripples as the wind picked up, Jim knew this was a new day that would change his life forever.

Gary arrived just as Jim was cracking eggs into the frying pan. "Mornin,' Gary. Welcome to the *Wolverine*. You like your eggs over easy, right?"

"Yep."

As they ate, Jim relayed the contents of the report to Gary. "What do you think?"

"Nothin' surprises me anymore. Da real question is, what are ya goin' to do about this?"

"That's why you're here. What do you think I should do?"

Gary set his napkin down and took a long drink of coffee. "Nothin.'"

Jim slammed his fist on the table. "Are you serious?"

"Yep."

"They can't get away with this."

"Dey already have. Nothin' ya do will bring back Alan." Gary pointed at Jim. "You cannot avenge his death. Only God can do that. You cannot administer justice; only the Almighty can do that. Are ya planning on playing God?"

Jim stared at him in anger and said nothing.

"If ya feel ya have to do something, then turn it over to Joe Maki. Murder will be hard to prove. Dat was never the plan. No matter how ya look at it, it was still an accident, even if it was part of a malicious plan to take over da mine. I understand yer anger. Don't let it cloud yer judgment. Take my advice. Put this behind ya. It's been a year."

Not wanting to hear any more advice, Jim changed the subject. "Did you do what I asked for the tour tomorrow?"

"Yep. But I don't like it."

"I didn't ask if you did or not."

Gary wanted to say something more but thought better of it. "Look, Jim, we better get ready to shove off. Elizabeth and Jack will be here anytime."

CHAPTER 75

This was the second time Jim had taken the yacht all the way across Lake Superior to Isle Royale. With the name *Wolverine* emblazoned across the back of the cockpit, everyone who passed the boat as it exited the upper entry of the Portage Canal en route to Isle Royale knew who was onboard. News of the wildly successful mining and refining operation had spread quickly, and Jim and Elizabeth were celebrities across the Keweenaw Peninsula.

Piloting the yacht from the fly bridge, Jim used his trim tabs to bring the yacht on plane and then cut the twin engines boasting over one thousand horsepower back to a comfortable cruising speed of just over twenty knots, making it a three-hour trip to Rock Harbor. There, they would rendezvous with Jack and Gary, who had headed out in Stallworth's forty-four-foot Hatteras in keeping with company policy of not having all of the key personnel traveling together in case of an accident.

"I haven't been to Isle Royale since I was in fifth grade," Elizabeth remarked. "Back then, we took the ol' *Isle Royale Queen* out of Copper Harbor because it was a shorter run and my dad knew the owner, who let me steer the boat."

Jim got up from the captain's chair and walked around the counsel to the lounge where Elizabeth sat. "I'll let you steer."

Seeing no one manning the helm, Elizabeth sprang up in a panic. Jim caught her and pulled her down on his lap. "But first, it's going to cost you something."

"We don't have time for that now." Elizabeth looked ahead to see if the boat had begun to turn off course, and looking back, she saw the steering wheel move by itself. She gave Jim a puzzled look.

"Autopilot. We have three hours."

After a quick flick of her wrist, Elizabeth's bikini top dropped on the teak deck. "Time's a wastin.' Nice day to get some sun up here."

"Yes, the view from the bridge is rather remarkable."

With the spray from the occasional four-foot wave in the open water cooling them from the July sun on a cloudless day, the ride to the national park for their off-site managerial conclave was as good as it gets. Jim didn't even care what the passengers in the National Park Seaplane may have witnessed.

CHAPTER 76

Sitting on the pier, the shareholders of Red Metal Enterprises were regaling one another with stories after enjoying an incredible fish boil put together by Jim and Gary. The sun had already set behind them, and they watched the rising moon over Raspberry Island light the ripples in the expanse of water across the harbor. They all felt quite content after the final course of chocolate cake and brandy made by the Franciscan monks north of Eagle River.

Gary was relaying an incident he had reported to him about a couple of Finnish miners who had shown unusual dedication during a recent power outage. "Dese guys were blasting a stope on level seven and were in da process of hoisting lagging or da timber used ta line the drift walls between sets of steel. Since da stope is about eighty feet off da track level, one miner operates a pneumatic tugger, or basically a compressed air-powered winch, while da other ties up a bundle of lagging to be hoisted vertically up the raise to the drift they are developing. Since there is a lot of background noise in da mine such as ventilation fans, we use light signals to indicate up, down, and stop. When da power goes out, Toivo, the miner up top, finds he still has a tank of compressed air and can keep working. So he yells down to his partner Eino, 'Blink, blink,' meaning he's taking up the load. A few seconds later, ya hear Eino screaming, 'Blink!' meaning stop as the supply car starts to lift off the track 'cause the line became tangled around a post in the dark. Fortunately, Toivo ran out of air pressure moments later anyway."

Not sure whether this was true or one of Gary's jokes, they all had a good laugh. Jack Stallworth spoke up. "It's been great working with you the last eight months."

"You going somewhere?" Jim asked.

"No, not on your life. I'm here to stay. I wasn't sure how this management gig would pan out, but so far, it's worked well. The first quarter of the year was good, but last quarter was even better. Production was up nearly twenty percent to over seventy million pounds, but profit was up thirty-three percent thanks to getting the Wolverine Mine up to capacity. Folks, we netted thirty-six million dollars last quarter. That's about twelve million dollars per month, which is where sales should settle in now that we are at full production and copper prices are holding steady. Ford Motor is taking everything we can give them for their electric motor division."

Gary was working out his share and figured it was about a quarter million dollars a quarter or a million dollars a year. That was a hundred thousand a year to the Mohawk Methodist Church, which was more than their annual budget. *Never heard of a preacher donating enough to more than double the church budget. Imagine what they could do with that,* he thought.

Since the sun didn't set until nearly ten o'clock and the moon had been up for some time, Jim was surprised when he looked at his watch and saw that it was eleven thirty already. "Hey, guys, it's pushing the bewitching hour, so I'm turning in. It's been a good day but also a long one."

"What time tomorrow, and what's on the docket?" Jack asked.

"We're working on a business plan for the remainder of this year and next. Then I thought we'd take a tour to the old Minong Mine. We'll take my boat and leave about eight o'clock. It's possible to get up close to the mine by water using McCargoe Cove," Jim said.

"Why your boat?" Jack asked.

"'Cause it's newer, faster, and a foot longer than yours, and I wanna drive."

"Boys and their toys," Elizabeth muttered.

CHAPTER 77

At seven thirty the next morning, Ray Edwards accepted Jim's invitation to come along for a boat ride. He made himself comfortable in the master stateroom while Elizabeth set out a continental breakfast for her other guests in the main salon.

Ray was the R.E. in R.E. Associates. He was Jack Stallworth's boss up until the beginning of the year when Jack exercised his stock options to buy out R.E. Associates' share of RMS after the disastrous year the enterprise and its predecessors had last year. He spent the time reviewing the PI's final report and RMS's latest financials that Jim had sent to him.

At eight, Gary took the last line off the dock cleat, and they were underway, heading past Scoville Point and then around Blake Point at the northeast tip of the island. It was a perfect day for boating, with waves calm to two feet and partly cloudy skies. Jim was monitoring their progress along a preprogrammed course at the lower helm. The electronics on the new boats did everything for you, including making your coffee in the morning.

Once everyone had settled into the salon with more baked goods from the monks, this time giant muffins with wild berries, Jim began. "Last night, we briefly went over the mid-year results, and we have exceeded our expectations by having Wolverine up and running at planned capacity and having a net profit margin of some sixty million dollars between both mines, producing over one hundred thirty million pounds of copper and almost half containing enough silver to produce the copper windings on the new high efficiency hybrid electric motors. All this in just over a year since the cave-in. My, how things have changed. Since Alan's not here to ask, then Gary, how much more high-grade ore reserves do we have?"

"I'd say we'll exhaust our reserves on level six in 'bout two more years, and we've got 'bout two years of the high-grade seam no one knew about on level seven. As I told ya yesterday, I've got Toivo and Eino working on punchin' in some drifts down there already."

"Based on the numbers we've generated so far, payback on the money MacIntyre invested in Wolverine will be in about two more years or when the reserves on six are gone. That means that whatever we find on level seven or lower is pure profit," Elizabeth said.

"I'd say you're right about a two-and-a-half-year return on investment," Jim confirmed. "Any venture capitalist would be happy with that. So, Jack, what about Kearsarge and Northern Michigan Refining?"

"Until this quarter, Kearsarge made up the shortfall from Wolverine's production. Now it too is running at capacity with Chicago Wire, adding to their contract this year and two new accounts I've brought in. Northern Michigan Refining has all it can do to keep up with producing the copper and silver alloy from Wolverine's production."

"So at this point you'd say we're maxed out?"

"Yes."

"Then good. Oh, and one last thing—you're fired."

"What?" Jack was astonished. "You can't do that. I own fifty percent of the joint venture."

"You're right. At the moment I can't, and the shareholders can't, but that's going to change right now."

Elizabeth opened the door to the master stateroom, and Ray Edwards appeared. "Hello, Jack. It's been a while. What, about six months since you finagled the buyout of our shares of stock in RME?"

"Yes, since I exercised my stock options."

"By submitting year-end financials showing Wolverine Mine as a questionable investment, not meeting its targets. The trigger for those options was a direct result of the cave-in and a prolonged recovery, which sped up exponentially after the stock was transferred."

"I cannot be held responsible for a mining accident."

"Oh yes you can," Ray said, tossing the report Jim had given him at Jack. "There's some interesting reading by a private investigator who links you to Jack Sanders and Eric Kramer, complete with confessions. Plus, the money trail leads right to you."

Without picking up the report, Jack asked, "What do you plan to do?"

"That's up to you. If you want us to mail a copy to Joe Maki, we can. You might be up on murder charges. Or maybe just manslaughter. Or you can sign these documents that revert your 50 percent ownership back to R.E. Associates. I'll even let you keep the profits you earned the last six months that you showed us would never materialize." Another packet of papers flew Jack's way.

Jack read through the first couple of pages on the packet and asked, "Does anyone have a pen?"

Ray handed him a pen and then signed the documents as a witness. Jim had slowed down the yacht and was approaching the old dock at the end of McCargoe Cove. Gary and Ray headed out on deck to tie up the yacht.

"Come with me, Jack. There's one other thing I want to show you," Jim said.

"I don't think so," Jack replied defiantly. "I've already done what you wanted."

Jim opened the drawer below the counsel, pulling out a 40-caliber semiautomatic pistol. "Mr. Smith and Mr. Wesson insist. Don't make me get blood all over my custom birch cabinetry."

Jack still didn't move.

"Talk to Andy MacIntyre lately? I'm really a pretty good shot, and I do love to shoot."

"Go ahead."

The retort was deafening in the confines of the salon. Their ears were ringing. Jack grabbed his left ear and, feeling something warm, pulled his hand back to see the blood.

"Superficial," Jim said. "The ones on your head bleed a lot. Now get moving before you make a mess. I'm not going to kill you, but if you piss me off anymore, you might be crippled."

Jack made his way off the boat with Jim and Elizabeth behind him.

"Follow Gary; he knows where he's going."

As they hiked up the trail, Gary gave them some background. "The Minong Mining Company organized in 1874 and worked two underground entries in this ridge. There are some really nice specimens of native copper and pumpellyite in here, but collecting dem is strictly prohibited by da National Park Service, and we don't want ta break any rules."

They picked their way carefully down the narrow trail to one of the mine entries.

"Well, Jack, since you missed the last mine tour, I'll let you be the first on this one," Jim said, waving his M&P 40-caliber in the direction of the opening. "Elizabeth, you may want to join your lover since you two were headed to the Cayman Islands to rendezvous with Mary D'Andres, your longtime friend and president of the Continental Bank, who turned down our original finance proposal. Something about buying a couple condos down there with all the money you and Jack were making."

Elizabeth tried to feign innocence, but she was too surprised with what Jim knew to pull it off. "What are you talking about?"

Jim turned and held her chin in his hand so he could look straight into those incredible blue eyes one more time. "It's time to quit playing the game. You have had an elaborate plan to take over the entire operation from the beginning. I wish I could say it's been fun, but up to now it's been more of living a nightmare than a dream."

"I still own 40 percent."

"It doesn't matter. Ray and I own 60 percent. Count on a change in your class of stock. If you have any sense at all, you won't push it."

Jim shoved her into Jack. "Get going. Both of you." They started down the incline where the remnants of the old rail haulage system were. After they walked thirty paces, Jim raised his gun and yelled, "By the way, you're fired." He took aim and pulled the trigger. The explosion brought down the roof at the entry, the old timbers easily giving way.

The three of them watched the dust settle. Jim asked Gary, "Do you think they'll make it out?"

"As long as der's no wolves in der, dey probably will. However, it'll be quite a challenge. Dis entryway goes in quite a ways, and der's seven years of old workings in der, but it does connect to the other entry."

Ray put his hand on Jim's shoulder. "Good shot there, partner."

"Thanks, partner." Jim smiled. "That detonator's only a couple inches in diameter. I joined the Keweenaw Sportsman Club this spring and have been shooting competitively."

Gary just shook his head in disgust as they headed back down the trail to the boat. "I didn't think you'd do it."

"That's the problem," Jim said. "Everyone underestimates my resolve until I prove them wrong. Come on. I'll give you guys a ride back to Ripley on my way."

"On your way where?" Ray asked.

"Home. I've got one more resolution to make happen."

ABOUT THE AUTHOR

Having started and run three companies, including one that made *Inc.* magazine's list of fastest growing companies in America in 1992, Mel Laurila has lived the entrepreneurial experience of turning a dream into reality. A graduate of Michigan Technological University with B.S. and M.S. degrees in metallurgical engineering, he is very familiar with the mines in Michigan's Copper Country.

Mel Laurila has published a textbook, *The Sampling of Coal*, and has written over one hundred articles and technical papers during his thirty-plus years in the mining business. He continues to consult with major mining equipment suppliers.

Mel and his wife, Anna, reside in Georgetown, Kentucky, and Republic, Michigan.